Under the Tree of Life

by

Ruben D. Gonzales

Men and Women of Valor

Cover Art by *Teddi Black*

The Wild Rose Press, Inc.
PO Box 708
Adams Basin, NY 14410-0708
Visit us at www.thewildrosepress.com

Publishing History
First Edition, 2025
Trade Paperback ISBN 978-1-5092-6314-1
Digital ISBN 978-1-5092-6315-8

Men and Women of Valor
Published in the United States of America

Dedication

To my wife, Sue Ann who, against her better judgment,
lives with a writer.

Prologue

Mustafa Bok walked among the dead. Not his dead, the others' dead. It could have been worse, but the boy and girl rebels fought bravely and without hesitation, so he counted only one major casualty among his little rebel army. The weapon smoke from the brief firefight still hung in trees, hugging the narrow jungle road.

"Gather every weapon," he shouted to his band of rebels.

With the small unit scavenging among the enemy bodies, he knelt at the side of the wounded girl. "Can you help her?" he asked Brother Denis, a friend for many years, who was busy packing the girl's wound with gauze.

"I'm afraid my meager skills will not be enough," the Catholic brother responded. "She needs a doctor."

"Shall we carry her to the hospital in Bandella?"

"It is too far. She would bleed out before we got halfway."

"Then what?"

"We must pray."

"What?" Mustafa said, putting his hands together in a mock prayer motion. "Pray to your Christian God for a miracle?"

"Pray that the doctor the Agency promised will soon arrive."

Mustafa took the girl's hand and gave it a tight

squeeze. She looked at him with defiance springing from her eyes. He nodded. Her returning smile was thin. She blinked.

The small group of ill-clothed teenage boys and girls fashioned a litter of branches to carry the wounded fighter away from the bridge and river crossing. They hiked along a winding African trail. Most flopped along on worn rubber sandals, but some made the trip barefoot. Branches from the bushes lining the path clogged their way and the boys used the barrels of their AK-47s to sweep any thorny limbs aside.

Mustafa mopped the sweat from his brow as he pushed his way through the last of the Central African jungle and stepped onto an outcrop of rocks that overlooked the great savanna to the east. After scanning the horizon, he said, "We will rest here."

They placed the girl in the shade of a giant Baobab tree. The large, exposed roots of the tree provided a circular seating arena around the fallen soldier. Mustafa looked out over the eastern plain where three million years before, man first walked and formed social groups. He often wondered why after all this time men still found it difficult to get along with each other.

"Will she make it?" Mustafa asked Denis.

"Not if we don't get her to a doctor."

Mustafa noted the girl's shallow breathing. "We'll be better off with a real doctor."

Mustafa and his teenage band of rebels lay on the ground with some resting their heads on their rifles. The early evening sun began its descent beneath the forest tree line. With dusk and the end of another day beneath the ancient tree known by the locals as *The Tree of Life,* their wounded soldier breathed her last.

Mustafa could only sigh at the irony.

Chapter One

Tommy Foster took the short center snap from Henry the ER orderly, and taking three quick steps back, set to throw a pass down the field. Dr. Jones from pediatrics, who'd played football at Brown before going to Yale Medical School, ran a post route toward the two green trash cans symbolizing an end zone. Foster planted his right foot, and shifting his weight, passed the ball between two defenders from the hospital sanitation department.

That was just before a big mechanic from maintenance plowed into him, knocking Tommy on his ass. Foster didn't see the completed pass, or the pretty pirouette Dr. Jones performed as he danced around grasping defenders, or the accompanying high stepping into the imaginary end zone.

"Dawg, man," Dr. Jones shouted, jogging back to where Foster spread prone on the fresh cut grass of the big square of yard in front of Mercy Hospital, "you still got an arm."

"Nothing wrong with my arm, man." Tommy rolled to his side, struggling to sit up. "It's the knee that will never be the same."

"Hey, guys, let's play some more," Dr. Jones called out to the dispersing team members.

"Man, I got to get going," one of the maintenance workers called back.

"Yeah, it's been an hour already!" one of the pharmacists from the hospital dispensary shouted as the teams quickly gathered bags, assorted satchels and sweats before heading back to their different departments inside the Mercy Health complex.

"Me too, Charlie," Foster said, "I need to make my rounds."

"Tommy," Dr. Charlie Jones asked while lending a hand to pull him to his feet, "why don't you let me look at that old knee of yours. I'm sure a joint replacement would fix you right up."

"Not this week, Doc. Thanks." Foster laughed and brushed off his sweats. "Besides, from what I hear, you like cutting into people way too much."

"Who's been talking trash about me?" Jones looked around the makeshift field. "I bet it was Sanchez from records, wasn't it?"

"Now, Doc…"

"That guy and his bum knee, I mean, I'm a surgeon not a miracle worker. Three other sawbones hacked into that knee of his before I even examined it."

"Take it easy, Doc, it's not that," Tommy soothed. "I've got a long list of things to do, and I can't afford to be off my feet."

"Okay, but you remember that knee won't hold up like that forever and the V.A. isn't going to help you anymore. One day you'll be walking along casual like, and it will collapse, and it just won't work."

"Right, Doc," he said grabbing the football from him, "I'll remember every time I take my ibuprofen."

Tommy stuffed the worn ball into his duffle bag along with his other gear. He donned a pair of headphones and grabbing the bag, limped across the green quad to the north employees only entrance at Mercy. He listened to a mix of his favorite old jazz. A cool spring air blew gently across the only section of the hospital grounds with a grass area large enough to afford a modified game. The buildings loomed out over the Atlantic with small patches of grass, shrubs, and palms strategically placed to relieve the eye of the solid expanse.

Foster swiped the security pad with his ID card and stepped inside the florescent light bathed north corridor, smelling the first hint of disinfectant. He hated the aroma. In fact, he hated everything about hospitals—and any medical facility in general. This came from experience. When he injured his knee playing football, he spent a long time in a rehab hospital and then again after an IED blew apart the Humvee he was driving during a tour in Afghanistan. His dislike came about honestly. It was a juvenile attitude to hold but he took a stubborn pleasure in it just the same.

Foster turned right at the third hallway and limped to the employee dressing room designated for the north wing of the hospital. Four rows of lockers filled the space with a narrow wooden bench between them. The bench sparkled under several hefty coats of polyurethane that protected the wood from wear and preserved some fifty years of graffiti and knife carvings. Once, during a lull between shifts, Foster counted some twenty hearts between the two thirty-foot benches.

He twirled the dial of his combo lock through the three numbers and once he opened the locker, pulled off his sweats and T-shirt over his headphones and toweled off his chest and arms. He weighed a good thirty pounds less than his college playing weight, but his biceps and stomach were still ripped with muscle, thanks to the good athletic genes he inherited from his African ancestors.

Foster pulled on blue trousers and matching shirt from the locker and slid into black socks and black shoes. Lastly, he took his belt and a holster that held the security gear he wore on his rounds. His beeper flashed yellow and displayed a series of numbers, code red for the laundry room.

"Damn," he said, sweeping the headphones off and tossing them into his locker. He slammed the door shut and headed out into the hallway, buckling the belt on as he walked. He lumbered to the service elevator that would take him to the basement. He cussed to himself again when he remembered he forgot to secure the locker and take his ibuprofen but just the same hurried along on a slight limp. *Nothing worth stealing in there anyway.*

As soon as he got off the elevator Tommy noticed the lighting in the basement appeared much dimmer. He figured the hospital administration kept it dark there trying to save a little money on electricity, but it didn't make his job any easier as he fumbled along in the dark. Along the back corridor he turned right and hurried to the laundry room. The big machines stood silent as the next shift didn't start until three PM. Still, someone set off the alarm that called a code yellow. In the hospital, security codes yellow signified a suspicious character or package. By the sound coming from the shelves with stacks of folded sheets in the far corner he expected to find a *character*.

Foster contemplated shouting out so that the intruder might run off, but realized he stood blocking the only way out. Thinking better, he moved forward quietly and took out his flashlight which weighed a good pound and bore a striking resemblance to those banned flashlights the police used to carry. The fact that they were outlawed because cops used them to subdue suspects by hitting them over the head with it, played a key role in that decision. Thankfully the letter of law did not include security guard level. He swept the beam around the room but stopped as it illuminated the smooth bare back of a tall, thin woman. Blue scrub pants rested at her feet and her narrow shoulders hunched against the temperature in the cold room.

"Don't move!" he cautioned as he slowly advanced.

"Don't shoot me, officer," she said in a child's voice, covering her naked chest with a green scrub top.

"Turn around slowly," he commanded.

As she turned, her deep brown eyes blinked under the glare of the bright light. She wore her black hair in several tight braids that fell to her shoulders. Deep dimples showed in the chubby cheeks framing her face. When she raised her hands to shield her eyes, the scrub top fell to the floor.

"Come on, Tommy. You know I hate it when you shine that damn light in my eyes."

Chapter Two

A crowd of some ten people waited in the freshly painted lobby of the Miami Gardens Neighborhood Clinic. Doctor Thema Atsu Book had formed the not for profit on the first floor of a vacant rambling building nine months before, opening the clinic under the watchful eye of her attending physician supervisor who understood how much it meant to Thema to help the less fortunate.

She had seen an old TV show rerun late one night and was so impressed with the lead character, she almost boarded a bus the next day to visit the doctor-clown in the West Virginia hills, only to discover the man's clinic had ended operations years before. The internet information on the real-life Patch Adams still inspired her. The physician who dressed as a circus clown preaching laughter and compassion as much as medicine had confirmed for her the spirit of life and nature's remedies contributed as much to curing common ailments as modern meds. She grew interested in natural herbs and remedies and experimented on her patients when she could. The patients sometimes laughed at the various green globs and other home remedies, but accepted nature's own, if only to please her.

"My God," Thema Book gasped to her clinic assistant after seeing the crowded lobby. The bright room with colorful oversized sunflowers painted on the walls and bright pastel soft stuffed furniture seemed a perfect antidote for her patient's normally drab existence in the inner city. "It's nearly eight o'clock on Friday night. Don't these people have lives?"

Marie Santiago smiled. "Don't worry. It's only the Gibson family. They came in with their little brother, Dwayne. He has something wrong with his arm."

"Well, show him in and I might as well see Mrs. Gibson, too," Thema directed as she slid a fresh sheet of protective paper onto the exam table. "Bring along the oldest daughter, ah, what's her name, Tanya? She makes sure Mrs. Gibson takes her meds."

Marie opened the waiting room door and called out to the family. Mrs. Gibson hobbled into the clinic's lone furnished exam room with her daughter and a glum-faced teenage boy. Thema smiled broadly to the elderly matriarch, and they embraced warmly.

"How are you, Mrs. Gibson?" she asked after pointing the boy toward the exam table. Marie took her post in the far corner, silent but available for anything Thema needed.

"Oh, okay I guess." Mrs. Gibson nodded vigorously while stifling a cough, "I just can't get rid of this congestion."

"Now, now, have you been taking the amoxicillin I gave you last week? Tanya?" she asked the daughter.

Few of her patients could afford any drugs, at least the legal ones, forcing Thema to rely on drug reps and the local Mercy Hospital pharmacy for donations to her medicine pantry. She acknowledged that the drug industry deserved their bad rap for many things, but all the reps earned an "A" from her when it came to giving her drug samples. She didn't mind that they helped in the hope that they would one day get her account. The clinic might be a work in progress, but they gave generously with an eye to future anticipated sales.

"Oh yes, Doctor, we make sure she takes it," Tanya said

"That's good." Thema gripped her stethoscope. To take the chill off the diaphragm she gently rubbed it against the sleeve of her lab coat. As she moved the scope with her right hand about the woman's back to listen to the woman's lungs, she moved her left hand, applying a slight pressure in unison. "Mrs. Gibson, it doesn't do you any good unless you take the whole prescription."

"Oh yes, Doctor," her daughter said again, "we'll make sure she takes the whole bottle, but Doctor, she doesn't sleep at all!" Tanya protested. "After she works her day shift at the plant, she goes straight to her house-keeping shift at the hotel and works all night. Honestly, I never see her sleep."

"Now, Mrs. Gibson," Thema gently scolded. "You promised me you would cut back on your hours until this cleared up."

"It's only a couple nights a week."

"No buts! Do you want to get better?"

"Of course…"

"Well, you need to rest."

"Doctor, it's that good for nothing Jackson," Tanya interjected.

Thema glanced at the younger woman. "Your brother?"

"Yes, he's in jail again, for fencing, and they are threatening to put him away for a long time. She's trying to raise enough money for his bail."

Redirecting her gaze on the patient, Thema asked,

"Mrs. Gibson?"

"It's only a thousand dollars," the woman said, and coughed again. "Just a couple more shifts."

"Doctor, she is going to work herself to death."

Thema frowned at her patient, the female one. "Is this true?"

"Of course, it's true, Doctor," Tanya said. "I told her she should just let him rot in there."

"Oh, no, I couldn't. Child, he's your brother, we must make his bail. He doesn't belong in there."

"Says who? Let him serve his time," Tanya said. "He'll be out soon enough."

"Tanya, how can you say such a thing. What if it was your son?"

"If my Jamison got himself arrested, he'd spend every minute he deserved, and I would think nothing of it. Is it his business, going around and fencing stolen property for somebody?"

"Well, okay now, Mrs. Gibson," Thema interrupted, then sat on her stool to make a note on a chart. "Your lungs sound much better than last week, so I think that medicine is working. Just make sure you take the whole bottle and by this time next week I think you'll be back to normal. If not, you can come back, and I'll take another look at you."

"And working," her daughter asked.

"Well, if it hasn't killed her yet, I guess she'll be okay. But Mrs. Gibson, it wouldn't hurt you to take a little time off. You'll get better sooner if you do. How much is that bail?"

"It's a thousand dollars. I need fifty dollars more."

Thema nodded. "Well then. How about I make a little contribution today to Jackson's bail fund to get him out if you promise to take a day or two off?"

"Oh no, Doctor Book, I couldn't take your money."

"Nonsense, let me make my little tithe, but don't let me hear from Tanya next week that you didn't follow through on your promise." She glanced at Marie as she maintained her spot in the corner. "Marie, help Mrs. Gibson out to the waiting area, and get fifty dollars from the petty cash box. Be sure to make a note of a donation to the Jackson Gibson defense fund."

"Oh, thank you, thank you," the woman said looking over her shoulder as Marie escorted them out into the waiting area.

"You're wasting your money, Doctor," Tanya called back as they left. "He'll be back in the joint next month!"

Marie herded the two women out to the waiting family, leaving Thema and sullen Dwayne alone.

"Okay, Dwayne," she said while closing the door for privacy. She noticed that the boy held his right arm high and close to his breast. "What seems to be the trouble?"

"Nothing," he said in a voice he tried to make older than his actual age.

"Don't worry," she said with a wink, scooting the stool on rollers closer to where he sat on the exam table. "If you don't tell me, I can't help you."

He squirmed on the table.

"Come on, now, tell the doctor."

The boy remained silent.

"Now look," she crossed her arms and looked at him. "I've been working since four this morning and it is very late on a Friday night. I'd much rather be at home with my feet up; instead, I am trying to help you. So, tell me what's wrong."

Dwayne hesitated a minute more and the two of

them struggled with the silence. Finally, he rose to his feet and began to wiggle out of his over-sized sweatshirt. He pulled it about halfway off and when it hung up, Thema stood and helped him to drag the last bit over his head.

A soiled loose bandage covered his upper bicep. A day's worth of dried blood caked on the material above more recent wet spots. Thema smelled a slight odor like bad lunch meat. She unwound the home-made bandage and revealed a six-inch-long festering wound running parallel to the humerus.

"You're lucky," she told him, not expecting an answer. "If you left your arm like this for another day or two it could have fallen off." She took a bundle of cotton and dripped some rubbing alcohol on it, then started to clean the wound. "This is going to hurt."

When the boy didn't flinch, she asked, "Are you going to tell me about this?"

He hesitated for a minute. "I hurt myself climbing over a fence,"

"Dwayne, it doesn't look like that type of wound. This resembles a knife cut."

"Fence."

"It doesn't matter. I'm not the cops."

"No?"

"Of course not. I may be a doctor, but I am not a snitch."

Dwayne just smiled but maintained his silence.

She used eight stitches to close the wound and took a small plastic container from an under-counter refrigerator. Using a wooden stick, she stirred a dark green moss like mixture.

"What's that?" the boy asked, when she brought the

container to the table.

Thema grinned. "Green slime I keep around for fence cuts like yours."

"Can't you just give me a shot?"

"Not to worry," she said, taking a sterile wooden tongue depressor and scooping a blob of goo from the container. "This is Goldenseal extract."

"What's that?"

"It's a plant that grows wild in places, but I order a jar online." She smeared the gooey concoction over the boy's wound. "The native Indians used it for medicine."

"No kidding?"

"No kidding. It helps with healing, especially on the skin's surface. I think it limits the scarring so your arm will stay nice and pretty."

"You can just go out and pick it, the plant I mean?"

"If you can find it," she said. She wrapped his arm in a clean dressing. Then taking her hand she placed it over the coated wound and applied pressure. She felt the heat from her hand to the boy's arm.

She then pulled a vial filled with a broad-spectrum antibiotic and a syringe from a medicine cabinet. She drew the clear serum from the bottle and cleaned a spot on his left arm with a swab of cotton and alcohol, then she inserted the syringe needle and pumped the drug into his muscle.

"This should fix you up," she told him while placing her hands on the boy's wound again and applying pressure. The extra-hands-on ritual was something she begun during her first shift as an ER resident. The small act of making a connection with the patients seemed to provide them with a moment of peace and the warmth generated by the connection appeared to cement the procedure. She enjoyed the interaction, and most patients did as well. "Now, if you take it easy for a couple of days your arm will feel better."

Dwayne smiled at the spot on his arm where she placed her hands.

"He's doing better, everyone," Thema said, as they came into the waiting room, and she met with ten pair of wide and worried eyes staring at her. "He'll be fine. Just make sure he gets some rest and keep that wrap on for a couple of days. You can let that green stuff sit there for a while. If he starts to run a fever, bring him back."

****

After the family swarmed around Dwayne, Marie ushered everyone out, said goodbye, and locked the door. She worked there every afternoon after her morning classes at the community college. She began an RN nursing program the previous spring and working in the clinic convinced her she chose the right profession. She didn't even mind the late hours. Most of the time she spent her evenings in front of the TV so working at the clinic kept her busy. Doctor Book worked hard and put in long hours; Marie loved working alongside the smart and dedicated woman. It amazed Marie how the doctor still found time to study. Studying always came hard for her.

Marie switched off the little electric coffee pot, pouring the last scorched bit into the adjoining sink, dumping the grounds from the filter holder in the trash and turning off the last of the lights. She returned to the service counter to begin filing the stack of the day's charts, but Dr. Book was still writing in one.

She could only dream of a day when the files could be kept on a computer like modern clinics utilized. Of course, that would take a lot of money, and money was something the clinic didn't have. It had lots of love but little money. Maybe there was a grant out there that they could apply for.

"Do you want me to wait and file those, Doctor Book?"

"No, I need to finish my notes. Why don't you run along, I'll lock up. You can file them tomorrow. Now that our residency is coming to an end, Dr. Mason will be in tomorrow and you might give her a little time in the morning. If she goes out to celebrate tonight, she'll probably be a little late."

"She's always late."

"Well, I usually cajole her into volunteering, so her heart is not really in it, but give her some slack, Marie, at least she tries. Besides, I can't work every shift, I still need to study, and I'd like a Saturday off occasionally."

Marie gathered her things and shuffled to the exit on two very tired feet. Just as she reached for the door, someone pushed the door in, nearly smacking her in the nose. A big man looked at her and said, "I'm here to see Doctor Book".

"Oh yeah, who are you?"

"I'm Mike Blanco, here's my card. Tell Doctor Book I'd like to see her."

Chapter Three

Tommy walked in the hall of the first floor of the south wing of Mercy Hospital. He liked the quiet atmosphere of the pediatric ward. When he first came to work at Mercy, he was stuck in the ER but the never-ending chaos over there added several layers of gray hair to his head. The doctors who worked in the ER deserved medals, and though he was not the squeamish type, he asked for a transfer after one weekend in the ER.

When a position opened in pediatrics the higher ups moved him over to the inpatient side of the hospital and he loved it. The kids there were captive, but most of them only stayed overnight or a few days at most. Occasionally, they'd get a bad case that required a longer stay, but most were what they termed ins and outs. He hated that any kid had to be sick, but pediatrics drew less blood than elsewhere in the hospital, so he was happy to be there.

The kid patients were too young to remember his playing days, but occasionally a parent or grandparent remembered his career at the University of Miami, and they'd encourage him to relive a few moments of past glory. Of course, it didn't take long before the surprise in their eyes showed as they realized the one-time big-name quarterback now worked as a gimp security guard in the children's ward of an old hospital.

He finished his route on the second floor without

incident then headed back to the security office. He usually worked alone on this rotation and at the tail end of his shift rarely ran into anyone from administration, or doctors for that matter. So, when he heard steps behind him just as he reached the office door, he jumped.

"Tommy Foster!" a familiar voice called.

"Mike Blanco!" Foster said recognizing an old teammate. "What the hell are you doing here, slumming? I haven't seen you since the reunion."

"Come on, Bro, it hasn't been that long," Mike said. "You going to invite me in or we going to stand out here flapping our jaws?"

As he unlocked the office door, Tommy thought about his pal. Last he checked, Mike was working for some private security company out west while Tommy bounced around, working construction until he landed at Mercy Hospital. The steady salary complimented his disability pay and together it allowed him to afford living in the city while he dreamed about finishing his degree.

Tommy let his old friend in and asked, "So what have you been up to?"

"I'm still working out of Colorado and staying sharp," Blanco said as he looked around the cramped office space and took the lone visitor's chair

"Sharp? What are you talking about? Sharp for what?"

"Look, man," he said, sitting back in the chair and crossing his long legs that seemed to take forever to fold. "I am on to a dream job. I've been working with Valor Security and Investigations."

He pulled a card out of his shirt pocket and handed it to Tommy. Mike's name was embossed over a background watermark representative of a law enforcement badge and VSI prominently displayed in shadowed font. The card had the normal contact information along with a web site that he made a note to check out. He couldn't wait to google the outfit and find out how they attracted his friend who, as he remembered, only enjoyed knocking heads around.

Mike leaned forward, resting his massive arms on his thighs. He drilled Tommy with a thousand-yard stare. "This group has contracts all over the world—and a big one in Central Africa just rolled out."

"Doing what?"

"Security, my friend," he said, slapping his hands and rubbing them together. "We provide armed security. And they're not afraid of spending money on the latest weapons and technology. I'm putting together a team to go over there."

Central Africa? Jeez. "I hear it's rough over there."

Mike shrugged equally massive shoulders. "Sometimes."

"Isn't that where that big Tutu–Hitu thing exploded?"

"That's Tutsi–Hutu, Tommy. Big civil war for a while, but that's settled. There's a new administration in place and things are looking up."

Tommy settled into his desk chair, crossed his hands in his lap and asked, "So are you visiting a patient at the hospital?" He got a whiff of an odd odor off his friend and noticed the man's suit could use a pressing.

"No, no, not this trip, ah, actually I came to talk to you."

"Oh, yeah? About what?"

"A job."

"Boy," he said leaning back in his chair and

motioning around the room with a hand. "I got a job."

"Oh yeah," Blanco said, glancing around the cramped office. "With all the cafeteria food you can eat, I'm sure."

"No," he said and made gagging motion, "they make us pay for that mash."

"I bet, and I bet there are a bunch of bills too?"

"What do you mean?"

"I'm sure the loans for your college years are increasing even as we speak. What are they now, a hundred thousand?"

"More," he said, blowing air out in a whistle through puckered lips, "a lot more with interest."

"What a hole that must be."

"What of it?"

"Say, I thought you were working construction?"

"Before I took this job, I spent plenty of time on construction sites, but its murder working outside and," he said, giving his knee a rub, "it gave my knee fits."

"What about the architecture thing you always talked about?"

"Ah, I'm taking some classes but it's slow going," he explained, fiddling with a triangle ruler he kept on his desk for doodling late at night when the hospital was particularly quiet. "Most of the architecture programs want you to go straight through, five years full time, then a long internship type thing. I've taken some classes at the community college, but one day I'll be looking into it again full time. So, what of it?"

"Well, like I said, man, I have a job for you. I want you on my team."

"Look, man," he laughed, "my soldiering days are long over, and even if I wanted another job there's plenty of places I can look at right here."

"Oh sure, at what thirty maybe thirty-five thou a year to start, or whatever construction pays now. Hell, it must be a struggle for you on what you make here. Why you should be able to pay off those loans in no time. That's of course, as long as this old hospital stays open."

"Say, Bro, take it easy on the critique, so what's it to you anyhow?"

"I told you, man," he said, leaning forward, like he had a secret to tell him, "I've got a job for you that pays enough that you can wipe out your debts and put a hundred thousand in your bank account."

"What kind of job pays like that?"

"I tell you, man, a job so easy you'll think you are on vacation!"

****

Tommy couldn't put his finger on it, but sensed his friend was holding something back. Not so much what he said but what he didn't volunteer. "So, are you telling me you want to offer me a job that can pay that much?"

"That's right," his friend said, settling in the chair, "VSI has money coming out the butt."

"Who runs it?" Tommy asked, a little more interested with the money out the butt comment.

"Couple of ex-soldiers, Green Beret, Special Forces type. They have a worldwide footprint, and they are putting a project together. I need someone with your experience."

"What kind of experience?"

"Your construction and military experience."

"Why construction?" Tommy asked, holding his hands out to the side.

"They want to build this clinic over there and tend

to the sick."

"In Africa?"

"That's right," he said, then smiled. "The Dark Continent."

"And I'm the only one who can do this?"

"Well, almost."

"What do you mean.?"

"Look," he said, taking out a handkerchief and wiping his face, "that country is locked tight, in order to get in, VSI put this clinic project together. And it is expensive, I mean there'll be some money changing hands, but being a health clinic project and all, they can make an exception, save some face and pocket a little change."

"So, that's the job?"

"That's just the cover. We'll have a doctor for the clinic. We need you there to build the clinic— but we are going over there to protect a local who is big into politics."

"Why does he need protection?"

"Some army dude staged a coup and took over the government and is going after any opposition. Guess who hired us?"

"Who?"

"The Agency."

"The CIA?"

"Yeah, the new government is backed by the Chinese so the Agency can't go covert over there. Instead," he said, motioning to himself with his thumbs, "they farmed out the job to VSI."

"Does VSI have the infrastructure to make this work?

"We've got the manpower, and the Agency will

provide intel."

"So, again, why me?"

"It's a little rough over there so experience with both construction and military is needed. The job description was made for you, Tommy."

"I was in intelligence."

"That's a plus," he said, giving Tommy the okay sign with his thumb and forefinger, "and since you're not exactly on a career path here, what could be better? Any other architect with a military background is in business and couldn't take a year off to help us out and if we found someone willing to take a year off, they wouldn't have the army intelligence." Blanco leaned back in the chair and grinned. "You, my man, are the perfect fit."

"It's nice to be wanted," Tommy said with a wry smile.

"Look, we are exploring other options, but it really takes a combination of skill sets and you fit the profile. Besides, wouldn't you want to get back into some action? You can't get back in as a soldier, but you can get in by the back door. Of course, there are a couple of challenges."

"Like?"

"Like you need to commit for a full year."

"Who else is involved in this?"

"There'll be a strike unit going over disguised as a construction crew and the doctor."

"Who?"

"That's not important now, but someone in the city."

"How did you get a doctor to agree to this?"

"The Doc is young and about to wrap a residency and needs the money, like you. It will be good cover and being Black, the doctor will stand in as the lead and give

24

us the *in* we need. So, unless you dream of staying in security the rest of your life, this is perfect for you. You possess the perfect set of skills," he said, holding up three fingers and counting them off as he checked off his points, "Army, construction, and you're Black. Look man, it's simple. You go over there, build the clinic, and the Doc works to heal the sick. The crew protects the would-be target, and we get a big pay day.

"You put in your time and in return the foundation takes care of your bills and when you get back you get a fresh start with money in the bank, and you can go back and get your architecture degree. It's sort of like joining the Peace Corps, but with money." After flashing another big smile, he said, "It will be just like a vacation. What could be better?"

"Come on, man," Tommy questioned, giving his old friend a sharp-eyed look. "What's the part you're *not* telling me?"

"This is on the level. We'll prepare contracts and everything and your lawyer can check them."

"Oh, don't worry about that, I'd have that done first thing."

"So, how does it sound to you?"

"I'll need some time to mull this over before I jump on your train."

Mike checked his watch. "The problem is, we don't have much time. I need your answer like now."

Chapter Four

"Some guy named Blanco is out in the lobby and wants to see you."

"About what?" Thema asked.

"He didn't say. Here's his card."

Thema looked at the card that displayed the letters, VSI, and listing an address in Colorado.

"Doctor Book," the man said when she came out into the lobby.

"That's me and who are you?"

"I'm Mike Blanco," he said, reaching out to shake her hand. His broad smile showed off a mouth full of natural teeth amid a short dark beard.

Thema noticed he filled out what appeared to be a new suit, sported a fresh shower scent, and stood well over six foot. Good looking, too. She was sorry she wasn't dressed nicer.

"So, what can I do for you?" she said, motioning for him to follow her to her office. "Are you a drug rep? Here to help us out?"

"Well, in a way, yes. An agency we work with suggested you for a job I'm overseeing, and you come highly recommended."

"I already got a job," she told him, moving behind her desk and taking a seat. She knew that the clinic couldn't afford to pay her, and she was a little worried about how they were going to keep the place going after she left the hospital. "Who recommended me?" she asked, pointing to an empty chair on the opposite side of her desk.

"We can't divulge our partners, Doctor," he said, taking the seat, "but they are well connected and mentioned you for the job."

"Why do I need another job? The clinic is all the job I need."

"You want to get paid, don't you? This job will pay you enough to clear up your debts and give you and your clinic a fresh start."

"What kind of job pays like that?"

"The group that hired us is building a new state of the art clinic in Central Africa. We need a doctor to run the old clinic during construction."

"Why me?"

"You have a unique set of skills and experience which are perfect for this opportunity."

"I don't know. I'm pretty set here."

"Yes, but your clinic," he said waving his hand around, "can't pay you and you are behind on your student loans."

Thema paused for a moment and peered at him. "How do you know about my student loans?"

"The group I work with flies beneath the radar," he said, glancing down, like he was avoiding her eyes. "But they are serious folk. Look, you are in transition and so the timing is right for you."

"What group wants to hire me?"

"MAM."

"Who?" she said, narrowing her eyelids.

"Medical African Missions. They are the client and paying the bills. Right now, they are doing research on childhood nutrition and want to dig deep in Central Africa, and they are starting with that clinic project."

"I'm not experienced in childhood nutrition."

"The bulk of the research will come later, after the clinic is built. They've been doing some research and have had some promising results there. In the meantime," he said, pointing at her, "you'll be manning the clinic and taking care of the local villagers. You know, generating goodwill."

"Where do they get their funding?"

"A group of the new philanthropic software rich are funding it. Duncan Technology is the lead group, and they contribute most of the money."

She knew of them, vaguely. "Duncan Technologies. The computer people?"

"That's them."

"And these people," she said, pointing a thumb at her chest, "want to offer me a job?"

"That's why I'm here, I mean, I like you, but I wouldn't be barging in on you if I didn't think you were a great candidate. I've been following you on social media and can tell you are passionate about what you do."

"So, why am I such a hot commodity?" she asked although she never remembered friending this guy or his group on any social media platforms.

"Because you are a perfect fit for what we need. I mean, you're going to fit right in."

"And" she asked, ignoring the attempt at a compliment, "what does this great opportunity pay?"

"It's a straight two hundred thousand dollars for the year, plus expenses. You'll never touch the two hundred, and there are other benefits, too"

"A year?" she asked, trying to not show how the figure took her breath away. With that kind of money, she could take care of those student loans and get a fresh start.

"That's the gig. They fly you over," he said, making a bird in flight with two hands, "put you up, cover the cost of the project, and then," he said, pretending like the pen in his hand he was waving was a wizard's wand, "you work your magic."

"That's a lot of money, I'm sure there are any number of doctors out there that would love to take this job."

This Mike Blanco person nodded. "It is a sweet deal, but it comes with some extenuating circumstances. You are the most qualified, but you also possess unique qualities for what we are trying to accomplish."

"What do you mean?"

"An African army dude just staged a coup over there and kicked out the white people. The only outsiders getting into the country right now are missionary types. Not only that, but only the Black missions. The Black Baptists are getting in, along with a couple of other groups, but he's selective, leaving us with only one possibility. He's given various groups a month to produce worthwhile projects and then he's slamming the door again. Given the circumstances, we were lucky to have been already working on a project which gave us an edge to get in, and like I said, you fit the perfect profile to lead this project."

"You mean because I'm a doctor?"

"Well, no, being a doctor alone doesn't get you in there."

"Then what?"

"Well, girl, because you're Black."

Chapter Five

Raised in white foster homes, Doctor Thema Book never adopted the Black persona. But when she applied for a couple of residencies, she wanted to be in an urban area that really needed medical access. Luckily, several positions remained available since no one wanted to work in the inner city. When asked about relatives, she always explained her foster home upbringing. She recognized it drove her. She never contemplated her past, there was usually just too much of the present to worry about the past.

"Listen, Mr. Blanco, I told you that child nutrition is not my specialty."

"No problem," he said. "Most of the research has already been completed. You'll be tending to the sick in the village and working with them on re-education."

"Re-education on what topics?"

"Eating better. Look, once the new administration knows we can run a clinic then we can start work on the next phase of the problem and get other people in there doing the heavy research countrywide."

"Isn't that a behavior modification problem? Why don't they just get the Peace Corps in there?"

"No, that's too white, too U.S. government thing. We are going to start simple with bandages and stuff, and work on a little community goodwill on the side."

"But why the Central African Republic?"

"The research the MAM people completed before the coup points to a correlation there with good health and the environment. That's what you'll be looking at, and at some point, carrying on with that research. In addition to putting band aids on cuts. Isn't that your side interest, in the areas of herbs and nuts, and all?"

"Got it figured out, don't you," Thema said, wondering how in the world he had gathered info on her natural supplemental remedies she utilized. *Damn social media posts.*

"All but the part where you agree, but the outfit I work with is serious about this and they are willing to spend some money to make this work. All you have to do is sign on and we can start feeling good about ourselves."

"So, your group, what is it…?"

"Valor Security and Investigations."

"Right, VSI. But why would MAM hire you?"

"We provide security and logistics worldwide and will be providing logistics for the project. Plus, we get the job done."

"So, what about these other benefits you mentioned?"

He hesitated for a moment, squinting at her. "If you agree to take the job, MAM will buy the building you're currently in and will complete the buildout of your clinic. If they can spend a couple hundred million in Africa, they can spend a couple of hundred thousand more here in the hood."

"What exactly would they do?"

He hesitated again, like doing an internal calculation. "A total rehab job. They'll buy the building, finish out the rest of the exam rooms, finish and furnish the lab as well. When you complete your contract with

MAM, they will donate the place to your foundation."

"That all? I just can't close the clinic down. We've established a real niche here. The neighborhood counts on us."

When he didn't say more, Thema said again, "Is that all, Mr. Blanco?"

"Okay, in addition to donating the building, to get you signed on, the foundation will fund the doctors who work at the clinic for the year you are away."

"Two years," Thema bargained.

"Damn, girl!"

"And my assistant," she added, nodding at Marie who until this moment, sat nearby, but stone silent. "She's full time, the clinic can't run without her."

"Okay, okay, two years and we'll fund Marie's *'part time'* position, too. But remember, it's a full year in terms of your contract."

Like a sudden storm, the opportunity laid out before her blew her away. She couldn't calculate the investment MAM was willing to make just to get her on board. She hoped it wasn't one of those things you find out is too good to be true, so she buried her worries about how much this guy knew about her life. Was it a coincidence he knew about her finances?

She always wondered about her African roots. She understood her name was different from the average Black name. When she researched the name online, she discovered the central African name meant *queen*, and she was proud of her heritage. Whoever her real mother was, she must have been proud of the African root thing, too.

It would certainly be an adventure and in the end, she'd come back to a better financial place. She could come back to the clinic, continue her work in the hood permanently, and not have to job hunt and work under someone else to make ends meet. She could be her own boss for a change. It seemed like a small thing to get so much in return. Still...

"Your proposal is enticing, Mr. Blanco, but I'm just not comfortable with the whole thing."

"Call me Mike, Dr. Book, just Mike," he said. "Listen, this project is important to the MAM folks. If you agree to the terms and commit to the year, I've got one more thing for you."

"What?" Thema asked the man with genuine interest.

"If you agree then MAM will pay off your student loans, the whole two hundred and fifty thousand dollars."

This deal was certainly a deal too good to pass on, but she still worried that he had so much information about her student loans and the clinic. "They must think I'm a miracle worker or something."

When she still hesitated, he said, "Look, I knew we'd have to give a lot to get you but that's okay. The group can afford it."

"Money is no object?"

"You'll be putting in a year, but MAM is serious about this. This mission is important for them and besides you, they are providing some other assets. We'll have a construction coordinator and a crew for the building project. You'll supervise and the coordinator will build the clinic. We'll have help from local labor, and you'll run the clinic with some local help. There'll be some experienced people going along and they'll be helping with a lot of things. I imagine there'll be someone with local knowledge on the politics who can iron out the red tape and keep the whole project moving."

"Come on, Blanco," Thema asked, "are you holding back?"

"Two things," he said leaning across the desk and pointing at her for emphasis, "One, I need your answer right away."

"Like when?"

"Like right now."

"I can't give you an answer right now, I need some time to think about it."

"We don't have time. You take this deal and you'll be on VSI time. If you don't take the job, we'll get someone else. They won't be as good a match or anything, but we are going over there with a team in ten days."

"Ten days?" Thema said aloud, "That's impossible!"

"Nothing's impossible. The plan has been in place for a while and most of the big equipment has already been shipped. It will be on the ground there by the end of next week. If you take the job, you'll be on a plane next weekend sometime."

"How's that possible?" Thema asked.

"Does it matter? Just realize that this might seem like a small project, but it is a big mission, with a lot of money and people behind it."

"How about a visa," she asked.

"We'll get whatever documents that are needed."

Thema realized that Blanco and his group were way ahead of her. That's probably why they had so much about her circumstances. Hell, they probably already had a passport and visa for her. "I don't care what your timetable is. I need to think about this, and I am not going to rush in. I'll need some time."

"Okay," he said, "I get it. I'll give you until Monday. You're scheduled for your shots and a WHO health card in town on Monday afternoon. Here's my cell number" he said, handing her a card. "I wrote the address for the doctor's office on the back. Call me by six PM tomorrow. If you don't want the job, don't call. If you call, I'll confirm the doctor's appointment and send you the contracts. You'll sign everything Monday morning and we'll cut a check to cover your first few months, and the first installments of loan payoffs. I'll get a contractor out for the clinic work early in the week, and you can go over what you expect. You'll have the rest of the week to wrap your personal affairs, pay off some bills, finish at the hospital, and you'll ship out next weekend. Then you'll be in that sun and fun in Africa. What more can you ask for?"

Thema basically sat there with her mouth open. The scope and speed of this thing was well beyond her experience.

"Well," he said, "I have a plane to catch. I hope to hear from you but if not, good luck to you and your clinic."

Thema walked him to the door and opened it. "Hey," she said to him before he started through the doorway, "You said two things, so what's number two?"

"Number two? Hmm, didn't I mention it? They've just settled a war over there so things might be a little rough, but it should still be just like a vacation with sun and frolicking."

Chapter Six

Mike Blanco looked west out of the wall-to-wall windows in the conference room of VSI headquarters. Located on the top three floors of a high rise, the view of the green Colorado snow-capped mountains was spectacular.

"Are you sure about this Tommy Foster for the job? his supervisor asked.

"He fits the profile."

"Does being an old friend have any influence on your decision?"

"Sure, we've been friends since high school. He's been through some rough times since he got out of the service, but I trust the guy with my life. With Vince starting this security business to help veterans, I think he'd approve of this pick."

"What about the doctor? Did you choose her because the Agency recommended her?"

"I probably would have picked her even without the Agency recommendation."

"Why?"

"The people she works with say she's a miracle worker in the ER. This project is going to need someone like that."

****

Brother Denis enjoyed sleeping out under the canopy of African stars. The weather in central eastern

Africa, though it could be blisteringly harsh during the day, turned tranquil in the evening. The humidity settled and a breeze rose over the dry savannah, cooling the air of the damp forest and making sleep easy. Carrying his hammock sling always seemed less intrusive than having to impose on the local villagers for a bed. The local tribes were proud people and were embarrassed by their meager accommodations and provisions. Besides, even if he found a sturdy bed long enough to rest comfortably in, the bed bugs would eat him alive, and he'd find himself outside anyway. This way he only needed a couple of trees or posts to string his hammock between and stretch his mosquito netting from.

Brother Denis accepted the jungle night, both the sounds and the dark. On a moonless night you couldn't see the hand in front of your eyes. But on a night with a full moon out you could almost read by the light. Thankfully, since they might need to travel at night, there would be more moon for the next week.

The tree frogs and toads croaked out a constant din and the occasional cry of a guinea hen or occasional big cat broke the monotony in the night. Only the monkeys and antelope still roamed freely. Most of the big game had long ago been hunted out in the region. Like adversaries to the current administration, here today gone tomorrow.

The moon appeared. Even at an early rise, moonlight lit the village, and the brilliant white crescent cast a long shadow over the humble grounds. It didn't matter. The government troops would not come at night, only patrolling during the day. When it came to fighting, they much preferred to battle in the light of day as opposed to the bush at night.

Mustafa came behind him. "The boys are ready, Brother."

"How far a walk do we have?" he asked as he swung out of the hammock.

"Couple of hours or so, we should be back before morning."

Mustafa led off, closely followed by three teenage boys, then Brother Denis, and a fourth boy at the rear. To guard against a sneak attack, Mustafa explained. Brother Denis appreciated the concern, but this night would be quiet. The real battles would not come for a week or so. They still had to bring in the doctor and supply the clinic. They promised him as much and he wouldn't fully commit the little rebel unit until a doctor assumed an active position in the clinic.

The only thing worse than a dying soldier without medical attention was a child soldier dying without medical attention.

****

The next day Doctor Thema Astu Book sat at her tall kitchen counter that doubled as a desk, making a few notes on a pad and running some figures through a calculator. Adding the loans for each of her school years, plus the estimate of repairs and the cost of furnishing the clinic, and paying the staff, it came to way above three quarters of a million dollars. A lot of money, Thema admitted, but to get what they obviously wanted the MAM foundation decided to pay. That's what worried her.

"This deal worries me," she said to Marie, who had come by to see if she had made up her mind. Marie was completely sold on the whole thing, but Thema kept her reservations, since it was her who was flying off to

Africa, the dark continent. She hated being so negative on the project, but an entire year away from the states seemed like a long time.

"Look, Doctor Book," Marie started and used her title, which worried Thema because they were always on a first name basis, unless they were talking about money. In addition to helping around the clinic Marie also took care of the books and when they talked about the precarious financial situation the clinic was in, she always called her Doctor Book.

"Come on now, Doctor Book," she said, "just think about the money and think about working in Africa."

"Ah…yeah, that's what I'm talking about."

"Don't you want to go back to your homeland, go in search of your roots? You'll fit right in there, in Africa."

"Okay, don't start with the Kunta Kinte stuff."

Marie smiled big. "You're the one with the African name. It will be like a home coming for you! What does your name mean, anyway? I don't think I ever asked you."

"No, you never have. It means *queen*, and having an African name doesn't mean I'm African, just like having an Italian name doesn't mean you can bake pizza."

"Are you kidding? You are going to fit right in over there. You can work your magic with your plants and things and perform miracles."

When she still didn't say she was willing to take the job, Marie said, "Well, if you're not going to do it for your heritage, do it for the money. I mean, Doctor Book, there are some serious financial obligations to deal with at the clinic, and it will take you a long time to get out of debt, if ever."

"We're not that bad off."

"Doctor Book, the other day I made some calculations, and it looks bad. This is your chance to get ahead and get a fresh start. Even with your doctor's salary, if we wait to get on your financial feet, it could be years. And that's with two jobs. You'll work yourself to death."

She did feel bad about the clinic's financial situation. The fundraising for the clinic had been a burden and robbed her of time. The prospect of running a fundraising campaign twice a year and writing grants for money to keep the lights on was overwhelming. When would she find the time to work with the sick if she was constantly fundraising?

"Look, Doctor Book, it's a big decision, sure, but you'd be working on a worldwide problem with a bunch of kids you'd walk across fire for anyway. You can do some more research into your little plants and mosses and think about it, I mean just think about it, Africa. The wide-open plains, elephants, zebra, fresh air and the sun swept savanna."

"Rain, malaria, amoebic dysentery, schistosomiasis, and snakes. Let's not forget the snakes."

"Come on, Doc, try to look at the bright side."

"Oh, I've been thinking about the sun. It gets hot in Africa."

"Thema, you were born for Africa."

"No, I was born in America."

"Come on, girl."

"If you love it so much, why don't you go."

"I'm not qualified, but apparently you are the chosen one."

Thema just shook her head.

"Well," Marie said, holding her phone up, right in

position to hit the dial keys, "Shall I call him? I mean it will be just like a vacation."

Thema couldn't imagine what it would be like over there. She wondered about the opportunity as she stood there in her worn kitchen that needed new appliances and a fresh coat of paint. She wagged her finger at Marie and took the phone from her before she dialed the number that held the key to their futures. No, she wasn't sure what it would be like over there, but she was sure it wouldn't be like a vacation.

****

Over the top of the tree line, above the dark jungle, a hundred miles to the east, the great Africa plain stretched to the horizon. The thick jungle lay to the south and west, open savannah to the north. The danger of fighting out on the open plain could have proven insurmountable, but Brother Denis reminded himself not to waste a lot of time worrying about that since the Mobassi administration's soldiers seemed to prefer raising havoc in the bush. The villages were full of evidence of death squads and rampaging former police. When Mobassi took command, he drove out the police administration and the security forces of the earlier government. The euphoria of new leadership and law and order only lasted a couple of months before the people realized the new leader harbored as vast a lust for securing his own fortune as the old one. And now, to make matters worse, many of the former police force had gone rogue and rampaged over the countryside with no security force in place to curb them. No, the battles to come will be in the bush right here.

Brother Denis found a place to sit and rest. Looking at the little rebel army he said, "I believe we could use a few more soldiers."

"Another handful," Mustafa said.

"Will the Buta come?"

"No, not yet."

"Well, it's a start."

"Yes, it's a good start," Mustafa noted. "Twenty already in camp and more arriving every day."

"They're so young."

"Yes, like that boy in your Bible."

"Which boy?"

"The story of the boy who fights the giant."

"Oh, you mean, David."

"Yes, yes, David, the boy king."

"But Mustafa, you must remember, God was on David's side.

"But Brother, is not your God on your side as well?"

****

After the moon set beyond the tree line, Brother Denis waited for his eyes to adjust, but even after nearly an hour he still couldn't make out his hand in front of his face. "Do you think he will come?" he asked Mustafa.

"Yes, he will come," the man answered.

"It has been some time now, at least a year, no?"

"He will come."

"Maybe he has abandoned the fight?"

"A man can never leave a fight."

"A man might not abandon a fight, but after a few years it is easy to forget what you fight for, even the stubborn. After time the reasons for fighting place a poor second behind the reasons for living."

"Careful my friend, you must remember," Mustafa advised, "these boys will follow us, but they will not die for us. We must give them a reason to die."

"They'll not be dying for us, Mustafa, I don't expect that. No, they must fight for their brothers, for their families, for their future, for you. I hope that is reason enough not to forget why you fight."

In the morning, the horizon beyond the eastern plain began to brighten in a red glow with the first rays of the day's new sun. Brother Denis marveled at the miracle each time. He wondered what the first thinking man created in this valley thought as he watched the ball of fire rise each day. Through the night did the man worry if he would see the sun again? Did he worry that the night might last forever? Did he pray then, pray that the light would come again? Did he promise his God that if the light did come, that he would be good? Did God give the first man thought so that the incomprehensible could be contemplated?

"There," Mustafa pointed into the valley below a narrow deep hog ridge.

A dozen or so figures in the shade of morning made their way in single file on a narrow path. They traveled in a half run, in a shuffling gait, approaching the hilly crest at the edge of the forest. Each teen carried a pack of equipment and held a weapon. A tall young man led the group and though he usually could be found to smile wide and full, on this day he only frowned.

****

"Okay," Thema told Mike Blanco when she called him. It had taken her a while, but considering everything, she knew it was one of those deals that were too good to pass up. "I'm in. I don't even want to think about the clinic for a while. I'm going to call Marie to fill her in on the details. I guess we'll have lots to do for the next few days…"

Over the next week, she busied herself with the preparations for the trip. She signed the contracts and took her shots on Monday and that afternoon she arranged a meeting with her hospital supervisor. She found the man smiling, though buried as usual behind a cluttered desktop. Already advised that she would be leaving her residency a little early, he acknowledged the administration's willingness to accommodate the MAM Foundation, especially since the foundation would be a new benefactor of the children's wing.

"Don't be silly," he said, waving off her concern with a flick of his wrist like he flicked ash from a cigarette, "We've had emergencies before that required us to bend a few rules. This is a terrific opportunity for you."

He sat low in his heavy desk chair that creaked audibly when he rocked back. "What a wonderful opportunity to tend to so many in need. Just what real medicine is meant to be," he explained. "I served with the Peace Corps in Kenya back in the late sixties, so I understand your trepidation, but it was one of the best times of my life."

"Yes, I think I heard someone say something about your service there."

"The Africa of old is quickly disappearing," he said, rather sadly. "Enjoy it while you can. I'm afraid it is losing much of its mystery and beauty and becoming just another festering Middle East."

Chapter Seven

After Tommy agreed to take the job with VSI, he started a list of things to do. First, he talked to his supervisor to tell him the news. Tommy apologized for not working out a long notice, but they'd manage to get along fine without him. His boss asked him about the gear in his locker, so Tommy told him to just give it away.

"Well, how about your extra uniforms?"

"Divide them among the guys."

"You may need them when you get back."

"Look, man, no offense, but when I get back, I am never going to go back into the security guard business. I'm going to be an architect if it is the last thing I do."

Tommy got up, shook the man's hand, and headed out of the basement where the staff offices were. He drifted out into the noon sunlight, closing the double doors behind him for what he hoped was the last time he ever used that employee entrance. He paused, then turned to face the tower building that housed patient floors. He never was good with goodbyes, and even though a few nurses may have appreciated a last word, he decided against it.

****

Brother Denis roused his little group of teen soldiers, and they formed a makeshift line, standing at a lax attention. The sun climbed steadily in the east and the day, not yet warmed by its coming, grew on. The newly arrived little party trotted into the forest clearing. The group leader stood tall for this region and had passed his mid-twenties birthday the summer before. He carried the big pack on his back and twenty scrawny teenagers followed him closely and no one spoke a word of greeting or curiosity.

"Sekou, my son!" Brother Denis greeted. "We did not expect you until midday."

"We met with no resistance," he said, coming to a stop and lowering the butt of the weapon he carried to the ground, "so we ran on through the night."

"That is pretty good time, my friend," Mustafa noted, greeting his comrade with a hug, "even for a man of the Masai."

"You speak good English for the son of a thieving Mandingo bush trader," Sekou retorted.

"And how is the cattle thief who fathered you?"

"He wanted to make this trip but the run along the falls trail would be too much for him."

Mustafa nodded. "It is better he didn't make this trip. He needs to save his legs for the later battles which I am afraid will not be taking place out on the field, but in the capitol."

"And how are you, Brother Denis?" Sekou asked. "Are you still wandering the bush and saving souls?"

"The Lord's work has no boundaries, my son. All we need to do is open our hearts."

"I don't know, Brother," he said with a smile and a hardy laugh, "last time I opened my heart some woman took a chunk and never returned it."

"Even so, Sekou, we are glad you came."

"Yes, Brother, although I wonder if this time will be

different."

"This time it is different."

"And so, they said this before."

"This time will be different, you see, we have developed a thorough plan."

"Still" he gestured about, "there is not much of an army here."

"Yes, and is this all that would come with you? I expected more."

"Brother," the man said, turning and waving a hand at his group of fighters, "this is all there is."

"All?" Brother Denis repeated, looking over the recently arrived recruits and noting a good many of them were young teenage girls.

"Yes, Brother. The days on the run have not been kind to my young charges."

"Are there no more boys among the tribe?"

"All the men and most of the older boys are dead, my friend, but do not worry, the young girls can carry more than enough gear and carry the burdens of their people as well."

"Still…"

"Remember, my friend, it is not whether a soldier is a boy or a girl, but whether they have a big enough heart for the fight."

"And do they?"

"Brother, if a people are to be measured by the size of their hearts, then my young comrades are great indeed."

****

The week sped along without pause and Thema wondered if she'd be ready in time. She kept busy packing and repacking the two trunks that VSI said she could ship. Those plus two suitcases. Not much for a year away. She'd never been a clothes person, preferring sweats and T-shirts, and for the last four years, mainly scrubs for working in various medical settings.

She spent Tuesday morning with a contractor at the clinic going over the renovations and he told her the company's construction division did quite a few medical offices and clinics and she'd get the best in modern planning and equipment. She finalized the construction contracts and pinched herself, making sure it was true. She couldn't imagine what a blessing it would be for the community.

After that she concentrated on the mechanics of subleasing her apartment, cleaning out the fridge, contacting her friends, and most importantly, completed the one-year schedule at the clinic.

On Wednesday morning she signed her VSI contract, and they deposited the first quarter's funding into the clinic's bank account and an advance on her salary into her personal account. When Thema counted the zeros behind the whole number it hit her that these people were serious. With money in the bank, she went shopping.

Thema grabbed her knapsack, locked the double locks, and skipped down the steps to the sidewalk. She pulled on headphones and strode three blocks to the bus stop and hopped on the number thirty-eight to the Army-Navy Store on Seventy-Second Street. Mike Blanco had told her the VSI was providing the supplies for the project, but she wanted to bring along a few personal items.

She remembered the army navy store carried a whole line of outdoor gear. The real stuff and not the fake stuff you saw in most places. Figuring she'd need a few outdoor things, she wanted to be prepared.

The streets flashed by and she rode to the beat of Jelly Roll's classic "Hesitation Blues." She must have dozed off because before she knew it, the bus pulled to a stop and the lurch of the brakes shook her awake. She opened her eyes and caught some dude eyeing her across the aisle, like checking her out. The dude looked away quickly when Thema caught him staring. She snuck a look at her reflection in the bus door window and winced at her clothes and natty hair. She wore her favorite sweats with pants that dragged the ground and needed washing three days ago. She meant to change out of them but in the excitement, she forgot about it. Although her hair was a mess now, she'd make sure to have Marie braid it tight for her before she left. Yeah, that would make sure she didn't have any African varmints roosting there in a new home.

Thema stepped off the bus to the beat of the *Crave* and headed north and found the army surplus store on the corner. She glanced both ways along the sidewalk and then entered. She grabbed a shopping cart and pushed it along an aisle of the store and began to fill it with gear she might need during the one-year sojourn in Africa. She began with the basics; a hunting sheath knife in case she had to skin a lion, a canteen in case she crossed a desert, a hiking lamp that you wrapped around your head in case she wanted to read at night, and some extra wool socks in case she went on a hike in the jungle. She already owned a pair of hiking boots, so she skipped that section of the store.

"How about a camo jacket?" the helpful store clerk asked her.

"What?" Thema said, trying to hear the man above the piano beat.

"A camo jacket?"

"Dude," she said, pulling the phones down around her neck with Jelly Roll, a faint melody, "I'm going to Africa not the South Pole."

"Girl, you'd better take a jacket. It gets cold at night in Africa."

"Dude, what part of Africa do you live in?"

"Listen, the Discovery Channel always has clips from Africa and although it's hot during the day those dudes are always bundled at night."

"Man," she responded, irked with the TV expert, "I already own a good coat. I'll make sure I carry it over."

"Then how about one of these water purification systems?"

"What for?"

"Girl, you can't drink the water over there right out of the river, unless you are fond of sitting on the john all day. You need to purify the water or boil it before you drink it."

"That bad?"

"Dysentery bad, my friend," he said and with emphasis he waved the box container with the pump purification system, "Unless..."

"Dude, I get it, I get it," she said, "but I'll just be drinking bottled water over there."

"How about a hat?"

"Un uh, I never wear hats."

"It gets hot in Africa, and nobody goes around without a hat of some sort."

"Oh yeah," she asked, "what kind of hat."

"I tell you, I have these old pith helmets the English

used to wear," he said leading the way down one of the aisles, "but they are heavy and hot as hell. But most people like these Australian skimmers, Crocodile Dundee type. They are supposed to be much better."

"Come on, man," Thema shafted the man, "what you going on about, the closest you ever been to Australia is the local steakhouse."

"Look, I'm just trying to help out."

"Well go on and find someone else to help out while I grab a few more things."

"Okay, okay, I'll be at the checkout."

Thema waited for the man to leave the aisle then put the hat on her head. She looked at herself in the nearby mirror and had to admit the Aussies had flair. She pitched the hat into the cart along with her other stuff. She walked to the end of that aisle and came back down the next, the one closest to the sidewalk windows. Heavy metal bars covered the street side windows, protecting the merchandise displayed there. The camouflage gear and an assortment of rifles, meant to attract the neighborhood customers, appeared safe enough. She looked through the window and caught a glimpse of a man out of place. A white man dressed preppy, certainly stood out in the neighborhood. Thema figured the man for a cop, but she had a hint of suspicion that she recognized the man from somewhere, but shook the feeling off since all white men looked the same to her.

Thema pushed the cart down the aisle and around another corner and headed to the checkout counter but remembered snakes. That area of central Africa was infamous for poisonous snakes, like the Black Mamba. With a vision of the ugly snake in her head, she swung the cart around. When she rolled her cart on another aisle she caught a glimpse of a man at the end of the row of first aid supplies. When he saw her, he stepped quickly out of sight, like trying to avoid being seen. Thema hustled to the end of the counter, but by the time she got to the corner to get a good look at him, the man had disappeared.

Glancing both ways, she found herself right in front of the first aid section of gear, so she started scanning over the inventory and saw a snake bite kit. The kit came in a plastic snap close box. There were several things inside including one of those suction cups, so it looked good enough for her. She had read that if a Black Mamba did bite her, no snake bite kit would help. For a lesser poisonous snake, it might come in handy.

Thema tossed it in with everything else and headed to the checkout counter and began to pull things out of the cart, piling stuff on the counter. The salesclerk didn't say anything when he waved the infrared scanner across the bar code of the hat.

"Got everything you need?"

"I hope so. There must be five hundred bucks worth of stuff there. What more do I need?"

"How about a gun?"

She took a step back. "A *what*?"

"Yeah, girl, a gun! I can get anything you want."

"Dude, I'm going over there to work in a clinic, not rob one."

"It's Africa, girl, everybody in Africa carries a gun."

"Dude, you…"

"Listen, girl," the clerk urged, "Africa is a dangerous place. Just turn the cable on if you don't believe me."

"Dude, even if I wanted one, there is no time. I'm

shipping out in a few days."

"Well, look, on the level. If you want a little Beretta automatic or a Glock, just say the word. I keep a private collection back in the office that requires no waiting period."

"Man, like I said," she tried to end the conversation by taking out her charge card and slapping it on the counter. "I am going over there to build a clinic. I don't think I'm going to have to worry about guns over there."

"That's what you say now."

****

When the sick of the local villagers heard that Brother Denis was near, they began to filter in for treatment. Used to providing rudimentary aid, he set up a makeshift clinic in an out of the way palaver hut under a wide limbed, heavily foliaged acacia tree sitting on the outskirts of the village in the shadow of the Kizi Mountains. The shade provided an oasis against the brutal sun above and the out-of-the-way location allowed a degree of privacy. He borrowed a table and a couple of rattan chairs from the village and set out his kit.

He didn't bring much besides several large bottles of penicillin and some alcohol. He packed along the normal bandages and aspirin. He carried a supply of chloroquine for malaria cases and some paregoric for dysentery. He really couldn't do much with their serious illnesses, but he could usually knock out an infection or a bug. The villagers brought the sickest to him first. One man sported a month-old infected wound. Brother Denis scolded him, in his simple native tongue, for not keeping the wound clean. He scrubbed it clean and gave him a big dose of penicillin. He warned the man that the wound wouldn't get better if he didn't keep the flies off it.

Later in the morning another young patient came with a similar wound, only fresher. The wound had been kept clean and well bandaged against infection. At first Brother Denis hadn't looked closely at his newest patient but when he looked to compliment the lad, he realized the lad wasn't a lad but a pre-teen girl. He still gave her a small dose of penicillin and after congratulating her on best practice sanitation methods, sent her on.

"Mustafa, my friend," Brother Denis addressed his comrade, "are we in a state now where just as many girls as boys will be fighting?"

"That was no girl, my brother, that was a soldier. One with battle scars as deep as any man, maybe deeper."

"Are there many?"

"Yes, many have answered the call to arms, some by volunteering others by force. I'm afraid the numbers of men and older boys have dwindled so that the girls are forced into their role. But do not worry, at this young age, the girls can be even stronger than the young boys."

Although many years had passed, the Buta tribe still waged war against the governing body of Central Africa. Six different administrations had come into power over the last thirty years; each of them had tried to wipe out the Buta. The tribe's ancestry was deep and had spawned many tributaries that flowed through the mountains and foothills of the Central African landscape, like rivers running downhill whose ebb may be slowed but not ended.

Brother Denis contemplated as he treated the sick and wounded. They needed a real doctor, not a poor nurse, he moaned to himself as he leaned into the work. When the sun finally set beneath the western forest tree line, Mustafa lit two gas lanterns so they could work on into the night.

****

Thema spent most of Thursday morning taking her final exams, although from the questions it was a foregone conclusion that she would pass and spent the afternoon at the clinic going over the accounts with Marie. Leaving the clinic in Marie's hands didn't worry her since Marie basically ran the place and took control of bill paying a year before. That night, she had dinner at Marie's and filled her in on the final details.

"Now, Marie," she counseled her friend as they sat in her small apartment in the Gardens, "you'll have to work around the construction but try to keep the clinic open at least a few hours every day. Maybe in the evening you can stay open a little later, like after the construction stops. The crews will likely knock off around three o'clock."

"I've been thinking we should stay open later," Marie said. "And now with the funding in place we could start that. Just a few hours at a time and then when the construction is completed and you are back in town, we could make it permanent."

"Good thinking."

Her friend began to tear up. "I can't imagine coming in every day and not seeing you."

"It's only for a year and I expect you to be another year closer to your degree. Besides I'm only a cell call away, so you can ring me occasionally and keep me posted. So don't worry about anything. I'll be back before you miss me."

"Sure." She smiled but it failed to reach her eyes. "It will be just like you're on vacation."

Chapter Eight

Mustafa led the small detachment of rebel children as they pecked their way on another seldom used trail. He made sure his young charges took care walking the trails and paths, teaching them to take a different route each time they ventured from village to village so their track and way couldn't be found. A few hours after stepping lightly through the thick underbrush, even the best of the Mandingo trackers couldn't follow.

"Mustafa," the young leader, Sekou asked the older man as they made their way through heavy vegetation, "we seem to be a bit short of ammo."

"I'm surprised you can still get ammo for those ancient AK-47s," he laughed, pushing through a low limb but careful to not mark it, "Those were left by the fleeing rebels in Uganda more than twenty-five years ago."

"We keep them clean," Sekou responded, "and in the bush, the weapon has proven it can perform under the conditions."

"Well, don't get anxious, only a few days more."

"Days? Are we not ready?"

"Almost ready," Brother Denis preached from the end of the line. "Remember, patience is a virtue."

"We've been fighting for ten years, Brother, isn't that patience enough?" Sekou asked.

"If you have fought for ten years to get to this day,

my son, then a few more days can be tolerated."

"But why?"

"Reinforcements are on route to complete the plan," Mustafa explained.

"Plan?" Sekou asked.

"Yes, my son," Brother Denis explained, "did you think we brought you to this moment so you can attack the palace gates with our handful of rabble, throwing rocks and sticks and yelling Allah!"

"Something like that, yes."

"No, no, my son," he said, continuing the hike through the deep underbrush, "this time there is a plan and the resources to make it work. It may take longer to put into action, but we will be more successful because of it."

"I hope it will be so, Brother, the palace gates are strong indeed."

"Oh, but my son, we are not going to the palace. The palace will come to us, and we will fight on the familiar ground of your ancestors."

"But Brother Denis, why will the administration come to us here?"

"Because, my son, because we possess a secret weapon, a valuable secret weapon."

****

Thema checked again for her passport, for at least the tenth time that Friday night.

"What are you looking for?" Maire asked her.

"My passport."

Thema had asked Marie to come over to distract her and help her settle her nerves. It was her last night, and she was feeling apprehensive.

"It's in your carry on," she said. "Exactly where you

put it ten minutes ago. Safely tucked into the inside pocket with your traveler's checks."

"Sorry," Thema said, smiling. "Just a little nervous I guess."

"I'd say. What you need is a good gang stabbing or gunshot wound to tend to. Something to settle your nerves."

"I *have* been out of my comfort zone. I like to be in charge of things and this deal, well, it's kind of running out front and it's like I'm trying to play catch up.

"I think I'll take these textbooks," she said, pulling from a shelf several of her reference texts, and putting them on the already crowded bed, "If I can squeeze them in."

Marie looked at Thema's gear and asked, "Do you really need those books? Isn't that kind of thing available online?"

"From what I understand, the internet won't be available, so I want to be prepared."

"What about this," Marie asked, holding a long wooden comb women used to tease out hair. "Don't you think the women in Africa are more into braiding?"

"Say, speaking of braids, how about you do my hair real tight."

Marie got behind Thema and started working her hair. "What is this other stuff for?" She asked Thema, when she saw a box of decorative jewelry Thema had out.

"I might need that, and what I don't use might come in handy as gifts and trinkets for the natives."

"What about that?" Marie asked, stopping to pull a small leather charm from the pile.

"That's something I've had since I was a baby. A

good luck charm."

"Okay, look," she said, pulling on her hair. "You've got one suitcase filled with long pants and sweaters. Now, I'm no expert but I think it's mostly hot over in Africa so I think you could take out about half of those and then you'll have room for your books. Then again, wouldn't there be some reference material there already?"

"So far, I haven't received much information. In fact, all I've received is a few shots and a wad of money. It seems a little amateur to me."

"What did you expect?"

"I expect a plan or schedule or something. I'd like an inventory of the clinic, and some construction plans for the new building too."

"You just worry about patients and childhood nutrition. Let them worry about the hospital, I'm sure they'll have an architect or someone along."

"And where will I be seeing patients until that happens?"

"I'm sure there's something there, clinic or straw hut or something."

"I hope so. I don't want to get there and work under a Baobab tree."

"What kind of tree?"

"The Baobab tree. It grows in that part of Africa and has many medicinal qualities. I can't wait to get there and study its many uses."

"Well, don't worry," she said, continuing to braid, "I'm sure they are carrying over the equipment you'll need."

"I just don't want to forget anything."

"Thema, you've got everything, there's nothing

more to do. Look, it's still early, as soon as I'm done here, let's go out for dinner and get a drink."

"I'm not ready.".

"After I'm done with these braids, you are ready, and you are starting your vacation."

****

After stuffing himself with chicken pie and greens Tommy began to say his goodbyes to the house full of relatives and started to work his way to the door and outside to the waiting van. The big family going away party reminded him of the sendoff he got when he shipped out to basic training ten years ago. Everyone was older this time but still shared the same mixture of happiness and worry for him.

In the back of the airport van, two other trunks and two suitcases crowded in the space. "Whose gear is this?" Tommy asked the driver as he helped him load his stuff.

"This is Doctor Book's stuff."

Then Tommy remembered. Mike had said there was going to be a doctor along on the trip. He'd completely forgotten. When he stepped around to the front of the van, he planned to get into the front passenger seat but when he found someone already sitting in that seat, he climbed into the back seat. "Hello, Doctor Book."

She turned and greeted him, "Mr. Foster?"

"That's me," he said, surprised that it was a pretty lady in the front seat. Mike told him there'd be a doctor on the job, but he didn't say it was a pretty woman. "You're a doctor?"

"Last I checked. Do you have a problem with female physicians, Mr. Foster? Or women in general?"

"No, no, I love women, I'm just surprised. Mike

didn't say anything about a woman doctor."

"Oh, are you and Blanco friends and share the same opinion of women?"

"Yes, we did play ball together, but I wouldn't want to say what his view of women is."

"Wait, you're Tommy Foster, the ex-college quarterback who works security at Mercy Hospital."

"I did, until I took this job."

"I'm one of the residents, or should I say, I just finished my residency. I've heard about you."

"How did you hear about me?"

She smiled. "I couldn't help but hear the nurses talking."

He wondered what type of gossip the nurses had spread about him and wondered if the mission to Africa, with the pretty doctor along, might just include romance. "So, Doc, how did Mike talk you into this job?"

"He said it would be just like a vacation."

****

Mike Blanco watched a burly young man checking gear spread across the airport hangar's floor beneath a huge retrofitted 747 emblazoned with the block MAM logo. The man took a plain black pen from one of two matching flapped breast pockets of his beige military style jacket. He flipped through several invoices attached to a big clip board with the words "Airport Maintenance Only" painted on the back side.

"Does this completel the gear?" Mike asked the man, working his way through a mental list of items he put together earlier in the week when the project got the go ahead, hoping he hadn't forgotten anything. Three other men worked around him carrying bags and hauling crates. They worked quickly and in silence with the burly man relaying instructions to the men with hand signals although the absence of noise in the giant hangar didn't require it. As he checked the items off the list the men lifted each item onto a conveyor belt that carried the article into the plane's cargo bay. Two other men, already on board, grabbed the items off the conveyor and stowed them away somewhere inside the big belly of the plane.

"So, is this going to do it?" Blanco asked. Though Blanco stood six foot two he always seemed to look up at the man. He couldn't tell if he stood taller or did the boots the man wore give him an edge.

"This is the last of it for now," he answered. "The supplies are packed in the storage area. What we couldn't cram on board will follow by C-130 transport."

"Where are the medical supplies?"

"We loaded them first. Enough to handle any circumstance. I wouldn't want to go into this action without medical."

"Good, now if our two birds will show up we can get on our way."

"What's their ETA?"

"They should be pulling into the airport now," Blanco said, checking his watch to make sure of the time. "How long will it take to get off the ground?"

"We'll be pulling out ten minutes after they arrive."

"Who's flying this bucket?"

"Captain Johnson, he's an old pro."

"Is he aware of the mission?"

"He's worked for VSI before."

"How about the crew?"

"The same," the man said, "they've been over before and are familiar with the process. What about customs when we land?"

"What customs," Blanco said, but it wasn't a question. "Ah," he nodded toward the hangar doorway, "here comes the good doctor now."

The airport van pulled into the hangar and approached the waiting plane. Blanco stepped to the door and slid it open.

"Why are you parked way round back here?" Thema shouted above the noise from an airport pushback tug starting to get into position to maneuver the plane out of the hangar.

"We are loading the supplies for the mission."

"This is quite an operation," Tommy noted.

"It's a well-oiled machine," Blanco said, moving off to help with the luggage from the back of the van. "MAM runs crews out of the airport a couple of times a month, so the company has the experience now."

"Is this a cargo plane?" Thema called out to the man checking off items.

"Mostly," he explained. "We've packed in quite a bit of equipment, but the plane has a couple of nice forward passenger cabins with all the comforts and two flight attendants. There's a bar and even a couple of beds just in case you get sleepy."

"And what is it you do?" Thema asked the man.

"I'm part of the construction crew," the man said. "I'll be working for you."

"Isn't Mr. Foster going to build the clinic?"

"Mr. Foster is going to design the clinic and supervise the construction. I am going to run the crew. I'm experienced working with the native population."

"You are, are you?"

"Yes, I've built quite a few things in Africa."

"What else do you do for this outfit?"

"Anything I can do to help out."

"He's the best," Blanco interrupted, moving the conversation along. "Well, let's get on board. It will be a long flight, and we'll want to get going."

"So, what do you think about this project, Mr. Blanco," Thema asked.

"Call me Mike."

"Okay, Mike, what do you think about going over to some jungle to build a clinic? What makes you think you can get it done?"

"I've been working for VSI for a while, and they never start a project they can't complete. This one is no different. We'll get it done."

A walk-up ramp connected the forward door to the hanger floor, and they climbed the long steep steps. Blanco stopped at the top of the platform to turn and look at the hanger floor to make sure they didn't leave anything behind. He didn't really understand how the different pieces were fitting together on this mission. On the surface it looked like a simple job, but in this line of work, looks could definitely be deceiving. No, he couldn't see the broader scope of the mission, but whatever it was, *it wouldn't be a vacation!*

Chapter Nine

After Thema and Tommy Foster stepped aboard the custom jumbo jet, they found themselves in a forward cabin furnished with an assortment of big chairs and a sofa. Tommy made his way to a more conventional row of seats and a pretty flight attendant directed him to a row with two first class size seats. "You and Doctor Book are sitting here."

Tommy wasn't about to argue about the seating arrangements. He could think of few nicer things than sitting next to the good-looking doctor for the next twelve hours.

"Ladies and gentlemen," a pretty brunette in a tight blue flight attendant looking outfit announced, "we'll be taxing to the runway in a few minutes, waiting in line before takeoff. We'll be serving a full dinner menu in a few hours, but in the meantime for your convenience there are complimentary beverages and snacks at the bar in the companionway between the two cabins. Please take advantage and we hope to be on our way shortly."

"Ah, Doc, I'm just going to get a little something for the nerves," Tommy said. "Can I get you something?"

She flipped the page of the in-flight magazine in her hand before giving him a glance. "No, I'm good."

Tommy sauntered back to the companionway. He counted out eight or so other passengers in the rear cabin and found a pretty blonde behind a counter dispensing copious amounts of liquor to other nervous looking passengers. He quickly joined the line behind several big men who dominated the entire space.

"What can I get you, Mr. Foster?" the blonde behind the counter asked after the men finally got their drinks and cleared out of the way.

"Rum and coke," he answered and downed the drink in one big gulp, then signaled for the blonde to start making another one.

"Ladies and gentlemen, this is your captain," an announcement came over the speakers. "We're loaded and set to take off," he said in a thick country drawl. "We'll be getting this big bird off the ground real shortly. Please make sure your little behinds are in your seats and prepare and pray for this takeoff. Our non-stop time in the air will be about twelve hours, depending on wind, putting us on the ground at nine hundred hours, ah that's nine o'clock, for the un-military types. The weather for tomorrow is going to be damn hot and damn humid. You all enjoy the flight. Flight attendants, pretty ladies, make sure everything's ship shape back there."

When Tommy got back to his row, he found Mike Blanco talking with Doctor Book. "You two look comfortable," he said.

"Just keeping your place warm," Blanco said with a big smile, then added, "Did you get yourself a little fortification?"

"Just something for the nerves." He motioned to Blanco to get out of his seat. "Now, if you don't mind."

"No trouble, brother," Blanco said. When he slipped past Doctor Book he said to her, "Just remember, whatever you need, ask me."

While Tommy got situated, the flight attendants

scrambled about the cabin, checking that the passengers had their seatbelts buckled for takeoff. Tommy noted the plush passenger cabin, in comparison to normal commercial accommodations. "What was Mike going on about?" he asked Thema.

"He was filling me in on the project timeline. I mentioned to him earlier that I was worried about the lack of a timetable, so he was telling me what plans they had made."

"Any plans for the clinic?"

"I'm sure there will be a construction schedule."

The brunette flight attendant cruised through the cabin, gathering the unsecured carry-on bags. She snatched Tommy and Thema's extra cases and moved quickly to the rear cabin to stow them in an out-of-the-way place. They dispensed with the seatbelt and emergency exit talk, but one of the ladies asked them to please read the emergency card instructions located in a pocket on the back of the seat in front of them.

The big plane taxied out from behind a row of hangers and joined a waiting line of departing passenger planes. The line moved quickly and before Tommy could arrange for one of those small pillows for his head the plane began to gain momentum. Thema's hand reached over and dug into his hand. When he turned to look, her eyes were clinched closed. As the runway sped by, the plane lifted into the air.

"My God," Thema said, letting go of Tommy's hand. "What in the world have I gotten myself into?"

Don't worry Doc. It's going to be just like a vacation.

****

Tommy remembered pulling his headphones on and

putting his head back but not going to sleep. He awoke with a stiff neck, a sore throat, and was hungry since he slept through the dinner meal as well. Having stuffed himself at his mother's house an hour before take-off, he fell right to sleep when his head rested on the seat back.

The air in the cabin had dried out his mouth and he didn't wait for an attendant. Pulling his headphones off, he undid his seatbelt and struggled up. He stepped over a sleeping Doctor Book and ambled off in search of a drink. He plodded forward in the dark cabin and found the two attendants behind a heavy curtain in a brightly lit galley area. The two were holding court with Mike and another man.

"Mr. Foster," the blonde attendant greeted him as he came through the curtain. They had been laughing about something, but they didn't share what with him. "Can I get you something?"

"A drink!"

"Bourbon and cola?"

"No, just some water this time, my throat's dry as a city sidewalk in August, probably from my snoring."

"Why do you think we are back here?" Mike joked and they started laughing again.

"Here you are, Mr. Foster. Here's a couple bottles" she said, handing him two ice cold bottles of water. "Don't pay any attention to the comedian here, you weren't snoring as far as I could tell."

"Who's your friend?" Tommy asked Mike after emptying half the bottle of water in a couple of big gulps.

"This is Bobby Raines, he's one of the construction crew."

"How are you," Tommy asked, extending his hand. Raines shook his hand and Tommy tried not to wince from the strong and heavily calloused grip. The man stood two inches taller than Tommy and weighed over fifty pounds more. Raines would make a good tackle on a number of pro teams, better than those tackles he had back in college that contributed to the condition of his bad knee.

"Man, where are you from?"

"Kansas," Raines answered."

"You play ball?"

"I played for a couple of years at a small school in the south, Furman."

"Did you play defense?"

"I played on the line, but it wasn't that exciting. I mean, it wasn't like quarterbacking or anything."

Tommy didn't react to the reference to being a quarterback. This group knew a lot about everything, so his college playing days wouldn't be a secret.

"I was a cheerleader," the brunette attendant volunteered.

"Oh yeah," Tommy said, as the attention turned to her, "where did you go to school?"

"I attended Alabama, and it was just divine there."

"It was," Tommy asked. "What did you like best?"

"The fraternity parties!" she answered and then smiled big.

That made the group start laughing again and Tommy took the opportunity to separate himself from the little pep rally and head back to his seat.

Tommy worked his way back to the darkened cabin. He noticed most of the passengers spread out in a variety of sleeping positions. By the crowd of bodies, he thought it looked like about twenty. He wondered how many people it would take to build this clinic. With that many people you could build a whole village.

When he returned to his row, he climbed over a still sleeping Doctor Book.

"Stretching your legs?" she asked after he brushed against her leg.

"I got a dry throat so got something to drink."

"Yeah, me too."

"Yes, it is sure dry in here. Oh here," Tommy offered, remembering he had an extra bottle of water in his hand.

She broke the seal on the bottled water and took three or four big slugs. Tommy watched her throat move as she gulped. "Thanks," she said, showing Tommy a big smile. "Look, call me Thema, I'm not used to Doctor Book yet."

"Doc, from what I hear, you deserve the doctor thing."

"What do you mean?"

"There was some stuff going around the hospital about you."

"Like what?"

"That you're a miracle worker."

"That's the training, Foster, just the training."

"So, what's your specialty?"

"It's family medicine and I've been working in an inner-city clinic."

"Wow, that's a missionary type thing if I ever heard of one. Is that how they talked you into this gig?"

"I have a soft spot for kids."

"I hear you."

"And they threw some heavy money my way."

"That helps."

"So," she said, "you're a long way from a football

field."

"You heard about my football playing days?"

"The nurses talked all about your playing days."

After a pause Tommy said, "Is there anything the nurses didn't talk about? And how is it, I never ran into you? I think I ran into everyone at Mercy."

"It's a big place, Foster, you couldn't get around to scoring a touchdown with every nurse there. So, what happened with football?"

"Oh, it was never a lifelong plan, playing football."

"I guess it's a long shot for most college players. What happened?"

"Second year on the squad I hurt my knee. They kept me on scholarship until I recovered, but by then it was too late for college ball, so I joined the army."

"So, how's the knee now?"

"Well," Tommy said, "it was back to normal until an IED tore into it in Afghanistan."

"That's tough."

"Well, if everything works out on this job, I might finish college."

"Architecture, right?"

"Right."

"So," Thema asked him, "what do you think about the mission?"

"I was reluctant at first," he answered truthfully, not sure how much of the mission he should disclose. "But they caught me in transition and talked me into it"

"Me, too. With my soft spot for kids and the project's main goal in childhood nutrition, it seemed like a promising idea."

"When I first agreed, it was about the money and a chance to start over, but now, the back to the roots thing is growing on me. That and I like to build things. I'm not an architect, but close enough, and then my military experience counted, too."

"Why?"

"I guess because the administration over there is a military one so it might come in handy."

"Do you think there is still some military trouble over there?"

"Mike said that's one of the reasons they wanted me. I was in intelligence."

"No one said anything to me about an ongoing conflict. Mike said everything was under control over there."

"I'm sure it is, Doc, I wouldn't worry about it. It should be just like a vacation."

"Well," Thema said, settling back into the big seat, "I'd better get some sleep, we'll have long day ahead of us tomorrow."

Tommy leaned back in his seat. Pulling on his headphones he checked his device for a new music track. Gazing out the window with the clouds streaming by, he marveled that in a few hours they'd be in Africa. Pretty cool stuff and with the pretty Doc and the support staff along on this mission, it might turn out to be just like a vacation after-all.

Chapter Ten

Brother Denis walked them through the night. The tired group never slowed even though, in addition to their normal load, they bore a variety of recovered arms and ammunition.

Heavy burdens—even for grown men.

"Mustafa," Brother Denis directed as they entered the town of Bonga, "have the party store the cache of supplies close by. Check if there is a hut available. I want to make sure we can always get at what we need. Plus, I expect a restock in a day or two."

Brother Denis then made his way to a thickly thatched palaver hut on the edge of town where many in the rebel group were already settling into sleep. He grabbed a stick and poked the embers of a dying fire and brought it back to life. He threw some more wood on the blaze and when banked, put on a big pot. One of the older girls came over to him and after shooing him off, filled the pot with water from an earthen jug. He pulled a burlap sack from a stack of supplies and handed it to her. She used a pint-size, leftover tomato can to measure out rice for the whole crew. Denis set out several large cans of mackerel and a small pouch of hot green peppers which he would add to the rice pot just before it set up.

"I wish we had some fresh meat instead of that canned trash," he said to Mustafa as the girl opened the cans with the point of a large knife. "The boys deserve better."

"One day, my fine Christian friend. But isn't it so that your ancestors lived on fish and bread? It must be a true sign the heavens are in alignment for our little venture."

"What are you talking about?"

"It is a sign, my friend. Your God partakes of the fish of the sea—and so do we. He partakes of the grain of the land—and so are we. He came to the world to bring the truth—and so will we. I tell you my fine Brother, the signs in Heaven couldn't be clearer that our little cause is both just and ordained."

"Mustafa, my friend,"

The big man smiled. "Yes, Brother Denis?"

"Sometimes you can be so full of …"

"Is that all?"

"No, send one of the girls to the village to find someone who can spare a little salt for our divine last supper."

The girl took a wooden spoon and stirred the rice pot. She threw in the peppers and after opening the cans added the fish. A second girl came back with the salt which was added by a palm full to the mixture. The pot was stirred again before it was pulled off to set on the side of the hearth where only a few light embers fell.

"So, my friend," Sekou asked when he approached the two men and squatted at the fire, "how much longer?"

"Twenty minutes or so," Brother Denis responded.

"No, I mean how long before our first action?"

"Oh, well, two, maybe three days."

"How many?"

"Two or three days, maybe more, maybe less."

"Why so?" he asked.

"We took a patrol two days ago. Just a small truck and four men. Caught them by surprise but we aren't ready for anything bigger. We might be able to take out a truck or two but not a whole column. We need a couple of days to settle in. If we can keep the boys under cover for a few days until we get a chance to bring in a few other fighters, we might get a chance at a bigger column."

"Any word from the Buta?" the young man asked, kneeling at the fire.

"No not yet but it is early," Mustafa said. "In the meantime, we could use the time to train the new recruits."

"Yes," Denis said, "We need to gather enough men and supplies to make a real fight of it. No telling how Mobassi will react to a little insurrection. If we can take out another patrol, we might get his attention."

"Will it be enough?" Sekou asked, picking up a stick and poking the fire, causing sparks to fly.

"Enough to make some noise," Mustafa admitted. "We can meet the patrols out at the Juarzon River bridge. It's a bottleneck."

"Yes," Brother Denis agreed, "we can dig in along the road. The bush is very thick there."

"Perfect!" Sekou agreed, stepping back from the growing flames, "Could be a real surprise, of course, it would be nice if I had more men."

"Once the word gets out that you will be making your stand in Bonga the men will come," Brother Denis explained, scooting away from the heat. "We'll be ready by then."

"How many men do you think we will need?" Sekou

asked.

"Oh, for the road ambush we can get it done with what we have. The next skirmish or two we might need a few more. Mobassi's army is not large and poorly trained, and we are far away from the capital. My sources say altogether about four companies with a thousand men. But he can't send them all and leave the south and the capital unprotected. After our first ambush he might send a platoon with forty men. We'll take that group at the bridge too. He might send two platoons after that. Maybe even the rest of the company, another two hundred men.

"Two hundred men," Mustafa said, followed by a low whistle.

"Perhaps," Brother Denis added, rearranging the coals in the fire pit. "It is hard to tell. Mobassi will send the big guns eventually. It would be bad press in the world news if he can't keep the peace in his own backyard."

"We'll need more men, my friend," Mustafa said.

"You don't sound confident."

"I'll sound more confident when we get more men, especially the Buta men."

"By the time the real fight starts we'll have the men."

"How do you know this," Sekou asked.

"Because of our secret weapon."

****

At about five a.m., the sun rose over the eastern horizon and started to break through cloud cover that turned a deep purple against the dark continent of Africa. Tommy opened his eyes and through his little porthole window got his first glimpse of his ancestral home.

Somewhere down there his people first popped their little heads out of the jungle and some dudes, looking to score big by selling some cheap slave labor to the white folk back home, took them captive.

"Are we there yet?" Thema asked, shaking her head.

"Probably close, another couple of hours or so," he said, removing the headset. "Take a look at this sunrise."

"Wow, is that Africa?"

"That's it. Somewhere, in the dark, in the dark continent of *Africa*. It gives me a funny feeling in the stomach."

"I got a feeling, too," she said, "but it's not about ancestors. Where's the loo?"

****

Thema jumped when the captain's smooth southern drawl boomed over the overhead speakers. "Passengers and crew, we are arriving at our destination. The weather looks tough right now, currently heavy rain with high wind. Better get on back into your seats and buckle in, it could be a rough ride. Reports from the ground tower advise wind shear at fifty knots but don't you all worry none, I've seen worse."

Thema leaned over Tommy to peer through the airplane window into a thick gloom and watched a rich green land appear below. She could make out a river snaking through the forest canopy as it wound its way to the coast. In the distance the rich green forest gave way to the wide-open brown savannah of eastern Africa but underneath them, she didn't observe much of a break in the vegetation for landing such a big plane.

"Looks like a jungle out there."

"Ah, yeah," Tommy agreed. "It's Africa."

"Where's that sunshine for the frolicking they talked

about?"

"Be patient, we'll hit the ground soon enough."

"Poor choice of words," she said, buckling her seat belt and pulling it snug.

Thema peered at the spec of an airfield the Corps of Royal Engineers built during World War II. In her research in preparation for this adventure, she read that the British Army made a variety of infrastructure improvements in the country, including bridges and the air strip in case the War overran the South Pacific and threatened Australia. Since then, the various airlines that used the strip modernized it and provided for its minimal maintenance.

The 747 swayed in the stiff wind that swept the little field. The wind roared about the plane and the interior lights flickered. The engines revved higher and then tailed off as the pilot began the descent. A series of turbulence hit the plane, and it dropped fifty feet in a second or two. Thema could almost hear the pilot yelling, *whoa baby*, in the cockpit. As the sound of whining engines filled the cabin, she gripped her arm rest and dug her nails into its surface. She looked around the cabin and from where she sat everyone else appeared calm about the whole thing.

Thelonious Monk filtered from Tommy's headphones as the whine of the landing gear moving into position sounded out. When the thud of the 747's tires hitting the runway echoed in the cabin, a short but enthusiastic cheer broke out. From their porthole window Thema watched the ground speed by and eventually the pilot hit the brakes, and the plane began to slow. Thick bush crowded the perimeter of the narrow runway. Several gaunt bull cattle stood on the edge of the black top gazing lazily as two small boys with long sticks kept watch.

Welcome to Africa.

"Ah, ladies and gentlemen," the captain announced as the plane taxied on the runway, "thank you for your patience and welcome to Mobassi Field. Sorry about the little excitement there; we managed to bring her around into the wind and brought her down. Hope you all enjoyed your flight over and we look forward to seeing you all again real soon. Please remain seated until this baby has come to a full stop at the terminal."

Thema scanned the low-profile cement block building standing about fifty yards from the edge of the runway. As the only building in the area, she assumed it served as the airport's terminal. No fancy stores and coffee shops here. She didn't figure the building would be featured in any issue of *Architecture Today.*

The ground crew pushed an airport ramp to the exit door and Thema realized they would be deplaning right onto the black tarmac. She noticed several armed soldiers stationed at various spots around the airport grounds. The attendant moved down the aisle, dispensing warm wash cloths from a tray and advised everyone to go ahead and make a trip to the plane's restrooms as the facilities on the ground were just barely adequate.

"What did she say?" Tommy asked.

"They said to freshen up, looks like we'll be getting off soon. As soon as they chase the zebras out of the way."

"What?"

"Nothing, I'm just rambling."

As if on cue the long-legged attendant appeared with

their carry-on luggage. Thema took one of the bags, joined several other passengers, and shuffled to the freshening facilities scattered about the plane.

****

"Are you ready to get going?" an approaching slender brown skinned woman asked Tommy. He figured the lady with enchanting green eyes was in charge of something. She wore a lightweight beige business suit, and her long hair was pulled straight back into a ponytail. He wondered if she straightened her hair or did that come from white blood circling through her veins. That might explain the flowing hair and *café-au-lait* complexion.

"I'm sorry?"

"I said, are you ready to go?

"Who the heck are you?

"Oh, I'm Annette Monson, I'm with…"

"Don't tell me," Tommy said, getting a good look at her, "you're with the team."

"Yes, I am. Where's Doctor Book?"

"She's freshening," he told her and plopped a floppy hat atop his recently shaved head.

"So, what's up?" Thema said to them when she returned from the lavatory.

Tommy saw she'd changed into a clean white blouse with those little flaps over the pockets and epaulets atop the shoulders, sort of safari chic.

"Doctor Book," the lady greeted and shook her hand. "I'm Annette Monson; I'm with the forward team that oversees communications, passports and press relations, and all."

"I'm pleased to meet you."

"No, Doctor, we are so pleased to meet you. Every

81

member of the team is thrilled to be on this mission with you. We are just so impressed with your work in your clinic and expect you'll generate a significant impact with the mission."

"Why, I hope so. Thank you for the confidence."

"Doctor Book…"

"Please, call me Thema."

"Oh Doctor, thank you and back in the states I would be delighted to, but we like to keep a level of formality here. It helps the group if we stay formal and hopefully professional. The local government appreciates the pomp and frills of important people, and we like to give it to them."

"Does that mean," Tommy asked, "I have to put on my shoes?"

"Oh, and just a heads up, Doctor Book," she said, ignoring Tommy, "there will be a small press conference after we get in."

"Press conference?" Thema asked.

"As such, yes," Monson continued. "The Mobassi people are very anxious to greet you and welcome you to the homeland to help rebuild the country. It's a happy story for the new administration here. Help them reverse some of the negative press going around. It is an important day for the regime. A chance to turn a negative into a positive."

"Of course." Tommy weighed in with a smile. "They might get a little more mileage if they stopped that Tutsi Hutu thing. I think that might work too."

Monson turned on him. "Mr. Foster, we need to be careful of the tone we take here. The tribal conflict is not black and white, and it is not inherent here. There has been wrong on both sides of that history and the Tutsi and Hutu refugees are only two tribes in a wider problem. What this country needs is someone to unify them, not more conflict between the sides that really are more alike than different."

She turned back to Thema. "But no worries, Doctor Book, the press corps is small, someone from the foreign ministry of course, then maybe one or two representing the international wire services. Remember it's the show that's important, not necessarily the substance."

"Well, if that's the case," Tommy said, "I'm going to fit right in."

Chapter Eleven

Thema noticed a line forming near the plane's forward exit as they worked their way over. The pilot's cabin door slid open and a stout man in a white shirt sporting captain's wings came out and started to say good-bye to everyone. Inside the cockpit, another pilot sat at the controls, pushing buttons and adjusting instrument things.

"Hello, hey, how's it going," Captain Johnson greeted those standing right before the doorway, shaking hands quickly, patting the men on their backs, squeezing the women's shoulders. "Everybody okay, sorry about the excitement coming down. Little bumpy there but we didn't lose anyone, did we?" Johnson stepped in front of the first person in line and swung the handle of the door round and about. "I think the rain has eased, at least long enough to get to the terminal."

The door broke its seal and popped open with a flush of air. He pushed it out and it swung away easily clearing the passageway. The damp African humidity flooded into the cabin and hit her like a wet blanket.

"Who turned on the heat!" Thema said aloud when the warm air smacked her in the face.

"Welcome to Africa," Mike Blanco laughed. "Here, let me help you with those bags."

Before she could protest, he snatched her carry-on bags and skipped out the door and took the ramp stairs to the ground.

Thema lugged camera cases toward the door but tripped on the exit ramp threshold. The captain caught her under the arm before she tumbled completely over. "Take it easy there, partner!" he joked, helping to get her stable. "Do you need a pack mule for that load?"

"I got it," she assured him and noticed the captain sported cowboy boots. "Say, captain dude, you handled that landing like a pro."

"Do them all the time, Doc," he answered as he waved goodbye to departing passengers. "Just last week I came close to losing one over the harbor in Cape Town, but I saved her at the last minute and brought it in. Talk about exciting."

Thema stepped out onto the platform, followed by Tommy, and they began the decent to the surface below.

"Everyone, everyone," Annette Monson directed the team into a line as they hustled fifty meters in a light rain to the terminal looking building, "take out your passports. It's just a formality, really, but make sure they are ready just the same. The airport customs desk likes to show how important their job is—so bear with them. We've already been cleared by the administration."

"Yo, Annette," Thema called, trying to get her attention. They were walking fast, and she struggled to keep pace with her load. The rain drenched them out on the black top and poured from her head. Steam came off the runway in thin waifs. "Yo, talking girl!"

Annette turned. "Yes, yes, Doctor Book, what is it?"

"Will they be searching through our luggage?"

"No, no," she explained, "they never do, why?"

"What's with you?" Tommy asked as they walked in the rain.

"I don't want them looking through my stuff. I don't like the look of these people. Armed soldiers, nappy headed airport crew, cowboy Roy in the cockpit. For some organization that is supposed to be top notch, they sure are missing on a couple of cylinders."

"Now, Doc," Tommy said, as they trudged along under the rain. "They just finished fighting a war here. Let's give the locals a break, okay?"

"Didn't Mike Blanco say they were way over that?" she retorted, looking around again and not liking what she saw. "There is no reason for these guns."

The group marched to the terminal and entered through the doors where they were met with even more stifling heat. The absence of air conditioning surprised Thema, but at least the rain didn't pelt them indoors.

"Ladies and gentlemen, ladies and gentlemen," a uniformed soldier with a lot of brass called out to them as they came into the building. "If you please, you must retrieve your luggage and move to the custom tables for inspection."

Thema looked at Tommy and rolled her eyes.

Before the group broke ranks, Annette rushed to the side of the officer and passed him an envelope. The officer smiled, saluted her before turning away and walking off.

"Everyone, yes everyone. Now—" Annette stopped to take a breath and continued with a big smile. "—now you don't need your luggage, but please get in line for a passport check, then you can claim your bags and head to the exit. Outside, there is a row of Land Rovers at the curb. We need to get everyone out there as soon as possible. Four to a vehicle with the construction team and Doctor Book in the three lead vehicles. The drivers and the boys will put your luggage on the top carriers."

The team formed a single file behind Mike Blanco who had somehow managed to be at the head of the line.

"Doctor Book?" Annette called.

"Yes, right here."

"Could you come with me? They arranged a room over there for a brief statement and questions."

Thema followed Annette. They entered a small dull gray painted room, more a closet than anything, and stepped to a beat-up wooden podium. Monson stood just to her side. In this room a window air conditioning unit churned out enough cool air to keep the small room bearable. Five or six people, sporting press badges around their necks, sat at a long fold-up table. One ancient looking television camera—which Thema doubted even worked—stood at the ready.

"Gentlemen," Ms. Monson began, "Dr. Thema Atsu-Book has agreed to make a statement and then take some questions. Dr. Book?"

"First off," Thema began after she took a position behind the podium, "I'd like to say thank you to the Administration of Health for letting us come on this mission. It is a wise and concerned government that realizes the importance of public health for their people. By allowing us to bring the needed health resources to the village people of Masango it shows the world that even though the new government has its challenges ahead it agrees that the public health of its people is at the top of the list of things to do. Thank you for allowing us to help in our small way.

"On another, personal note, thank you for welcoming me. Although this is my first visit to Africa, I find it feels quite familiar, and I hope to help the people through this year ahead. My knowledge of the country and people may be limited at this moment, but let me assure you, I will be doing everything I can to make my stay successful for everyone."

Appearing unimpressed, the media table sat expressionless. Thema attributed the lack of response to the language difference since the former British colony, and most people, still spoke a sing-song dialect of the old-world brogue.

"Doctor Book?" a Black gentleman raised his hand, "May I ask how you feel about your place in the new revolution and what we are trying to do?"

She nodded. "Of course, my only expertise is in medicine. I committed one year to this project, in one village, and no more. The rest of the country's hard work will be in capable hands. I'm afraid all we can do is work on the clinic project and make that one piece successful."

"Doctor Book, if you please," another asked. "Is this only an isolated project for Medical African Missions, or are they prepared to bring more aid as needed?"

"Again, I am only a doctor, but of course the success of this one project should bear on any decision to offer more, both for MAM and the current administration."

"I can expand on that," Annette chimed in as she stepped to Thema's side at the podium. "Medical African Missions is prepared to make a multi-year commitment to the country here. There could be many more clinic projects if the administration feels it is worthwhile. Also, MAM is proposing to include schools in its building program if the administration agrees."

"Doctor Book," a third media person asked, "I should think it is perfectly clear that the only reason your mission received an invitation to come here is because you are a Black American. How do you think the people of Masango, and the country should accept you?"

"I hope as a doctor first and a friend second."

"But isn't it true you are being paid to work here for this year?"

"Yes, it is. But let me say, I would not have taken any other job in Africa for any amount of money except this one, with the chance to work in childhood nutrition."

"Ah, forgive me Doctor Book, one other question," the same media rep asked. "Since Masango is on the very edge of the resistance that so threatens this government, even as we sit here, what do you hope your presence will mean to the people there?"

"I'm not sure," Thema started to answer, surprised at the question, and turning to Annette Monson continued, "but as I said, we are strictly concerned with building the clinic and serving the people of Masango. We won't get involved with the politics of the area. We'll just be trying to fit in the village and I'm sure the administration has everything else under control."

****

In the morning Mustafa took a count of the number in camp and noted their numbers had grown with new recruits, mostly boys but a sprinkling of girls. He walked among them, stirring from their sleep. Just children, he reminded himself but hardened by plenty of action over the years. Even the oldest couldn't remember a time before war.

"What's for breakfast?" Brother Denis asked, swinging out of his hammock.

Mustafa said, "One of the boys climbed and dropped several Baobab ponds."

"What, no canned mackerel?"

"That will wait until dinner. There is a full stalk of bananas hanging there. Our new visitors brought it with them when they came in last night."

"How many more do we have?" Brother Denis asked, pulling a banana from the stalk.

"I count twenty now."

Brother Denis smiled. "Good!"

"More would be better."

"Yes," he said, then finished eating his banana and added, "and we will get more. How about pineapples?"

"You think pineapple will help the fight?"

"No, but it will help my empty stomach."

"Is this a hotel?"

"Mustafa, my son," Denis said while taking another banana, "remember that an army travels on its stomach. Men cannot fight on an empty stomach."

"Denis, my brother, the stomachs of my little crew are always empty. Isn't that what this war is about?"

"Yes, food," Denis agreed, "one can fight a war for food."

"And medicine, medicine as well."

"Yes…medicine…"

"And schools," Sekou said, joining the discussion, "don't forget schools! They are also worth fighting for."

"Yes, yes, they are. And you, Mustafa," Denis asked, "what is the fight worth to you?"

"For me, it is easy, for me it is for those who have already died."

"Yes,…yes, that too is worth it, for them."

"Sekou," Mustafa ordered his second in command as the crew began to stir about noisily, "get them together. Take them for a little run out in the forest and back. Get them awake, lots to do today."

Sekou stomped about the sheltered hut waking his soldiers and then led the group out into the dense bush. "Catch me if you can!" he yelled. He started out on the path but after a hundred meters jumped off the trail and started through the underbrush.

"Brother Denis," Mustafa said as he watched his little band jog off and disappear into the bush, "twenty teenagers will not be enough to wage any kind of a resistance, much less a war."

"Oh yes," he said, taking a banana and peeling back the green skin, "but we will grow in strength once the word circulates."

"Yes, you mentioned that before. Just what word do you think will bring people out to face such odds?"

"It's a surprise."

"Oh, is this the surprise we spoke of earlier?"

"Yes," he said as the group came back from their jog.

"Indeed?"

The group returned to camp. While the older ones were hardly winded, the younger members seemed to have found the pace difficult and trailed as they came in.

"Sekou," Mustafa directed the young leader, "this is not a sprint to the finish. We must prepare for the long journey. Take them out again but slower and have them carry their weapons. They need to train with them."

"Yes, sir!"

"And Sekou," he added, "run them longer, to the road this time. Give them a good look at the path. Take your time so no one struggles."

"Will there be action today?"

"Perhaps but do not be in a hurry my friend," he said, taking a piece of the juicy Baobab fruit, and waving the young man off to continue, "the time will come soon enough."

"He is impatient," Denis said, watching the group head out again. "It is a good thing."

"Impatient to die?"

"Anxious to get on with it, to finally fight back, to stop running."

"We will be into it soon enough," Mustafa said, leaning back against the hut wall. "Let us take our time and be prepared."

Denis said, "The support team just arrived, my friend, so we are at that point, only days now."

****

Tommy shuffled along in the middle of the party as the line slowly moved in front of the bored-looking officials. Barely glancing at them as they drifted by the table covered in a dirty blue cloth, three scowling custom officials manned the process. The first man took each passport, flipped to an inner page, and handed it to the second official who pulled a fancy seal from a long wax sheet and stuck it on a page. After affixing each seal to a passport book, the official passed the book on to a third official who hit a blue stamp pad and stamped over the seal before giving the passport back to its owner. They repeated the process with the next in line, and the next, and so on.

Annette Monson stood behind the officials with a grin on her face. She was speaking with a smiling army officer who gently nodded his head at each in the group as they passed. Although no one told him directly, Tommy figured Annette was the Agency asset that was responsible for logistics and intelligence for the mission.

Finally, the last of the line moved out of the terminal

and onto the walkway out front of the building. Now with the rain stopped, the sun baked the group and steam floated off the concrete. A line of six vehicles that used to be white, before mud covered them, stood parked conspicuously along the curb, their engines running, but looking welcoming to Tommy. The teams split into fours and started to find a ride.

"Everyone, everyone," Monson shouted again, "before you climb aboard. This is where my little group leaves you. The first three rovers will carry the mission team, Doctor Book, Mike Blanco, Tommy Foster, and the construction crew. You will go directly on to Masango from here, with the truck. Unfortunately, that is a ten-hour drive. The rest of the cargo will come off the plane and after it clears customs will follow you by truck sometime over the next couple of days. You can stop as many times along the way as you need. But you should try to get there before it gets dark. It is just after nine o'clock now so you should make it.

"Each of your drivers is familiar with the way, so don't worry. Mike has experience in the area and will function as your guide. I've given him a large bank of Central African funds for expenses. He'll pay for whatever you need to buy for the trip and any incidentals. Mike, don't forget to give Doctor Book her spending money."

"How about me?" Tommy asked.

"Mr. Foster, too," she said. "Now, the village is expecting you and I'm sure preparing a nice warm welcome."

Tommy raised his hand, "If I got to pee or something, is there a convenience store somewhere on the road to stop at?"

"No, Mr. Foster, but there are plenty of trees along the way, and I'm sure you are quite familiar with using trees."

A young boy and a driver helped each group get their gear together and stored. Most of their luggage was stowed on top in roof carriers, the other stuff in the boot. The drivers tossed the bags to the boys and pushed the trunks up one at a time. The boys, no more than eight or nine years old, scrambled along the roof rack storing the bags and gear in the most efficient arrangement.

Each of the rovers carried two spare tires atop and the boys arranged the luggage around the tires. They stuffed as much as they could on top then pulled a heavy canvas tarp over the whole package and tied it together with rope. After getting squared away the boys assumed a position on the back section of the roof along with the rest of the gear. The boy with Thema and Tommy's rover sat on the rear of the roof with his feet dangling over the back.

"Boy," Tommy asked the skinny youngster, tossing him a package of peanuts he snatched from the plane, "what's your name?"

"Alex!" he said, looking at the bright foil package, unsure whether to open it. His arms and legs resembled a two-inch iron pipe, thin but strong.

"Well, Alex, I'm Tommy and this is Doctor Book."

"Hello, Tommy," he said in a big smile of white teeth, "and welcome Doctor Bok for finally coming!"

"You knew Doctor Book was coming?" Tommy asked.

"Oh yes," he said, tearing the package open with his teeth, "everyone has been waiting for Doctor Bok."

"How's that," Tommy asked.

The driver came around and interrupted, "We've been waiting for Doctor Bok's arrival, Mr. Foster. When the people found out a doctor was coming, they celebrated."

"So, my man," Tommy asked, "who are you?"

"I am Kimo," the stoic young man said, "I am your driver."

"Say, Kimo," Tommy asked the young driver in a white shirt and blue khaki shorts, "tell me, why do you guys call the good Doctor Book, 'Bok'?" He pronounced the name as in the English *balk*. "And not *book*, like something you read".

"Bok is tribal name, Mr. Foster. Dr. Bok is African person."

"I guess I've been pronouncing it wrong all this time," Thema said.

"And another thing," Tommy asked, "why is every Tom, Dick, and runt of a boy ready to celebrate Dr. *Book's* coming?"

"It is a great day for the revolution, Mr. Foster," he said seriously. "The new administration said that when good people start to come here then it is a sign that we will one day be a prosperous country again. There have been many stories about Doctor Bok coming and we are happy for it."

"Okay, people," Mike Blanco interrupted, coming around the rover, "let's get started. If you don't mind, Doctor Book, there's a long way to go and not a lot of time. I'm sure you don't want to be out on the highway after dark. It is not a pleasant thing, I assure you, and there is no auto club in the area."

Reviewing the boy's precarious positions atop the rovers, Thema asked, "Are they going to ride there?"

"Sure," Blanco said, "where else?"

****

Blanco strode over to the rovers to check on the team members. He looked like he was familiar with each person in the crew, and he fist bumped every man.

"Are they really going to ride there?" Thema repeated to Tommy, as she regarded the boy's position on top of the rover.

"Now, now, Doc," he said, "the locals have their own way of doing things."

Trying not to worry about the boys, Thema followed Blanco and took a good look at their crew. She counted eight other members of the traveling team, all men, most of them about the same size as Blanco. Big dudes, and she imagined they were capable of swinging a hammer.

"Men," Thema greeted as she approached the group. Several crew members gathered around a laptop. "What's happening?"

"Doctor Book," Mike Blanco greeted her, snapping the lid on the computer closed and pulled away from the little circle. "Looks like we made it, right?"

"I didn't think we'd ever make it, to tell the truth. You folks did an awful lot of planning in a brief time. So, who's on your crew here?"

"They are good men," Blanco said, motioning to the men to step up. Thema noticed they automatically fell into a straight line. As in a *precision military line.*

"This is Bruce Richards," Mike said. "He's our foreman and will run the construction crew."

"Richards," Thema greeted him with a stiff handshake.

"This is Wade Billups and John Page, they are the mason crew and can build any kind of brick or stone structure you want."

"Men," Thema greeted with a nod.

"These next two characters are Frank Barnes and Willy Gray, engineers in the group. Barnes used to work with USAID and Gray worked for the Army Corps of Engineers before joining us."

"Barnes, Gray," Thema greeted the men, extending her fist and getting a fist bump back in return.

"And these last three clowns are Jimmy Phillips, Bobby Raines, and Marc Frisco, they'll oversee the framing. Phillips came over from CARE. He's built several schools in different African countries."

"Men," Thema greeted the last of the team. "You boys look capable. With this manpower you could build a whole town, not just a clinic."

"We can build it, Doc," Blanco agreed, "but that's not the only point. We got to get the villagers to join the effort. If they put some skin in the game, they'll tend to take more pride in the project and be more supportive of others. If we can teach this first group how to do it, then it will make the others easier. That's where you come in, Doc. These people won't follow us, but we hope they'll follow you."

Annette approached them. "Well, people, it looks like you are packed so let's get this show on the road."

Thema asked, "What about our medical supplies?"

"Don't worry, Annette said, "those supplies will follow you tomorrow,"

"Are you sure? I don't want to run a clinic without supplies."

"Don't worry, Doctor Book. You'll have enough supplies to fight a war."

"Okay, men, and doctor," Mike said to the group.

"You heard the lady, let's move out."

He directed Thema back to the lead rover and stopped to talk to Annette and after a short conversation left her and rejoined the group.

"Take care, Annette!" one of the men shouted out as he climbed into a rover. "Don't get lonely without me!"

"Hey, Annette," one of the others called, "put a big cooler of beer in one of the trucks when you send them tomorrow. Ice cold!"

Annette waved at the crew and headed back into the airport, Thema hoped, to take care of their supplies. She hoped their medical supplies and equipment would get through customs.

Thema got back to the idling rover but held on to her carry-on stuff because it didn't look like they would be getting to any of the top-side gear for a while. The back of each rover had space for a few more items, so she put her knapsack back there and her makeup kit but held on to her camera bag. Blanco sat in front with Kimo, the driver, and Tommy climbed into the back with her. Thema quickly noticed the welcoming air conditioning going full blast.

"What do you think about the team?" Tommy asked, getting himself squared away.

"Pretty big dudes," Thema told him.

"Big?"

"Big, like in linebacker big."

"Well, it's going to be heavy work."

"I suppose."

"Hope you are comfortable back there," Blanco asked, turning around in his seat to address Thema, looking over the rim of a pair of aviator sunglasses. "The rover is the only way to get around the back roads."

Then, popping a Miami Dolphins cap on his head he said, "We'll get a chance to stop along the way. It's a pretty drive as drives go and this rain will keep the dust at bay. Quite a country here, with a varied ecosystem. Something you should be interested in Doctor Book."

With the rest of the team squared away, the little caravan headed out. About a hundred meters outside the airport grounds the paved road ended, dropping off onto a rutted dirt road, no wider than a single lane.

And Thema got an odd feeling in her gut.

****

The four-vehicle caravan skirted the outskirts of the capital on its way inland. Tommy didn't think they missed much by skipping a city visit. From a distance the city looked pretty beat up.

"Well," he said as they drove past the city, "after a couple of years of civil war, there isn't much left to fight over, is there?"

"No," Blanco agreed, "this used to be such pretty country. When the British pulled out, they left enough people in place to run things, but the different native groups couldn't work together. Plus, five different civil wars over a span of thirty years haven't helped the situation."

"Let's hope this last one was it."

"No chance," Blanco said on a laugh. "These people will never get along."

"Oh, yeah," Tommy squawked, "which people are you talking about?"

"Take it easy, home boy, I wasn't talking about you."

"Brothers are brothers, dude."

"Look, Foster, I've been working in Africa for a

while. There are six major tribal groups and fifteen tribal dialects in this country. Hell, these people can't even agree on whether to shit in the river or not, even when their lives depend on it.

"What's that supposed to mean?"

"Ask Doctor Book."

"What's he going on about?" Tommy asked Thema.

"Basic sanitation," she said, bringing her camera to eye level and using a zoom lens to check out the city as they sped by. "Pretty serious diseases are spread through fecal material and when a village group shares the same source of water for hygiene and drinking, diseases can spread, sometimes in pretty devastating ways. He could have been less graphic, but I assume our good team leader is referring to the sociological challenge of getting the villagers to stop using the same river for both hygiene and their source of drinking water."

"I don't know about you, Tommy," Blanco said, "but shitting in one's drinking water is a serious thing. Back in the states, you'd probably get shot for that."

At the edge of the city, just before the rovers turned inland, they passed the city dump where refugees from other countries shared the dirty ground with the country's poor. A rusted tin roofed city spread out over the dump and hundreds of people scoured the newly deposited trash for both sustenance and income. The mission team watched in silence as they drove by. Several children stared at the cars when they approached. A few waved dirt-crusted hands as the caravan pulled by.

As the rovers sped, Tommy glanced at Doctor Book, who was fiddling with her camera. It was just as well she didn't get a good view of the dump and the children there. From what she told him, if she had seen the desperate situation of those kids, she probably would have stopped the caravan right there and started her mission. No, he was glad they weren't stopping there. Even a village in the jungle would be better than a city dump—and living there would be no vacation.

Chapter Twelve

The central African landscape of rolling hills, thick bush, and forest rolled by as the caravan of vehicles turned east and left the city behind, making their way into the interior of the country. The winding rutted road punished the passengers as the vehicles managed to find every pothole and rock in the road. The dense bush crowded the red dirt highway, blanketing the view of anything but trees and underbrush. Every hour or so a convoy of trucks and military vehicles would storm past going in the opposite direction. Their drivers would route the vehicles off on the shoulder and wait for the convoys to pass.

"What's this military escorted truck traffic mean?" Tommy asked Blanco.

"This war's not over yet. There are pockets of resistance scattered over the back country. It will take years to root it out. By then some other group will take over and it will start again, the killing, refugees, displaced farmers, the dead cattle. In the meantime, the military protects the ore trucks headed to the port."

"Ore trucks?" Thema asked.

"Ore, Doctor Book," Blanco said. "These mountains are full of valuable minerals."

After three hours on the go, the caravan made a quick stop by the side of the rutted road. Little Alex hopped from the top of the rover and, joining the other boys, they disappeared into the bushes. The men took turns going into the trees while Kimo and the other drivers waited behind their wheels. Thema and Tommy stepped out to stretch their legs although Thema refused to join the parade into the trees and swore she would hold it for as long as it took.

"Don't worry," Blanco advised her, "There's a small town a little over halfway to our destination named Bandella. We'll stop there for gas. There's also a Lebanese couple who run a little shop there. We can stop, grab a cold drink, and you can use their facilities."

"Lebanese?"

"Yeah, plenty of Lebanese expatriates run the shops and inland businesses. Good people, heavy drinkers. Their own country was blown to hell, so they make their way all over Africa trading and running general commerce. At least until some army clown decides to take over the country. Then they get reamed a new one for their hard work."

Thema wandered over to the thick tree line. This side of the road stood in the shade of the forest and the air hung heavy with humidity. Thema didn't find it uncomfortable. The trees stretched to the sky although she noticed the under bush did not appear as dense as it seemed from the road.

"Is this the African Tulip Tree," she asked aloud, seeing the tall broad tree.

"I guess," Blanco said. "It has those tulip-like flowers the kids like."

"What do you mean?"

"The kids, they pull off the flowers and the stems hold water, watch." Blanco said, plucking a thick stem from the tree. "See," he showed her, and when Thema leaned in to examine the flower, he squeezed the stem firmly and a shot of water squirted out hitting her in the face.

"Hey!"

"Yep," he laughed jogging away, "that's a tulip tree. Kids love them."

"They are more valuable than that," she called after him. "I hear the stem bark has healing power."

"Pretty red flowers, too," Tommy added.

Thema ignored the men and while kneeling at the base of the tree to examine the bark, movement behind the first growth of brush caught her eye. When a young woman came walking out of the trees along a path she hadn't noticed, she jumped. Several women followed balancing baskets atop their heads, and many carried babies strapped to their backs with several layers of long bright flowered cloth.

"Whoa!" Thema yelled, stepping back as the first women marched past, but the next woman in line slowed and then stopped in front of Thema, looking her over. The women sang a song in rhythm with their walk, but the singing turned to a native dialect chatter. The first woman turned and came back to the group and closely examined Thema. The chatter escalated and soon each woman was trying to argue a point with each other.

Thema took another step back, trying to put some distance between her and the native women who appeared to be discussing her as in turn each woman shouted something at her and pointed to her in not too friendly gestures. The woman moved with Thema, the chatter escalating again, the women shouting now. Suddenly the second woman, with a stiff finger, poked Thema violently in the chest. The force surprised Thema and she stumbled back. The first woman jumped between Thema and the second woman and started to shout. The other women in the line shouted back. The second woman reached around the first and tried to poke Thema again, but ready for the movement this time, Thema stepped away and avoided the jab.

The other women came then, their voices in virtual shouts, waving arms and pointing fingers at her. They surrounded Thema and she let out a scream barely noticed above the shouting.

"Doctor Book," Blanco called to her as he entered the fray.

He pushed past the ring of bright colors and grabbing Thema by the arm pulled her to him in a hug. With the women arguing, he led her away from the commotion. By then a couple of the crew came over and intercepted the native women following Thema and Blanco. One of the women came out of the group and mocked the retreating Thema by putting her hands to her face and shrieking loudly. The other women joining in mock gestures laughed hysterically and like the second woman, put their hands on their faces and mimicked Thema.

The woman who started the whole thing took three or four steps forward to the group of men and withdrew a long machete style knife from beneath the folds of her full dress. She waved it at the men and thumped her chest with the flat side of the knife and spit violently at the men's feet. She turned back to her friends, shouted something which made them all laugh again, and with a wave of her hand the group started off and crossed the road.

Thema watched the women disappear in the thick

bush, their way again accompanied in song, their voices stubbornly fading in the jungle. "What was that about?" she asked Mike Blanco from her safe position in his arms.

"They saw you are a Tutsi woman," Blanco said.

"Say what?"

"Tutsi," Kimo said, moving to them.

"What do you mean, Kimo?" Thema asked.

"You Tutsi woman, Doctor Bok," he said again. "They Hutus; they no like Tutsi people."

"But Thema is American," Tommy said.

"Yes, Doctor is an American Tutsi woman. You are American now, but she Tutsi, her people are Tutsi."

"And Hutus don't like Tutsi?" Thema asked.

"Yes, they no like Tutsi."

"Are you Tutsi, Kimo?"

He looked horrified at the question. "No! I no Tutsi… I am Masai!"

With the episode over, and a little embarrassed about the way she reacted, Thema reluctantly pushed away from Blanco."

"Listen up, everyone," Blanco ended the conversation, letting Thema go, but still gazing at her. "We've got a long trip to go if we want to get to Masango before nightfall."

Thema and the others got back into the rovers and Alex climbed back atop his perch and the little caravan continued its journey. Thema kept a watch out the rear window for the dangling feet of their little friend. After a moment, she asked Mike, "How can you tell I'm of Tutsi heritage?"

"You have the physical appearance; thin boned, narrow nose, pretty face; easy to pick out. The original

Tutsi were out of Ethiopia before they settled here. The locals consider them outsiders even after six hundred years, especially after the 1994 war."

"Is that the kind of reception I'll get in Masango?"

"No," he said, twisting back in his seat, "the northern end of the country is Tutsi. You'll fit right in there."

****

The road curved only slightly during the trip although it narrowed dangerously at several river bridge crossings. Eventually, the heavy tree landscape thinned, and the caravan approached a wide clearing in the forest. Bandella spread out before them. Beyond the eastern end of the town a wide savannah spread. The single lane split the small town in two and several shops lined both sides of the road. A line of tin roofed houses formed a second row of structures behind the first row and then garden spaces and fenced in areas for cattle and other livestock after that.

Tommy counted maybe thirty structures altogether, reminding him of what the old western towns looked like in those late-night movies he watched. A recent rain left six inches of mud formed ruts in the road, dried hard by a high sun. The people crowding the street stumbled along on their way to market or shops.

The rovers slowed and crawled their way to the end of the road. "The Lebanese shop is at the end of the street," Blanco said. "We'll stop there and get a cold drink and a snack."

"Is this Bandella?" Thema asked.

"This is it," Blanco said, "frontier outpost."

"Outpost?"

"Yeah, back in the day this town brought in traders

from as far away as a thousand miles. The great savannah lands to the east transition here with the western forest. We'll be swinging back west into the forest. This used to be one of the biggest trading centers in Africa. Of course, the jungle is in decline now, deforestation, erosion, and progress adding to its deterioration."

"Deforestation?" Tommy asked.

"People still farm in the ancient slash and burn mode. They'll walk into an old growth forest section and burn all the trees just to plant a little rice. I've seen a rich stand of ebony trees burned to plant fifteen dollars' worth of rice. Trees like that on the European lumber market would bring ten thousand dollars or more, if you could ship them there. There's a couple of European outfits in the country that spot lumber and haul out the best hardwood available and send it back to make furniture."

"Do they have electricity here?" Thema asked.

"Some, but nothing town wide. The small towns can't afford to run a generator during the day for power. The local hospital has electricity and some of the shops that can afford the fuel oil generate their own. Just a few hours during the day though. At six o'clock they shut off the power. After that it's kerosene and hurricane lamps unless it's a special occasion. It can be rough here, but they seem to make do. Here's the shop."

"There's already a hospital here?" Thema asked.

"Sure…a nice one," Mike said, "but it's here and they don't do house calls out of town. The area west of here is too dangerous for them so if you want help you have to come here. That's why the Masango Clinic is so important.

The three rovers pulled to the side of the curb less

street and idled while the paneled truck continued to move. Tommy started out, grateful as he swung his long legs out and climbed out of his seat, stretching his back, and rotating his neck in a circle. The sun beat on him, and he plopped his hat on his bald head. He already missed the air-conditioned vehicle. The rest of the team climbed out and the boys abandoned their perches. The drivers took off while the boys headed off in different directions.

"Tommy," Thema called to him as she and Blanco ducked through a low hung door and into the dark shop where the heat dissipated about twenty degrees.

"Mike," Tommy asked, "where are those guys headed with our wheels?"

"Take it easy, Bwana," he said, "they are going to fill up. This is the last gas before Masango."

"What are we going to do for gas once we settle in?

"There's a fifty-five-gallon drum in the van and more coming up. That'll be enough."

"Check it out, Tommy," Thema said. "You can get an ice-cold drink here."

"Make it two." Tommy corrected, coming to the counter.

"Make it three and one for each of the men," Blanco said.

"Three and more it is, my friend," repeated an older man of middle eastern appearance from behind the wooden counter. He pulled bottles of cola from a squat cooler and placed them on the counter. Taking an opener, he popped the caps off each bottle and slid them across to the waiting travelers.

"Do you run your own power here?" Tommy asked, then gulped the cold drink.

"I can but this cooler runs on kerosene, my inquisitive friend," the Lebanese man explained. "Who are your companions, Blanco?"

"I'm sorry, Sunil. This is Doctor Book and Tommy Foster. And the other men are a construction crew. We're traveling to Masango to work on the mission."

"A pleasure meeting you and so, this is the famous Doctor Bok?"

"Yes, it is. Did the word reach here already?"

"Oh yes, my friend, the word reached us for some time now."

"What word?" Thema asked.

"Why, the word on you, of course. It isn't so often a doctor ventures out into the bush. We have our small hospital of course, but the smaller villages do not have as much."

"How long has the word been out?" Blanco asked. "We only just landed this morning."

"Even for some days now and here you are!"

"Well, I am very glad to meet you, Mr. Sunil," Thema thanked him, wondering how anyone knew they were coming.

"It is Sunil, Doctor, just Sunil and this is my wife, Fatima." He introduced a burka clad lady hiding behind a veil and the sales counter. "Say hello, my dear."

"Hello!"

"Now, now, my friends, you must forgive my lovely Fatima, that is not the extent of her English, believe me, for she possesses quite an aptitude for languages, although she pretends to be a bit shy."

"Why, how are you then?" Thema greeted the lady with a short bow.

"Say, Sunil," Blanco asked the shopkeeper, "do you

think the young lady could use your facilities?"

"But of course, how rude of me, forgive me Doctor Bok. I am sure you would like to freshen up. Fatima my dear," he asked his wife to approach, "please show the good doctor to the washroom."

"Thank you, Sunil," Thema said.

****

Thema followed the man's wife into the rear of the building. She stepped over a rough threshold that separated the living quarters of the home from the business section. There Thema found a wide, attractive, and airy room stretching the length of the building. A small kitchen area occupied one end of the room, and a sitting area sat on the opposite side. There were three doors across the back of the room. Fatima guided her to the one in the middle.

Thema entered a bright whitewashed room, illuminated by a skylight above. The room contained an old claw foot bathtub and aluminum sink set in a wooden cabinet. A rack held two faded, but full yellow bath towels and a matching hand towel hung on a hook near the sink. A clear vase of plastic flowers sat on the back of a sparkling clean water tank of the toilet, which sat in the far corner of the space.

"Thank you," Thema said when she came out of the bathroom, "That was quite a relief."

"Yes, indeed," Fatima said in an English accent. "That drive is very long. I am afraid I am still not used to it."

"So, you haven't lived here long?"

"No, only a few years, we only just married. Of course, my husband arrived many years ago, but his first wife died, so he married again."

"I'm sorry for him," she said, surprised at her conversation, "malaria?"

"Some disease, amoebic dysentery, I believe," she said, leading the way back to the front of the shop.

When Thema walked back out to the customer area, she found Tommy in conversation with the shopkeeper.

"Look here," Tommy said to the man, "what do you mean that refrigerator runs on kerosene? Kerosene is for making fires, flames, and other hot things. How can you get cold from hot?"

"Come on, Foster," Blanco said, "you need to get out more. We brought one in our equipment supply. We'll get it operating this week. It even makes ice."

"Get out of here!"

"Basic chemistry my friend," Sunil explained with a thin smile. "All refrigeration works on rapid evaporation. So, the unit has a kerosene flame that heats the refrigerant coil causing the evaporation. You see—" he pointed beneath the cooler "—no need for electricity. You are used to your electric run refrigerators at your home. In those the electricity runs the condenser which in turn creates the evaporation, but here the unit employs a kerosene flame. Of course, our unit is absent the small light that goes off and on as you open and close the door. It is simple yet complicated at the same time."

Thema understood the concept from her high school science, but the practical application remained a mystery to her.

"Sunil," Blanco asked, "did you bake some fresh bread this morning?"

"Of course."

"Could you wrap one for each of us, a dozen altogether."

"Yes, of course," he said, heading off to the rear of his shop.

Blanco took the opportunity to confer with his men. The tight group kept to themselves and didn't appear to be the social types.

"Here you are," Sunil offered a bundle to Tommy. "This should get you to Masango."

"Oh, hey, don't worry," Tommy said, "I'm sure we'll find another shop along the way."

"Well, actually you won't, my friend," he said, "Bandella is the last big town on the road before Masango. Oh, there are a few villages along the way. The market in Sawaana might still be open when you pass. If you do stop, make sure you only eat from the hot coal grills. Don't worry about the skewered meat, if it is hot, you'll be okay. But stay away from everything else and don't drink anything but bottled water."

"You mean we won't pass much else along the road?" Thema asked as she watched Blanco laughing about something with the construction crew.

"No, you won't, my friend," Sunil answered. "Tell me, Doctor Bok, what will you be building in Masango?"

"A clinic."

"Oh, but of course," he said gesturing to the outside, "we have a hospital here."

"This one will be right in the village," Tommy explained. Then finishing his drink said, "You know, to take the place of the old missionary clinic."

"And this project requires such a crew?" Sunil asked motioning to the men in the shop.

Thema said, "I assume once we get going, we will move on to other projects."

"Other projects?"

"Yes," Thema said, "Mike Blanco spoke of a school."

"A school?"

"Yes, why?"

"Why, forgive me my friend, the current administration doesn't encourage education I'm afraid, at least not here. Ignorance is bliss for them."

"Why do you say that?"

"Why, my friend," he said, with a slight smile, "the army has burned every school within one hundred miles of here."

"Okay, okay," Blanco said, finishing his bottle of drink, "if the chemistry lesson is over and we are finished freshening up, we better get going if we are going to make Masango before nightfall. How much do we owe you, Sunil."

"On the house, as you say in America," Sunil answered, "In honor of Doctor Bok here. May your stay in Masango be long and fruitful, Doctor."

"Why thank you, Sunil," Thema said, "but we couldn't." She motioned to Blanco to give her some money. He in turn poured out a handful of coins and gave them to her.

"No, no," Sunil protested. "It is a little game we play, being gracious in an inhospitable land. One day you can return the favor."

"Okay then," Thema responded, handing the coins to Tommy and bowing slightly. "Blessings upon this house and your family," she said with a nod toward Sunil's wife.

Sunil thanked her with a bow in turn.

The party headed into the sun. The boys came out of a different shop and together they waited for the rovers to return.

"How are we doing on time?" Thema asked Blanco.

"Despite the chemistry lesson, I think we'll make it before dark. We've got three hours more to go and the road improves a little this way. There's a big mining company operating nearby and they take good care of the road so they can transport. Plus, there is less traffic altogether beyond Bandella, mostly Tutsi people along the way to Masango. Not a favorite of the current administration. They patrol the area as much as possible for security, and they are not afraid to engage the people."

"As long as we make Masango before nightfall," Tommy said. "I'd hate to be out on the road after dark."

"Our ETA should be about eighteen hundred, just before dark."

Tommy stepped back as the rovers pulled to the shop. The boys scrambled atop their perches and the other men climbed aboard. Tommy handed the bread to Blanco, and he handed it out to the crew, saving some for their rover. He switched places with Thema for this part of the ride, giving her the window seat on the passenger side.

The three rovers and the truck headed out of town at a fast pace. The coolness of air conditioning welcomed Thema, and she much appreciated it again. *God this country is hot as hell,* she thought as the thick forest countryside speed by. She'd underestimated the heat; it was a lot hotter than she was used to. She underestimated the rain, too.

The fact is, she underestimated quite a bit about this little adventure.

What else might she have underestimated when she let Mike Blanco talk her into this gig?

Chapter Thirteen

In the fading light Kimo slowed the caravan to a crawl before they rumbled across a plank-based bridge over the Juarzon River. The Royal Corps of Engineers built bridge narrowed to a scant one lane and Thema noticed the tight squeeze even for just one vehicle and how it would make for quite a bottleneck if a morning rush hour traffic ever materialized.

"Are we there yet?" she asked Kimo as they crossed over the bridge. The darkening jungle looked like the end of the world to her.

"A little farther," he said and added without emotion, "longer by the road but shorter by the trail."

After they crossed, Thema saw what she thought were several bodies on the ground but just off the road. "Do you see that?" Thema asked aloud, pivoting in her seat to peer through the window. In the dim light it was hard to tell, but the forms were not moving and could have been dead bodies. "Back there, along the road… stop!"

"I didn't see anything," Tommy said. "Mike?"

"Back there!"

"I didn't see anything," Mike Blanco said, "and we are not stopping. It is already late."

"Kimo…did you see anything?"

"The bush can make strange shadows, Doctor Bok. There was nothing to see."

Thema settled back into her seat. She knew she saw something and from his driver's seat, Kimo must have as well. "Are you familiar with this area?" she asked him.

"Yes, my family stays in Masango."

"I thought you said you were Masai?"

"The Masai are a wandering people, Doctor Bok. We settled in this area many years ago, but we are all brothers and sisters in Masango."

****

Brother Denis rocked the bucket at the end of the rope before flipping it expertly into the bottom of the deep well. From the sound he knew the bucket hit the water on its open side; after tipping, it would quickly begin to fill. He pulled on the rope and first feeling the weight drew a bucket of water from the village well. He lifted the line and pail and deposited the cold water into a bucket at his feet, then headed back to the fire pit.

He added the bucket of water to a big pot of water sitting on a fire he started earlier. The water in the pot heated to a nice warm temperature for a shower/bath. He grabbed a fresh change of clothes from his knapsack and a clean though thin bath towel. He rubbed at his beard growth but decided against a shave. He didn't want to look too civilized for his first meeting.

He walked to a rough latrine area. A square of reed mat panels on end surrounded a flat stone pad the village women laid for the occasional use as a bathhouse. The attempt at privacy amused Brother Denis since at the slightest occasion the village women would drop their lappas and expose sagging breasts without the least embarrassment. Still, he welcomed the few minutes of solitude.

After taking off his dirty clerical shirt, the only sign

of his once affiliation with the church, he stripped to his bare butt. Taking a large one-quart tin can, he dipped warm water from the bucket and poured it over his head. The water felt just wonderful. He dipped again and repeated the pouring starting with his head and working his way to his feet and continued until well doused. He couldn't remember the last time he took a real shower. Sometime last year when he holidayed briefly in Geneva, he supposed. Since then, a bucket bath had served as one of the few luxuries he allowed himself.

Denis took a bar of soap and spread suds around his body, especially the groin area, and worked a lather. He messaged the soap into his hair, noting the creeping thinness there and scrubbed his legs. He remembered a long-ago mission doctor reprimanding him for not bathing more, but most days the opportunity to do so eluded him. A couple times a week seemed to work out best. The villagers laughed at his routine since they bathed freely in the many rivers that crisscrossed the jungle.

Finally, he ladled the last of the water over his body, rinsing thoroughly before shaking the excess water out of his hair.

"You bathe like you are going on a date?" Mustafa joked from in front of the fire as his friend came back to the hut, his hair still dripping from his bath.

"I am, with a lady."

"What lady?

"The chosen one."

"She has arrived?"

"She'll be in Masango tonight," he said, while drying his hair with the worn towel. "I promised chief Kulu I'd be on hand to help greet her."

119

"Shall we come along?"

"No, this is just a low-key visit. I wouldn't want to scare her off after only a few hours in the country."

"Shall we post a lookout?"

"No," he said, glancing around the quiet village. "No need; it is too soon yet."

****

Mustafa watched his old friend disappear into the bush. He sent Sekou with him even though Denis insisted he could find his way there blind folded. "I appreciate the concern, my friend," the brother protested, "but I am quite capable of finding Masango without the need of a guide."

"Yes, yes, bwana," Mustafa joked, "the great white brother is at home in the jungle, but it is still wise to travel with a companion."

"And this is for what reason?"

Mustafa paused to search for a plausible reason. "You could get bitten in the leg by a black mamba."

"And so?"

"And you will need someone to cut off your leg before the poison travels to your heart and kills you. They say once bitten by a mamba the poison can kill you in less than a minute."

"So I have heard as well."

"Do not worry, my friend," he said, "I directed Sekou to act especially quick in removing your leg, so you do not suffer needlessly."

"You are a bit morbid for so early in the game."

"Remember, my friend, you are not on vacation."

****

Twilight clung to the surrounding trees as the tiny caravan pulled into Masango. Shadows from the forest stretched across the forty-hut village while cooking fires threw out light from thatched roofed kitchens. A low haze of gray smoke hung over the village like a fog. Villagers ran to greet the vehicles when they pulled in.

"Welcome to Masango!" Kimo announced as they parked just off the road in front of the compound.

The children arrived first, their voices raised in a singsong chant and their arms in the air. The adults came next with the elders leading the way. The smiles of the children brightened the dimming day like the stars in a night sky.

"Whoa," Thema shouted as she tried to force her way out the door of the rover, "what a crowd. Where'd the people come from?"

"It is you, Doctor Bok," Kimo explained, shouting above the din of laughter and singing and coming around the vehicle to help Thema get out, "They come from all around to welcome you."

A flock of children rushed forward and took hold of Thema 's legs and waist, holding fast, preventing her from walking normally, forcing her into a little slide and dragging step as they led her away amongst the crowd. Kimo came to her side and peeled the children off one at a time so she could use her legs. One stubborn child would not let go and after trying gently to pry her loose from Thema's waist, Kimo raised his hand quickly and struck the child across the face, forcing her to the ground.

"Kimo, don't!" Thema cried then helped the young girl to her feet. When the girl rose a big smile stretched across her face. Thema smiled at her.

"It's okay, Doctor. Bok," Kimo explained away, "she is only a village girl. Not smart!"

"Kimo," Thema scolded, holding the girl about the

shoulders, "she's not hurting anyone, don't you raise your hand like that again." She turned to the girl. "What is your name, child?"

"Girl no speak English, Doctor," little Alex explained.

"Ask her name."

Alex said something to the girl; she spoke back. "Her name is Nuru," he said.

"Nuru," Thema repeated to the girl. "What does it mean?"

"It means 'light'," Alex said. "It is village name."

"Come, Nuru," Thema said to the girl as she allowed the other children to gather around her again and lead her off.

"Where are they taking you, Doc?" Tommy called after her, as the throng swept her away.

"They are taking her to greet the chief and the elders," Kimo explained, following quickly.

The group paraded through a line of thatched roof huts and separate gazebo-like structures. Whitewashed stones lined the walkways between the village areas. Fires burned in some of the structures, so Tommy figured they were the kitchen areas. The huts were arranged in a big circle surrounding a square with a large gazebo palaver hut. Several men stood beneath the tall, thatched roof of the hut and waited as the crowd approached.

At first, Tommy could not make out the greeting party but when closer he picked out the individuals by the center fire pit light, including the tallest in the group, some white dude in a religious collar, and a lone woman dressed in military fatigues and carrying a weapon.

"Greetings, greetings," Kimo called out and when they narrowed the distance between them to speak, he greeted the group again, "Chief Kulu, this is daughter Thema Atsu Bok" he said in English. "Come from America to be the doctor in the clinic."

The chief spoke a few words in native dialect which Kimo translated. "This chief says, welcome, Doctor Thema Atsu Bok."

"Tell the Chief, thank you," Thema said to Kimo, and bowed slightly to the elder. "Tell him it is good to be here."

As Kimo translated to the fleshy-faced man, Chief Kulu's smile showed a great many missing teeth. He wore a lappa cloth around his big waist and an animal skin draped across his shoulders.

Pointing to Tommy, Kimo spoke again. The Chief's return came back in a husky voice. "This chief says, welcome, Mr. Tommy Foster."

The advancing crowd greeted this announcement with another round of laughter, song and singing. Tommy smiled through the further formalities and finally the last of the introductions.

"And finally, this," Kimo began, "is Brother Denis Collins, of the Irish Missions. He has worked for many years in the clinic while ministering to the villages in the mountains."

"A doctor?" Thema asked, shaking his hand.

"No, barely even a nurse, Doctor Bok," he explained in a thick Irish brogue obviously untouched by his years in Africa. His words appeared to come out of the side of his mouth. "I'm afraid our mission cannot afford to send out a real doctor or nurse. That's why we are so happy you have arrived. I'm afraid my skills are confined to bandages and shots of penicillin."

"It is so nice to meet you all," Thema said. "Please,

Kimo, tell everyone how thankful we are to be greeted so warmly."

Kimo launched into a long speech that raised many peals of laughter and another round of chanting before Chief Kulu raised his arms and brought a quick silence to the whole affair.

"Dude," Tommy asked Kimo, "what kind of stories are you telling?"

"I told them what they want to hear."

"And what is that?"

"That Doctor Bok has arrived to save their lives and make them well?"

"Doctor Bok?" Brother Denis asked as the din of laughter and chanting started again, "would you like to walk through the clinic? Look around your new job site?"

"I guess," she said, "but what about the chief," she asked.

Brother Denis spoke to Chief Kulu in native dialect and the big man laughed back and waved them off.

Brother Denis walked off in long strides calling ahead in native dialect to several other villagers who ran off toward a thatched roof structure standing at one radius from the central core of the village. "It is a simple clinic," he pointed as he went. Thema and Tommy followed a swarm of children. "Outside of the hospital in Bandella, the clinic is the only medical facility in this part of the country and is isolated from the rest of the land. The Brotherhood of Catholic Missionaries founded the first clinic."

As they approached the old clinic, a few villagers rushed ahead lighting hurricane lamps in each of the rooms. "There is one room for surgery," he continued, "and another for examinations. The old place has seen many patients over the years."

"Brother Denis, how long ago did you come to Africa?" Thema asked as they climbed the steps of the clinic to a wide porch rimmed by a low solid stone wall.

"A long time ago," he answered, stepping into the first room along the walkway and pausing to adjust the wick in a lamp that lit up the room, the one arranged for examinations. "There have been many different stations but not long here." The wide porch surrounded three quarters of the building. "I was first assigned to this area in the nineties," he explained as they navigated between rooms via the porch, going from room to room, "to work in the Congo then drifted over this way after the war there, been in and out since, depending on the need. This is great land here and wonderful people."

"Yes," Thema agreed, her arm still wrapped around her new friend Nuru. "The people seem very friendly."

"Oh yes," he said, moving off to the second room, "very much so. Especially for you of Tutsi heritage, but you must be careful, Dr. Bok."

"Careful of what?"

He looked at her and smiled warmly. "That the children do not steal your heart away."

"Yes, I can see that happening," Thema said, glancing at the little girl hugging her waist. "Tell me, Brother, do you tend to the village as well?"

"Some, not much, but of course the old man, Imamu Neo, is in the village."

"Who?"

"Imamu Neo, he's the village shaman, a medicine man."

"Medicine man?"

"Yes, quite an old fellow, with his own home-grown remedies. An expert in plant life about the area, quite remarkable really, several of his potions really work. He's got one for a laxative that will clean you out in a hurry and another for a migraine headache. Much of his expertise bears recording if you find the time, Doctor. It would be a shame to lose his talents, both the medicinal as well as spiritual."

"Speaking of the spiritual, Brother Denis," Tommy asked, "do you hold church services for the people?"

"No, no, of course not," he answered, stopping to give Tommy a direct look, "I am only a brother, not a priest. I do not say Mass."

"Oh, that, right," Tommy continued, "With the collar you look like a reverend or something."

"No, I am just a brother."

"I don't understand," Thema said, "what's the difference?"

"Well, brothers don't know book. We are called upon to minister to the people via our skills."

"And just what skill do you bring to the people?" Tommy asked.

"Healing, Mr. Foster," he answered and walked out onto the porch to access the next room, "healing."

****

Thema and Tommy followed the tall Brother Denis as he toured them through the village clinic. "This is the exam room and the next over is the surgery room."

The clinic rooms looked to be in good order, Tommy noted. The walls of the surgery were smooth and even; several layers of white glossy paint covered every inch of surface. Unlike the other mud walls and floors of the clinic this one looked sealed tight. He noticed a drain in the sloped floor where he imagined the wash water flowing into as they cleaned up. An eight-foot stainless steel table sat in the middle of the room. It looked like one of those tables you find in restaurant kitchens, but Tommy imagined it served as an operating room table. Overall, it looked to be a functional space for such a small village.

"And this is Zuma Lua and Mudiwa Chiumbo." Denis introduced two young village girls dressed in white blouses and khaki shorts. "Zuma and Mudiwa will work in the clinic, Dr. Book, and Zuma will be your assistant."

"She will?" Thema asked, her eyes twinkled at the prospect.

"Yes indeed," he said, squeezing her chin in his hand. "Zuma is a fine assistant. She trained for two years in the capitol some time ago and the last resident missionaries sent her to Belgium for one year of training as a nurse assistant. She reads and writes English and can speak as well, once you get used to the dialect, but more important she can understand every word so is an immense help around the clinic."

"That's wonderful," she said and to Zuma, "I am pleased to meet you, Zuma. I am Doctor Book."

"Yes, Doctor Bok," the young lady greeted with a handshake, "I am most happy to work with you here. You are a real blessing for us."

"Well, thank you, Zuma," Thema said, smiling wide, "I am very thankful for an assistant, especially one who can communicate between the villagers. I look forward to working together."

"And Mudiwa will be your all-around help in the clinic, sort of complete maintenance staff in one," Denis further explained.

"Pleased to meet you," Thema said, offering her hand to the girl.

"I'm afraid our little Mudiwa does not speak much English," he said as the young girl only smiled, "but she'll keep the place operating smoothly."

"And here's your office, Dr. Bok." Brother Denis directed the party as they came to the end of the porch tour. "Here's your desk and several file cabinets and the small dispensary closet, but unfortunately there is no medicine or drugs here now."

"Anesthesia?"

"No, I'm afraid. They ran out some time ago. Nothing much really but I hoped you would be bringing a supply of everything you'd need?"

"There's a small supply in camp now, Doctor," Mike Blanco said, joining the group, "and more on its way. There'll be three trucks full coming tomorrow and there'll be plenty of supplies. Enough for an army."

"Tomorrow, you say?" Brother Denis asked.

"Yes, everything that came over with us. It should arrive sometime in the afternoon."

"Oh, Mike," Thema said, "this is Brother Denis…"

"Brother Denis Collins," he finished for Thema, holding out his hand and getting a firm handshake in return. The men stood at equal height although Blanco outweighed the good brother by what could have been a fifty pounds.

"Good to meet you, Brother Denis; I have heard much about you."

"You have?" Tommy asked, "From who?"

Giving Tommy a hard look, Blanco hesitated before responding. "All the drivers and small boys know

Brother Denis," Blanco explained. "You been kicking around for a while, Brother Denis?"

"For some time, my friend."

"And just who sent you?" Thema asked.

"The Society of Irish African Missions," he explained. "They assign us to live and work in solidarity with our African brothers and sisters who struggle for justice and peace amid political turmoil and social disintegration. Our members are prepared to dedicate ourselves to stand by our troubled flocks throughout Africa.

"So, what do you think of our little clinic?" Brother Denis asked. "But of course, the new clinic will be a great gift for the town and the surrounding area. I'm sure you can't wait to get busy, Mr. Foster?"

"Oh, I'm not so sure about that," Tommy said, "you seem pretty set here."

"Yes, but just the same I'm sure you are anxious to get to work," he said. "But wait, forgive me. You all must be famished after your long trip. Chief Kulu has a special feast in store for you tonight. I understand he has killed one of his prized hogs. A great honor, really."

"Hog," Tommy said, "like in barbecue?"

The Irishman grinned. "Without the sweet sauce you Americans like. And do be careful of the spices here, quite potent by anyone's standard. Shall we?" he asked, directing the group to the village center.

Tommy and the crew found a table with the cooked hog, steaming bowls of white rice and several selections of cooked vegetable stews. A large basket of roasted corn in their husks made its way about the table and Tommy tried his best to hold back, but hunger got the best of him, and he started eating. The construction crew joined the party and sitting around a long outdoor table of bamboo board tied together, the group ate and talked into the night as Chief Kulu talked and laughed heartily, Kimo translating between mouthfuls.

An hour later the crew began to yawn and nod. One by one they excused themselves and made their way back to the vehicles in the black night.

"How rude of us," Brother Denis finally recognized, "You must be exhausted after your long drive. How stupid of me." He spoke quickly to the Chief who laughed again and said something to the group. "The Chief says you are welcome again and to sleep well tonight for tomorrow the work begins."

Thema spoke quickly, "Tell the Chief thank you and that I am ready to go to work."

After Brother Denis translated, the village erupted in laughter again and appeared to wave and say good night.

Chapter Fourteen

"Come," Brother Denis called, treading briskly along the path, "let me show you where your quarters are. This is a small village, but the earlier missionaries left a nice house there on the rise above the clinic. It has a common room, two bedrooms with good beds, and a small kitchen alcove."

"Doctor Book," Blanco said to Thema as they walked, "the crew erected some tents back by the road on the far side of the clinic. We'll be there if you need us, but we are calling it a night. We'll see you in the morning."

"Wait," Tommy said, stopping his friend, "if the crew is bunking there and the Doc is here on the hill, where am I sleeping?"

"You'll be in the mission house with Doctor Bok," Denis said. "There are two bedrooms there."

"Now, wait," Thema said. "Not that I mean anything by it, but did you say we'd be sleeping in the same house?"

"It's a big house."

"You are welcome to bunk with the crew, Tommy," Blanco said. "We can fix you a nice cot in one of the tents."

Tommy started warming to the idea of bunking close to the Doc. "I didn't sign up for a camping trip, I do my best sleeping in a regular bed."

"It is a big house," Denis said again, looking at Thema. "You both should be very comfortable there."

She gave Tommy a stare. He figured she was recalling his reputation at the hospital, and probably didn't want him under foot, even if he was here on business. "Okay with me, Doc," Tommy said to her. "What do you say?"

"What will the village think?" Thema asked.

"I wouldn't worry about the villagers," Brother Denis answered. "They are lax as far as marriage conventions go. The chief himself has several wives."

Question answered, Thema shrugged, then followed Brother Denis along the path with Nuru clinging to her side.

Before Blanco got away, Tommy stopped him. "What's with the sleeping arrangements?"

"We need someone to keep an eye on the Doc. Security is our mission. She's key to the project, so I need someone I trust to watch her. The other crew members and I have specific jobs, and I can't spare a man. This is one reason I brought you along."

"It is?" Tommy said, thinking about the pretty doctor and the proposed sleeping arrangements. He might get somewhere with her if she'd only forget about his reputation with the nurse's back home.

"Come on, man," Mike encouraged. "Pretty woman like the Doc—what's wrong with that duty? In fact, I'm a little jealous, and thought about sleeping in the house myself, but I've got too much to do to spend my time babysitting. Get it done, Bro, and that's an order."

Tommy was never so happy to follow an order.

****

"The mission home once belonged to a group of

132

Belgian priests," Brother Denis explained as they ascended a slight rise in the path, about fifty meters from the clinic. "They were the ones who built the clinic and staffed it until the late sixties. Unfortunately, in a rampage after a civil uprising in 1961, the ruling government beheaded the two clerics. They buried the good men nearby. The children take care of the graves and put flowers there."

"No one has been here since?" Thema asked, looking in the direction of the phantom cemetery.

"Oh sure," Brother Denis explained, "several groups, a Baptist doctor, and his family not too long ago." He pointed to the makeshift cemetery. "They are over there as well."

"Dude," Tommy interrupted, grabbing Brother Denis by the shoulder to spin him around. "Do you mean to say, every doctor that comes here gets buried here?"

"Yes, my friend," he said, pulling his arm away and straightening his tunic, "but weren't you told this was a dangerous place when you signed on?"

"They didn't tell us much about the trouble here," Thema said, looking around, but Mike Blanco had already disappeared. "They said the government had taken control."

"Ah, I see. Well," Brother Denis said, moving toward the cabin. "That remains to be seen."

At a motion from Brother Denis, little Alex ran ahead of the group. "I'm afraid this country has seen not much but violence," he continued, leading the way. "Of course, we hope for peace one day, right?"

The mission house appeared out of the approaching dark, light coming through its windows. It stood on an elevated platform and stretched longer than wide. A corrugated tin roof covered the structure, and a wide slatted wooden porch circled the whole house. Thema climbed the sturdy steps. Struts braced the shutters that covered the windows and screens. The entry door opened into the common room, furnished with comfortable looking wood framed furniture with thick cushions. Wide, tall windows on two sides of the room supplied a nice flow-through breeze and kerosene lamps bathed the room in bright light.

"Why, this is very nice," she said.

"Oh, quite," Brother Denis said. "In the early fifties, a French priest finished out the house and put in the loo and plumbing."

"Plumbing?"

"Yes, there is a high platform out back with two fifty-five-gallon water drums. You use a hand pump to fill the drums from the well and then the pressure runs the water into the house."

"Running water?" Tommy asked.

"Yes, quite simple really, just gravity, but for the best bath make sure you take an afternoon shower."

"Why?"

"In the afternoon, after the sun has beaten on the barrels, the water gets almost hot. There is a line that runs into a bathroom in the rear and the shower head. Just turn it on and the hot water runs right on you quite nicely. Don't do it right after a rainstorm though, rainwater can be quite cold. Well," he said, looking around, the tour completed, "I should think you'll be fine here."

"Wait," Thema said, "where are the bedrooms you mentioned?"

"Yes, of course. At the end of the hall, one on the left and the other on the right. The bathroom is between.

You'll have to share the bath. That's okay, isn't it?"

"I haven't shared a toilet with anyone since my football playing days," Tommy said, "but I guess if the Doc is okay with it."

Both men turned to Thema and waited for her response.

"We should be able to work out a routine," she said. "We're both adults."

"Wonderful, you are both going to fit right in here," Denis said. "Alex has brought your luggage so you should find your belongings. I supposed he can stay in the storage room off the kitchen. They don't require much, so don't worry about him.

"How about Nuru? Thema asked, nodding to the little girl attached to her waist. "Will she go home?"

"Kind of doubt it, looks like you're stuck with both of them," he said, moving off to the door. He paused and ran a finger along a tabletop that stood by the entryway as if checking for dust. "Don't worry, they are quiet. You won't even know they are around. Quite handy really, what with the washing, cleaning, and cooking. Handy indeed, almost indispensable, and now with two little helpers, the place should be ship-shape."

"Both?" Tommy and Thema said in unison.

The brother answered with a blithe, "Oh, it should be fine. There's nothing in the storage room right now so it should make a nice sleeping room. The small kitchen is there in the alcove and is quite adequate. You should find several more of these lamps. Just light as many as you need, barrel of kerosene out back, and Alex can handle any day-to-day needs." With one last glance around, he said, "Well, now if that's all, I'm off."

"Where do you stay, Brother Denis?" Tommy

asked.

"Oh, didn't I mention? I'm staying not far off, in Bonga."

"Bonga?" Tommy repeated.

"Yes, a little village five kilometers from here, on the edge of the border. I've only been there a short while, but I like it. Good people."

"So, we are close to the border here?"

"Oh yes, northeast of us, close by the path." he said, stepping out onto the porch. "Rain coming in," he warned, glancing to the sky and sticking his nose to the wind. Descending the steps into the fading night he added, "Better get the boy to shutter the windows or you'll be wet in the morning."

A low rumble in the distance highlighted the brother's warning and before he could call out to them, Alex and little Nuru ran to shutter the windows. Almost immediately the room temperature in the little space soared since closing the shutters stopped the breeze through the windows and room. Thema rushed around the room turning off the hot lamps except for one, which she adjusted to a dim light.

"Well," Tommy said, moving to the screen door and looking out into the enchanting scene before him. The lights in the village huts shined like stars in the sky night, "here we are."

Thema joined him at the door. Large insects of different shapes and sizes busily flapped into the screen, attracted by her lamp light. An approaching storm brought a cloud cover that passed before the moon like a heavy curtain and the night sounds subsided.

Anything much more than a few feet from the doorway stayed invisible. Then a crack of thunder rocked the house. With a shriek, Thema jumped into his arms. "Whoa, sorry," she said. "I've always been afraid of lightning."

"Don't worry, Doc," he said, holding her tight. "I got you."

Thema looked up at him and smiled. When she gently tried to push away, Tommy said, "Hold on now, I was just getting comfortable."

"Ah, let's just keep this professional, Tommy" she said, pushing him away.

"Well," he said, letting her go, "You might need a warm body to snuggle up to."

"Ah, Tommy," Thema said pivoting, "this is Africa. It doesn't get cold enough here for *snuggling*."

****

The first room they came to held a full-size bed and a set of sturdy cabinets. A mosquito net surrounded the bed and a new looking mattress. Though spartan by western standards it was adequate for their mission in a rustic way.

"This looks comfortable enough," Thema said and moved off to the second room, where they found the same bedroom set-up and her trunks and luggage.

"What do you think of the accommodations?" Tommy asked, following behind her.

"Hard to say," she answered as a heavy wind blew around the house. "I'm not sure what I expected but so far I'm not impressed by this MAM project."

"We just got here, Doc. Let's give it a few days."

Thema put the lamp on a table and opened the lid on one of her trunks and searched through the contents. "Here, Alex," she directed the boy, handing him a set of sheets she had pulled from the trunk. "Why don't you get these two mats from the floor, and you can make a space in the room by the kitchen for you and Nuru."

"Yes, Doctor Bok," the boy said and kneeling, rolled up the thick bamboo mats, "We will be okay. We never sleep in bed."

"Well," Thema said as it started to rain. The drum on the tin roof overhead made it hard to hear. "Can you please tell Nuru about the arrangements."

Tommy followed Thema and the two children to the storage room where she put the lamp on a small wooden table and then showed Nuru how to spread the sheets over the woven mats. She felt guilty about the arrangements. She'd have to talk to Blanco about the bed situation.

When tucked in, she kneeled over the young girl and smiled at her. When Nuru raised her arms to her, Thema bent to the girl and accepted a good night hug that spread warmth from her toes to her head. When she pulled away Thema noticed a leather wound charm around the girl's neck. A charm that seemed familiar.

She gave the girl a small kiss on her head, then said, "Come on Tommy, let's get you situated. Did you bring any sheets?"

"No, but I got a great snake bite kit."

"Just in case you run into a Black Mamba?"

"Got to be prepared, Doc," he said, as Thema pulled a second set of sheets from her trunk.

"Well, here," she offered him, handing him the sheets. Her hands touched his, and a spark traveled through her. "Ah, you go on to that other bedroom and settle in."

"So, what about you, Doc? Do you think you'll settle in?"

"I'm going to give it a while," Thema said, digging in her trunk again. "I might be overreacting. I mean this is such a peaceful little village. What on earth is there to worry about in a place like this?"

Chapter Fifteen

First thing the next morning, Tommy woke with a dull ache in his head and a sore neck from sleeping without a pillow. Of all the things he could have packed, a bed pillow never once crossed his mind.

After looking around at the rough mud plastered walls, open beamed ceiling, and thick layered mosquito betting surrounding the bed, he remembered. "Oh, right, Africa." He usually slept soundly, but if he didn't, he could always blame a missing pillow.

Aromas wafting from another room meant someone beat him to his first fresh brewed cup of coffee in his new African home. He had a momentary vision of the pretty Doc floating around the house in a flimsy night gown. He pulled himself out of the bed and worked his way out from under the netting. He wandered about the room barefoot and pulled a pair of cargo shorts from his trunk. He walked into the hall and to the bathroom. The western toilet there in the far corner hugged the outside wall. Water filled a third of the bowl. He decided to use the installed facility and reminded himself to only think about where the plumbing emptied later. Wherever it went, he was sure there were no building code requirements directing the flow.

He washed his face with water that ran from a garden faucet positioned above a shallow tin basin imbedded into a hole in a wooden tabletop. The water, piped from the barrels out back, provided a rustic convenience he appreciated, otherwise he might have to wash in a bucket. He dried off using the lower end of his T-shirt, reminding him that in addition to not bringing his pillow he didn't pack any towels either.

Out in the kitchen a single thick mug sat on the counter beside the three-burner kerosene stove, so he poured coffee from an old pot and searched for the good-looking Doctor Thema Atsu Book.

"Morning!" she said to him from where she sat snuggly beneath an old house coat on a short bench made of rattan with a thick cloth covered cushion. She had her feet in a pair of old slippers and had them perched on the porch rail facing east, she soaked in the morning sun as it came over the horizon. Her new friend from the night before, Nuru, sat close to her, resting her head on her shoulder.

"Morning," he said, noticing again how pretty the Doc looked dressed in a rag of a house coat first thing in the morning. "Thanks for the coffee."

"I thought you might appreciate a cup your first morning in Africa. Looks like someone stocked a few things in the pantry. But don't get used to it. I didn't come three thousand miles to wait on a man."

"Why did you come?"

"I came on vacation."

"Where's Alex?" he asked, settling in a nearby chair.

"He took off across the village, saying something about food."

"You think he'll be back?"

"I imagine," she said, taking a sip of coffee.

"I don't suppose there's any room service around

here?"

"Kind of doubt it."

"Well, do you think we should check with the crew, I'm sure they brought along some supplies."

"Let's give Alex a chance, I think he expects to provide."

"What do you think about this view?" he asked. "I didn't get a good look at it last night but in the morning light it is quite remarkable."

From the porch they could view the entire village and the surrounding dense bush, thick enough to hide an elephant. The road to the right lay beyond the clinic and the rest of the village was to the left. Beyond the clinic the construction crew's camp sat snug beneath a giant Baobab tree.

"It's nice enough," she nodded, non-committal about the view or their situation.

"Doc," he said, spreading his arms out wide, "it is breathtaking! I never dreamed it could be so spectacular. I mean just think," he said, "Africa in all its wonder."

"Yeah, well if it's okay with you, I'd like to withhold judgment on the wonder part until after breakfast."

"And how about that welcome last night?" he said, stretching out in his chair.

"Yeah, well, what about it?"

"Didn't you just get the warmest feeling?"

"You mean from the heartburn caused by the spicy food?" she said, peeking at him over the rim of her coffee mug.

"Come on, Doc, everything I ate tasted good."

"That's because you only ate meat."

"Got to eat whatever is on the menu, Doc. You

wouldn't want to offend the chief after he killed the prize hog, would you?"

"I pick a little more from the veggie side of the menu."

"From what I see, that won't be a problem around here."

"Hey, here's our boy now," Thema pointed.

Alex jogged swiftly across the compound. The little boy balanced a small basket on his head and sang a song as he moved closer. "Good morning, good morning," he said, "I brought some things for your breakfast."

"Hot bagels?" Tommy asked, looking into the basket.

"Bagels?" Alex questioned the term awkwardly, trying to pronounce the word like Tommy did. "No, but I have hot peanuts and fresh fruit."

Tommy took the basket and pulled out a rolled brown newspaper cone that contained some newly roasted peanuts. He poured a handful into his palm and twisted the top closed. "Hot peanuts in the morning," he said, "what can be better?"

"Thank God," Thema said picking through the basket and taking a banana and an orange, "I'm about starved." She handed Nuru a banana and starting to peel the orange.

"So, what do you think," Tommy asked, "pretty nice, no?"

"What," she said, "a few peanuts and fresh fruit. I can get that back at the local corner market."

"Yeah," he half agreed, pointing out over the village, "but can you get this view?"

"Well," she said putting a section of orange into her mouth, "I suppose that is one thing you can't get at the corner store."

"Doctor Bok," Alex said, "Mr. Blanco wanted to know if you would meet with him when you are ready."

"Okay, Alex, go tell Mr. Blanco we'll be right along as soon as we get dressed."

Tommy watched the boy dash off in the direction of the crew's camp, everyone anxious to get off to an active morning.

"Are you coming, Foster?" Thema asked, going inside to get ready, Nuru following closely behind.

After they washed and dressed, Thema and Tommy trekked to the old clinic with the little girl ever at her side. On the opposite side from the clinic, the construction crew made camp and built a latrine out of scrap bamboo and rattan mats. Kimo worked alongside Blanco, lashing some bamboo together.

"Looks like you boys are right at home here," Thema said, finding the crew settled in.

"This isn't our first mission. So," he said, looking at Thema, "did you two sleep okay?"

"I don't know about Tommy, but I was dead to the world. How about you?"

"I could have used my pillow," he said, looking at her, "but I managed."

"So," Tommy asked, interrupting the morning chit chat between the two, "when are the rest of the supplies coming in? I could do with more than a fruit breakfast."

"This afternoon," Blanco said, not taking his eyes off Thema. "But get used to the local food, Tommy, you're not here in vacation.

Thema said, "So what's the plan?"

Getting back to business, he pointed to the front of the clinic. "You'll need to get the feel for the clinic so you should be busy breaking things in."

Thema turned and noticed a few people milling about the front of the clinic. "I guess it's been a while since anyone in the village has seen a real doctor."

"Some time, I suspect," Mike said. "I think you'll be a busy bee for the next few days."

"Guess I'll get started," she said then asked, "Foster?"

"Doc, that's your thing there. I wouldn't be any good for you. Besides, the crew and I need to do some planning of our own."

"I can go," Kimo volunteered. "I can be of great assistance."

"Right then," she agreed, waving to him to join her and grabbing Nuru by the hand, "let's get started."

"Okay," Tommy asked, rubbing his hands together when they were alone, "what about us, what's the plan?"

Blanco said, "we've got pre planning to do before we start moving any earth, but it's straight forward."

"I didn't mean the construction cover, I meant the protection detail. When do we start that."

"We haven't reached the start point yet, but in the meantime, we need to keep up appearances with the construction project."

"Okay, then what's the plan on that?"

"First, we locate the available materials, timber and stone in the area."

"Stone?"

"Yeah, we'll need to set the building on a solid foundation. Without concrete, we'll use stone. There is some granite around, especially along the rim of the nearby range. The Royal Corps of Engineers used it on the bridges they built back in the early 40s. Of course, the locals use stone whenever they build. Those palaver hut knee walls are built with the stone. That's an old stone tradition. Ever hear of the Great Zimbabwe?"

"The Great Zimbabwe?" Tommy asked.

"Dude, don't you know anything about Africa?"

"Come on, man. It's too early to be busting my balls."

"Dude, the Great Zimbabwe is a series of ancient stone structures south of here. History says they could be a thousand years old. They aren't exactly the Pyramids but still impressive. Stonework is an old tradition in their blood."

"No kidding?"

"No, I'm not kidding. We'll get it hauled in, stone by stone, and Page will set the foundation. He's a mason by trade and there are plenty of ant hills in the area."

"Ant hills?" Toomy repeated, thinking he didn't hear him right.

"Sure, that's where we get the clay mud for the mortar. They don't use much, just enough to set the stone level. Good solid material, ant hill mud. It's simple really."

"Right," Tommy said, with raised eyebrows, "so when do we get started?"

"This is where you come in, Foster," Mike said, pulling a set of plans out of a cardboard tube and laying them out on a bamboo tabletop lashed together over bamboo leg posts. "Before that we need to look for some timber for the pilings and structure beams. We shipped over some four by eight plywood for the floors but for the joists, beams and roof supports we'll make do with local timber. We've even got some tin for the roof, but everything else we'll get local. You'll design the clinic like a post and beam structure. Look at these sample plans designed with post and beam. No two by four walls, but a larger size, wide open floor plan. You need to scale it to our site. We can come in later and put in some divider walls using stick and mud technique, but the post and beams carry the load. There are plenty of post and beam materials out in the woods. We'll start scouting around today and inventory what's available. There is good mahogany here, lots of sturdy hard wood. Some of this timber could last a hundred years."

"A hundred years." Tommy repeated.

"Maybe two hundred," Blanco said, "Just think of that legacy."

"That would be something."

"So, what we need from you is a fitting design that matches the location there with the post and beam structure. The current mission house is a small example but of course we need something larger."

"How large?"

"Whatever the Doc needs, but within reason. We'll build it for her after you draw it. You can do that, right?"

Tommy hesitated a second, reviewing in his mind the task at hand, "Sure, I can draw it. That's the easy part, just tell me what I am going to be working with. But what's the plan for the security mission?"

"We are getting right on that," Mike said. "We have to make contact with the local rebels."

"Why?"

"The rebel leader, a guy named Mustafa, is hiding somewhere around here. He calls the shots when it concerns the administration's military in the area. In the meantime, we need to move ahead with the project, stay busy, and not blow our cover.

"Now, I'm taking a crew and heading north along the Mt. Kizi range. There are several granite veins there and we'll check them out, as well as talk to some of the locals. Page will take a crew and scout out the timber. We'll be out most of the day, but we'll be back by nightfall. Willy and Barnes will stay in camp to meet the trucks getting in this afternoon. We just heard they started out late and will get here later today."

"Heard," Tommy asked, "how'd you hear? I didn't think there was phone service here."

"There isn't but we have a satellite phone link that VIS set up."

"Who's your contact?"

"Annette Monson, who you met her on the plane, works with the Agency and will be feeding us intel from the capital."

"That pretty little thing works with the Agency?"

"Yes, her public relations cover let's her snoop in difficult places. She'll keep us informed of anything important."

"Well, hey," Tommy asked, "how come we're not hooked up?"

"You will be," he answered, "plans call for a full communications room when the clinic is built. That's part of the equipment we did get on the plane."

"So, why can't we get hooked up sooner?"

"Well, we've only got a couple of handhelds for now and I hadn't planned on it until we built the clinic but tell you what. We'll put something together in the mission house after the trucks come in. There's extra space there, right? Soon as we get settled in and get our equipment in order, we'll get you sorted out."

"How long?"

"In a couple of days, why, you need to call someone?"

"I could call home, check in and tell them I got here okay."

"Look, the phone is for operation use. You're not on vacation here. Besides, you have got some designing to do, and we need to start hunting. So, what do you think?"

Tommy grabbed the set of plans, "No problem, give me a couple of days."

"Okay then," Blanco concluded, "I think we all got something to do so let's get busy."

Tommy took the plans and headed back to the mission house. He paused at the clinic and noted a few villagers lingering nearby.

When a quick question about the size of the foundation popped into his head, he spun about to retrace his steps to the crew compound, but the men began to leave, entering the bush, carrying big packs with extra gear. He guessed they wanted to be prepared for anything.

Tommy continued to the house. This time when he climbed the home's steps, he paid closer attention to the construction technique used to build it. He was disappointed that he hadn't noticed the post and beam structure. He wondered about his architectural skills when he neglected to grasp the basics of the design the project required. The lack of available materials and what wouldn't be available locally should have crossed his mind, but it didn't. No, he didn't expect to find a lumber yard around the place.

Once inside the house he examined the underside of the roof structure. Exposed beams spanned the length of the rooms and others zigzagged to the ceiling. It looked complicated. For the first time on this trip, he began to get a weird feeling in his gut, a feeling that he underestimated something on this adventure.

Chapter Sixteen

That night, as he contemplated the demanding weeks ahead, sleep eluded Mustafa. During the day he worked his mismatched charges for several hours and took advantage of the preliminary stages of the operation to get in some target practice. There would be no government troops within ear shot of rifle fire, so he didn't worry about that. And after the action started, it wouldn't matter.

In the meantime, everyone got to fire off some extra rounds. Usually, their low supply of ammunition prevented any form of target practice but with a resupply imminent they could now afford the luxury. Although they took out that patrol at the bridge, he wasn't particularly satisfied with his little army's performance. And now with new members to integrate into the force, they could use a little practice together.

"You slept long and hard, my friend," Mustafa greeted Brother Denis at the first sign of movement from the hammock. "Did you enjoy your walk in the woods?"

"One thing for sure," Denis said, "it is a bit longer to Masango than I anticipated, especially if we make the trip during the night."

"We'll manage."

"Yes, and the river crossing is very deep, as you said, even more than I imagined."

"It always is."

"Is there anything to eat?" Brother Denis asked.

"Bananas and cold rice," Mustafa said.

Brother Denis slipped out of his hammock and stretched his arms above his head.

"What is she like?" Mustafa asked.

"Who," Denis said, stepping across the hut and looking for the wash pan.

"The good doctor, of course"

"Oh, she is fine," he noted blandly. Denis poured some water into a flat plastic pan and dipped his hands in and started to wash off the sleep.

"Fine?" Mustafa said. "*Fine* is all you can say?"

"Yes, she is fine!" he said again, grabbing a towel from a peg set in the near post.

"She must be more than simply fine, my friend, so what else can you tell me?"

"Well," Brother Denis began again after taking a banana and peeling the meat free, "she is rather pretty. Of course, my experience in such things is limited, but I'd say, yes, rather pretty."

"Is that all?"

"No, no, I'd say very smart as well."

"Tell me something else, my friend, she is a doctor after all."

"Yes, but there is something more to her smarts, I think. She appeared tentative with her surroundings as she arrived, but little hesitation in her as she contemplated the tasks ahead. I think she will adjust to any situation and is already in love with the children."

"Is that so?"

"Yes, and that will be of value to us. Don't you think?

****

Tommy spent the rest of the morning bent over the wood table near the kitchen, going over the sample plans of the post and beam structure. The temperature in the back room rose steadily as the morning wore on; sweat flowed down his brow and ran into his eyes and dripped on the plan's blueprint paper. The design was for a spacious home, but it could be adapted. At lunchtime Alex came in with a basket of fruit, a bowl of soup, and a plate of rice.

"What's this?" Tommy asked him when he saw the bowls.

"Lunch," the boy said.

Tommy bent over and took a sniff of the hot steamy bowl of soup that Alex placed on the table and grinned. "Smells hot?"

"It is," Alex said, "it is village favorite."

"What is it?"

"Greens and peppers," he said, "very good."

Tommy smiled at the boy and nodded his head. As soon as Alex left, he picked an orange out of the basket and although he never cared much for fruit, he started to peel it back.

About halfway through the afternoon Tommy decided he needed some paper and headed out the door yelling out to Alex who was banging away on something in the kitchen, "I'm going to the crew's camp. Be back in a little while."

****

Thema puttered about the clinic. Her two assistants took care of the small tasks of cleaning and maintenance. Only a couple of actual patients came by. A young man showed up with a broken wrist which she set using a splint made from a sliver of bamboo. She set it and gave him a sling to carry the load. One older woman came in with a bad tooth ache. Although it wasn't her specialty, Thema extracted a rotten molar, packed the socket with gauze, and gave the woman aspirin for the pain.

Along about noon Thema asked Mudiwa, "Where is everybody?"

"The village is not used to Doctor Bok yet."

"What do you mean?"

"Village people must trust doctor first before they come."

"How long will that take?"

"Village will come when ready."

"But when will that be?"

"Subria, Doctor Bok."

"What?"

"*Subria*," Zuma said, "it means patience."

Nuru came running, calling to Thema in native dialect.

"What is she saying?" Thema asked Zuma.

"Nuru says a visitor has come."

"Who?"

"Imamu, he come to visit," Zuma told her, jumping from her seat and going to the doorway to peer out.

"Who?"

"Imamu Neo."

"Oh yes, Imamu Neo, the medicine man."

"Yes," Zuma smiled, "he medicine man."

"Well, please invite him in," she instructed.

"Imamu no come in clinic, Doctor Bok".

"No," she asked, "but why not."

"Imamu says *forest is his clinic*. He no come inside this clinic."

"Then we must go out to him?"

"Yes," Zuma agreed, "we go."

Thema led the way outside to the clinic steps, Zuma and Mudiwa following close behind. She found a thin old man there, waiting just off the bottom step. He wore a bright colored cloak that resembled a narrow weave Kente cloth pattern of gray and green geometric colors that stretched to his bare feet. He wore a necklace made of beads in different colors and shapes as well as a piece of wood wrapped in leather hanging from his neck. Though larger, the wood piece seemed similar to charms other villagers wore. Thema sensed it must be some sign of the village.

The Imamu held a long walking stick in a withered hand and leaned heavily on it when he shifted his weight.

Zuma spoke to the old man. "This man say welcome, daughter."

"Tell him, thank you," she asked Zuma.

The man spoke several words and waited for Zuma to translate.

"Imamu Neo, say, you must go walk about with him."

"Where?"

"Into forest," Zuma explained.

"What for?"

Zuma translated. "Imamu Neo says, *'There is much to learn of medicine in the forest. Not all in book.'*"

"Well, sure, okay then, when?"

"Imamu Neo say, you go now."

"Now?"

"Yes, he says now."

The Imamu Neo turned and walked slowly away, past the mission house and stepped onto a barely visible trail at the edge of the forest. Thema followed at a slow pace and Zuma followed behind. As Thema stepped into the forest shade Imamu Neo raised his hand and said something to Zuma.

"This Imamu say I no go."

"But who'll translate?" Thema asked.

Zuma asked the Imamu. "This Imamu says you understand what he will show you. No need other."

Imamu Neo stepped onto the faint forest path and quickly disappeared within the jungle depth.

Thema looked at Zuma and repeated, "He says I won't need you?"

"He says I no go, no need."

"What do you think?" Thema asked.

"I think Doctor Bok must go, quickly."

"Yes," Thema said, "oh, yes," she said, realizing she was being left behind and she rushed off to follow the Imamu.

Thema trotted along the path and caught the old man. He trekked lightly and made good time. She guessed his age to be somewhere in his eighties but remembering the difficulty in calculating age in native populations he could be one hundred. He kept a steady pace, and his footfalls made no sound. When the bush spread across the trail with limbs or vines, he seemed to flow through the obstructions with noiseless grace like wind through your hair.

The path led through dense undercover and thick forest alike and the pair walked in silence for only a brief time when the Imamu stopped and bent over at the waist, pointing to something on the ground. Thema looked at where the man pointed, and he said something in native dialect, and encouraged her to examine the vine he pointed to. He motioned for her to pull the vine. She yanked the vine from where it clung to a bush and examined it. It resembled a creeping Native American vine with wide leaf.

The Imamu took the leaf, placed it between his palms and rubbed vigorously, turning the leaf to a green pulp which quickly formed a sticky mass. The Imamu said something else, then, using his own arm as a visual aide, demonstrated how to massage the pulpy mass into the skin. Thema remembered reading that creeping vines in this part of Africa could be used as an anti-inflammatory.

"That's wonderful," she said.

The old man smiled and handed her a beaded bag and motioned to her to put the vine inside the bag, which she did.

The Imamu started off again, but they walked only another short distance when they came to a clearing in the woods. A tall tree stood before them, and a blanket of bright orange/reddish leaves covered the floor beneath the tree's grand limbs. Thema recognized the African Tulip tree and its bark that held natural healing powers when used as an antibacterial cover and in some forms even served as an anti-malaria medicine.

Moving to the base of the tree, the Imamu broke off several crusts of the tree's lower bark. He waved one hand over the other with the bits of tree bark and he made a squashing motion indicating how to grind the bark. Thema figured probably in a mortar of some sort, pulverizing the bark for use as a topical or maybe after straining in a liquid. He handed the pieces to her and motioned to her to put them in the bag.

Smiling and nodding, Thema thanked the old man and followed his directions. The Imamu continued to lead in this way, and they made slow but continual progress under the jungle canopy. Around another turn in the path, they came to a large growth of thick forest trees bordering a narrow river. The old man paused and pointed along the bank and into the canopy, showing Thema a rich thick woody vine that spread into the limbs of the trees some fifty feet above the ground. The twining vine bore pinnate leaves, quite large, in clusters of three. The bowl-like clusters bore purple-colored flowers in bright bloom, hanging wisteria like from the tree limbs of the forest foliage. The flowers past bloom held six inch long, brownish, yellow-colored seedpods, some ripened on the vine and split, revealing about two or three fat, kidney-shaped, maroon-colored seeds.

Thema recognized the dark, one inch long, Calabar beans. They contained chemical properties, but she also remembered the fine line dividing its beneficial medical properties from the known poisonous properties of the bean. Meanwhile, the Imamu continued talking rapidly about something and again gestured Thema to put some of the seeds into her bag.

Their little journey continued so, and the Imamu stopped a dozen times and after each explanation, Thema put the talked about sample into the bag. Finally, as the afternoon wore on, she realized they had walked full circle because upon a short rise in the landscape the village appeared below. The Imamu stopped and saying more knelt at a round clearing with a small fire smoldering in a shallow circular pit and a giant Baobab tree loomed over them. The Imamu bent over and blew lightly on the embers bringing the fire back to life. He took a couple of uniformly cut logs and placed them carefully to bank the fire.

Thema listened and nodded when she thought it proper. Finally, the Imamu motioned to her to open the bag and take out the sample leaves, bark, and seeds. As she drew each item, he spoke briefly about the sample, summarizing the qualities of each and pantomimed the usage, either topical or by the mouth. For one of the samples, he made a drinking motion. Of course, it was too much to remember all he told her, but she could do some research later and complement the nature walk with scientific resources.

Finally, the man paused and smiled. He said something to Thema and getting up, he motioned for her to follow. He walked to the edge of the clearing where another giant Baobab tree loomed over the man's little compound. He put his left hand on the tree's trunk and put his other hand on his chest, near his heart. Then he touched her forehead with his right hand, then her chest and held it there. Almost instantly, Thema felt heat beneath his hand. Then the man closed his eyes and relaxed, then chanted out a few words, *Imani – Dawa*, over and over for a minute.

At the end of his chanting, the Imamu took Thema's hand and placed it upon his breast, held it there, and began chanting again. The heat returned to her palm and grew as he chanted louder and louder to a point, she wanted to pull her hand away, but she let him hold it there. When the heat reached a level, one she couldn't take a second more, the Imamu released her hand and he at once slumped in exhaustion.

Thema covered the spot over her breast with her hand. A remnant of heat still burned there. The Imamu rose from his slump and when he gazed at her, he smiled wide and said something. Thema pointed to the man's charm dangling from his neck and asked about the leather amulet, which reminded her of something. The Imamu gestured to the great Baobab tree above them and said something she of course didn't understand, but his motions indicated the amulet came from the great tree.

Thema smiled at the man and nodded agreement with whatever he was saying to her. Then she stepped to the giant tree and placed her hands on its great trunk. Research on the Baobab trees of Africa found many medicinal qualities in the tree, not the least of which suggested enhanced fertility, and equated the health of the local children with their environment, which was dominated by the great tree. The natives in the regions where the trees grew referred to the tree as the *Tree of Life,* and the birth rate in the villages where the tree grew was higher, and also, twins were born in greater number than in other places not gifted with the tree.

According to legend, the circumstances of the tree's gnarly root like appearance, came about because of the tree's vanity. Apparently, when God created the Earth, he created the Baobab tree and endowed it with great beauty and healing powers. Unfortunately, the tree began to think of itself as greater than the other plants of the earth and began to brag to the other trees that God had favored it above others. When God heard what the tree was saying he got angry. As a punishment for the tree's vanity, God uprooted the tree and turning it over, planted it back into the ground with its roots in the air but it's lush branches of greenery was buried beneath the soil where no one could see. Since they were a gift from God, he let the tree keep its healing powers, but the tree could no longer brag about its beauty.

The veracity of the legend was debatable, but Thema

felt the healing powers of the ancient tree. The Imamu smiled broadly, and saying something more, finished the lesson. She expected the man to lead the way back, but he only stood in the same spot and smiled. She finally noticed that there in the outcrop of the rocks, a short round cave opening hugged the green ground cover, probably the Imamu's home.

The Imamu smiled again, and waved to her, signaling the end of the day's lessons. Gathering her samples together she stuffed them into the bag and stood up. Scanning the clearing she found an opening in the lush bush which she hoped led to the village below.

Just before she stepped on the path Thema turned to wave goodbye to the man but only found an empty camp site. She couldn't be sure if he tramped back out in the woods or had retreated to his den. In any case, tired and ready to get back with her little treasure of native fauna, she faced back to the path and started.

At the bottom of the rise, she found herself back in the thick underbrush of the jungle. She veered to her right and found a path that appeared to lead in the direction of the village, but the path soon disappeared into the lush forest. Thinking she had turned the wrong way she retraced her steps. She passed the cross trail that led back up the hill but walked on ahead. That trail ended at a wide shallow stream bed. She remembered crossing water on the way here but then again, the direction appeared different than when they started out.

Thema retraced her steps again looking for the first trail that led from the Imamu's hillside home but after walking for several minutes she couldn't find it. Looking first left and then right she could not pick out the path that led to the rise. She slogged on, to see if she could see the village again, wading through the thick underbrush. The vines along the ground grabbed at her feet as she stumbled, making it difficult to walk on the hill. Branches and limbs choked the trail forcing her to use her arms to protect her face. She stumbled and fell to her knees. Struggling to her feet, she pushed ahead and kept climbing, hoping to attain the high point and get her bearings.

A low limb from a tree reached out and tripped her, forcing her into an awkward gait, and as she staggered forward, she stumbled forward, approaching a running lurch, then she burst out of the bush and rolled into a clearing, settling on her back.

The first pangs of panic began to set in her stomach, but she stayed on the ground, breathing heavily, holding back the fear, determined to reason it out. She heard a faint rustling in the undergrowth below and wondered what animal approached, man or beast. The sound grew louder, and Thema could only stare in the direction of the sound. She struggled to her feet, but her legs, like lead, refused to move. She couldn't see which way to run, so she doubted she would get far. The noise grew louder in the bush.

"Help!" Thema called out when a tall village woman emerged from the thick bush. "Thank God!" she continued speaking although the smiling woman said nothing. "I think I'm lost. Could you help me?"

The woman said something in dialect, scolding her, but Thema didn't care, rushing to her side, thankful for the friendly face. The woman smiled broadly at her and with her hand she gently squeezed Thema's cheek. She nodded and with her large, callused hand she touched the spot where the Imamu raised heat on her breast. The woman nodded and smiled again, saying something to her. The women stood tall like Thema, with thick broad shoulders. A two-inch piece of wood wound tight with leather in a familiar twist, hung from her thick neck.

Thema recognized the woman from somewhere, but she had seen so many people the last few days she couldn't place her. The woman spun around and with a small laugh and wave of her hand beckoned her to follow. Thema hurried after the woman as she led the way to the village. At the village edge the woman separated the limbs of a thick bush so Thema could step through and clear of the dense under growth.

Once through, Thema turned to thank the woman, but she'd disappeared.

Chapter Seventeen

With a brutal sun beating down, the air hit him like a wet towel when Tommy stepped out in the open. The clinic stood silent, not a patient anywhere. He detoured to amble over to the clinic steps and climbed onto the wide straw roofed porch where the temperature dipped at least twenty degrees. He walked along the stone rimmed porch in search of Doctor Book.

He found Kimo and Nuru in the office, holding an animated conversation in their native tongue. "Mr. Foster," Kimo greeted him. "Welcome!"

"What's going on, Kimo," he asked, "this place looks deserted. Where's Dr. Book?"

"She go walk about."

"Walk about?" he asked, "with who?"

"She go with Imamu," he said. "Walk about."

"Oh…the medicine man?"

"Village medicine man."

"How long ago?"

"They left sometime, but back soon."

Tommy wanted to ask more but figured he'd probably gotten as much as he would and decided to save his strength. He wandered to the crew's camp and found Willy Gray sitting at a table working on some electronic device. The little device appeared miniature in the big black man's hands. Gray stood some six foot four and by Tommy's reconning, weighed at least two sixty.

"What's going on, Bro?" Tommy shouted to the man, greeting him from a distance since he didn't want to surprise him.

"Dude," Gray jumped, clearly surprised by Tommy's approach. "You scared the shit out of me," he said and quickly pulled a scrap of canvass over the table work area.

"Sorry," Tommy said coming the rest of the way into their little camp, "what you got your head into?"

"Just taking a look at a water filter, we're going to get a system operational along the river as soon as we start construction."

"Filter system? Don't you just drink bottled water?"

"Sure, but we'll need water from the river for washing and cleaning. The water system filters out most of the bacteria and saves the trouble of boiling water. We got the newest technology for large scale filtering but your boy at the house should have a table model for your personal needs."

"I think I'll stick to bottled water or hot coffee."

"You'll be safer for sure, but we can't truck in enough bottled water for our needs."

"Will there be a load on the trucks?"

"There'll be a couple of pallets but not enough for an extended stay, so we'll filter for the long run."

"When are the trucks getting in?"

"Sometime this afternoon, could be anytime now."

"Do you think there'll be any paper on those trucks."

"Paper?"

"Paper for my design work," he explained. "I wanted to work on a few sketches of the clinic design, and I'd like to get them on paper while fresh in my mind."

"There might be some pads or something but nothing special. Hey, Barnes," he called to the other crew member, "you got any paper for Mr. Foster here?"

Barnes came out of one of the tents and snapped his fingers, "Got just what you need Foster." he said, motioning for him to follow. Tommy noted Barnes's slighter frame that boasted quite an assortment of tattoos displayed across some heavily muscled arms and chest.

"I noticed some blank blueprint paper in that set of plans you took earlier," he explained. "I stashed them in the back of the rover."

Barnes pulled several sheets of the blueprint paper out of the back of one of the rovers and handed them to Tommy.

"What's that?" he asked, seeing a football tucked in a back corner of the rover.

"That's my ball," he explained. "Say, Mike told us about your playing days. He said you had a rocket for an arm."

"That right?" Tommy said, finding some common ground with this member of the crew.

"Here," he said, tossing Tommy the ball, "I'll run an out and you hit me."

Barnes ran out about twenty yards and turned sharply to his left. Tommy anticipated the turn and let go a perfect spiral that led the man perfectly and he snatched the ball right out of the air.

"Damn," he said excitedly, "I wish I had someone who could throw it like that when I played. I might have made the pros."

"Just what the pros need," Willy Gray said, "another pipsqueak receiver."

"Don't mind him," Barnes said, tossing Tommy the

ball and heading out on another route, "he's just a fat out of shape defensive lineman that never fulfilled his dream."

Tommy watched Barnes make a quick stop and go and then sprinted longer. Tommy threw the ball about as far as he could, giving him a chance to settle under it and he caught it in stride showing some soft hands. Quite a trick seeing as the man wore a pair of thick jungle boots and managed to dodge a couple of little kids as he dashed to the imaginary end zone where he spiked the ball into the village ground.

"Don't mind him," Willy apologized, "he's never gotten over his glory days."

"Used to be pretty good?"

"Yeah, in his mind."

"That all?"

"He made a couple of pre-season scout teams, but never broke in."

"And you?"

"I gave it up."

"What happened?"

"Long odds, man. I finished my degree then signed on with the Marines. After that duty I took the Foreign Service Test and have been working ever since. I've been with a couple of NGOs before signing on with VSI."

"What are you guys jawing about?" Barnes asked coming back from his scoring catch.

Tommy started to explain, but a rumble of trucks approaching interrupted him and the three men turned to watch the mission's supply trucks crossing over the Kagera River bridge.

"Looks like the supplies are here," Tommy said. "I'll leave it to you to unload."

Tommy left the two men and lumbered to the mission house. He passed the clinic on the way, and it didn't look any different. He hurried on, determined to get some sketches done before Thema returned from her walk. From the top of the stairs, he observed a variety of village people heading in the direction of the road and trucks. Help for unloading.

Tommy took refuge in the mission house and thanked the Lord for the relief from the sizzling sun. Compared to the one hundred degrees outside, it felt like air conditioning. He spent the rest of the afternoon sketching out some ideas. Little Alex sat at the table and kept him company. Tommy gave him a pencil and let him draw on a yellow legal pad. Demonstrating a keen eye for detail, Alex worked on several renditions of the village. Tommy and Alex worked until the light began to fade in the room, then Alex lit a lantern and disappeared into the kitchen. That's when Tommy realized he hadn't seen Doctor Book yet. Despite himself, he started to worry.

"Alex," he said to the house boy.

"Yes, Mr. Foster," he answered from the kitchen. He had pots on the three burners of the kerosene stove while at the same time chopping something on the cutting board.

"I wonder where Doctor Book is?"

"There are lights in the clinic, Mr. Tommy, she must be there."

Tommy strolled to the doorway and indeed, the clinic lights burned bright in the coming night. Surely, she would stop for the workday soon. He pushed open the door and wandered to the clinic.

As Tommy approached the clinic, he heard a

whining sound in the crew's quarters. It sounded like a generator, quieter than most, but a bright light confirmed it for him. Loud talk and laughter filtered from the camp, marking the return of the two search parties. He wondered what type of trees they found and hustled over to find out.

"Mike?" Tommy called as he approached the lighted area.

"Come on in," Blanco replied. He and his men were spread out around the camp. The men had a light bulb plugged into a cord that illuminated the whole area. The men looked beat to Tommy but smiling just the same.

"Looks like you folks are right at home now. Where did you get a generator?"

"We packed a couple away with the equipment that came in the trucks. It's just a small voltage, barely enough for one light bulb but it's okay. Got one for the clinic too if Doctor Book wants to work at night by a real light as opposed to a kerosene lamp. Tell her we've got one.

"Sure, I'll tell her about the light. So, any luck today?" Tommy asked.

"We got a good view of the land," Blanco explained. "There's a nice stand of virgin forest not two clicks from here. I think we could get everything we need right there. It will take some doing to haul in, but I think we'll be happy with what we get."

"Did you get everything you expected on the trucks?

Willy Gray said, "we unloaded everything, and they left a panel truck with a couple of barrels of gas and the plywood. They took off right after that, said they didn't want to be out in the boonies after dark."

"Any beer?" Tommy asked.

"Cold and ready," Barnes said pointing to a big cooler. "We got to thank Annette for that, I didn't think she'd remember."

Barnes handed Tommy a can of beer.

"What's on tap?"

"Mostly German lager."

Tommy held the cold bottle to his forehead. The ice-cold glass cooled his sweaty head.

"Drink it while it's cold, boys," Mike said, "it'll be tomorrow before we get our kerosene frig running."

Tommy asked Mike, "Did you make contact with the local rebel leader?"

"We met him and dropped them some supplies. They're organized and have seen recent action."

"Is he coming in so we can protect him?"

"No, he and his merry band like it out in the jungle."

Tommy stayed awhile and enjoyed the crew and their camaraderie. Barnes got out the football and they tossed it around.

"Foster," Mike said to Tommy once the commotion died and the crew began to settle in, "how are the plans coming?"

"I've got some sketches done and details by tomorrow."

"Great," he said, "soon as we get a line on enough timber, we'll start hauling it in. I think I'll take a crew out tomorrow morning and scout along the river and make sure there's nothing closer we can use. Page will lay out the site area and stake out the foundation tomorrow. So how big did you decide to go?"

"I haven't spoken with Thema yet."

"Come on man, we got to plan."

"I haven't talked to her much. I checked on her once

this afternoon, but the ladies told me she walked about."

"Walk about," Mike said. "She doesn't need to be walking about."

"She took a guide."

"Who?"

"Some Imamu dude."

"Imamu Neo?" Mike asked.

"Yeah, that's him."

"Tommy, that's the local kook medicine man."

"What of it?"

"Man, that's who she came to replace."

"Well, from what she told me, the Doc is into that native stuff, and she says it might come in handy here."

"Look, if she needs help, just tell me because Willy Gray can lend a hand any time she needs it."

"Gray?"

"Yeah," he repeated, "he's a navy corpsman. He used to be with the marines."

"Oh, you mean Willy Gray?"

"Yeah, that's right, did he tell you?"

"No, no, he only said he did a tour with the marines after college. He didn't say anything about being a medic."

"Corpsman," Mike corrected him, "in the Marines it's corpsman. And Richards was a medic in the army before he joined the Rangers. Anyway, they didn't come over for that kind of duty, but if needed they are available."

"Well, okay," Tommy said ready to leave, "I'm sure the Doc would welcome the help."

"Listen, Tommy, you're supposed to keep an eye on her. What kind of a security guard are you?"

"What's the fuss? I think that lady can handle a walk

in the woods."

"Listen Tommy. Doctor Book is a big key to this operation. No doctor—no mission. I put you there to keep an eye on her."

"Chill, dude, no harm no foul."

"Well, get it done," Blanco repeated, turning and looking toward the clinic. "She's in your hands. We've got a job to do here, and you need to babysit the doc."

Tommy retraced his steps in the approaching night and passed the dark clinic. The sounds of the croaking frogs and the wild night noise of the jungle at sunset, accompanied him on his route.

When Tommy entered the mission house, he called out, "Doctor Book?"

"In here," she answered from the table.

"Doc," Tommy said coming into the room, seeing the table covered in a variety of leaves, roots, and seeds. "What do you have there?"

She looked up at him and smiled. "The most wonderful things."

"Like, what...?" he asked noticing she had out a stone mortar and pestle.

"Well, around noon Imamu Neo came by, and we walked about."

"Yeah, they told me at the clinic. Blanco told me the man's a kook."

"Well," she said sitting back in her chair, "he might be a bit unorthodox, but he really is a sweet old man."

"Yeah, well okay," he said. "So, what did you and the old man do?"

"He was showing me the locations of these natural remedies.'

"Is that what you are grinding there?"

"Yes, I've been reading about these different plants and uses and comparing them with the Imamu's remedies."

"What do you mean?"

"Well, a number of these plants do contain healing properties."

"For real?"

"Yes," she said, pointing to each one in turn. "This root is used for treating malaria. This one when ground to a paste, can be used as an antibacterial. And these seeds when ground can be mixed with water and drank as an anti-inflammatory, amazing stuff. Of course, Imamu doesn't understand the chemical forces here, but this stuff works, and he uses it. I'm thinking that's why the clinic is slow."

"Slow, what do you mean?"

"I expected a crowd today, but only a few villagers showed up."

"I suppose they have to get used to you. It'll pick up."

"I'm not worried," she smiled getting back to reading. "If all I ever got to do this trip was research on the natural plants around the village it would be plenty for me."

"Long way to come for research?" he commented.

"I had my hopes about doing some research," Thema said, "and now that I see the environment here, I think it might be worthwhile."

"What do you mean?"

"Now don't think I'm weird or anything, but I think it has to do with the Baobab tree."

"What?"

"Healthy people. The tree and the people have a

relationship that promotes physical health."

"The tree?"

"Well, not just the tree but the area environment and fauna are a perfect mixture for supporting a healthy lifestyle. We've only been here a little while, but I haven't seen a sick child anywhere. Have you?"

"No, not really."

"Well, research points to the positive environment as the basis for healthy living and I think they are right. If I don't do anything more than confirm such findings it will be worth the time."

"What about the building a clinic project?"

"You can build it and then maybe that school too. That will be a good year's worth of work for anyone. Say, what about you?"

"What?"

"What did you do today?"

"I've been working on some drawings for the new clinic. Let me show you."

"So that's what that was. I put them over there."

Tommy gathered the drawings, and Thema cleared a spot on the table. "Blanco wants us to decide how big a place you think you'll need, the square feet you'll need and all."

"Well, I'm not sure," she said, "what do you think?"

"Well, how big was your clinic back home?"

"About three thousand square feet."

"So, about, fifty by sixty?"

"That was it."

"Would that be big enough?"

"Should be, I'd could tend to a lot of people in a place that size, properly equipped."

"Okay then. But we'll make it longer than wider

since finding one-piece beams to span a narrow width is easier."

Tommy and Thema talked and worked on into the evening. He liked working close to the Doc. He couldn't help being attracted to her. Even with her interest in that nature stuff.

Nuru and Alex stretched out asleep on the little sofa hours before and finally tired themselves they decided to stop for the day. Tommy shuffled around the room turning off the lamps and the Doc roused the two children and herded them off to their makeshift bedroom.

Tommy started to shut the front door but stopped when he gazed out at the moonlit village. He could easily make out the clinic below. Strange thing, the medicine man, Imamu. He wondered about the fuss for building a clinic in a town where apparently the neighborhood witch doctor already took care of the villagers, and a tree kept everyone healthy. Well, the clinic project was only a cover for the security contract. He guessed it didn't matter if a new clinic ever got used as long as the mission was completed.

When the Doc came back, she joined him at the door. "Another beautiful night," she said, taking in the view of the village.

"That's not the only beautiful thing here," Tommy said, gazing at her.

Thema regarded him and said, "Is that a standard line from your repertoire?"

"What do you mean?"

"Don't forget, Foster, over the past couple of years, I heard a lot about you around the hospital."

"Come on, Doc…" he said, moving closer to her, "you're not going to believe a bunch of rumors, are you?"

"No," she said, wagging a finger at him, "I think we need to keep this professional."

"Do you know what I think?" Tommy said, leaning in, their bodies touching, ready to kiss her. "I think we need to keep this...*personal*."

Chapter Eighteen

Tommy's second morning in Masango broke like the first: alone in a strange bed without a pillow, but different, since he hadn't gone to bed alone. He and the Doc got caught up in the romance of the place and ended up in bed. He didn't know how he felt about that. After getting his bearings, he dug himself out from beneath the mosquito netting. The Doc was nowhere to be seen, so he imagined she was off to an early start. He wondered what she felt about spending the night in the same bed.

"Where's Doctor Book," Tommy asked Alex when he found the boy in the kitchen.

"Doctor Bok gone to clinic," Alex said offering Tommy a cup of coffee. "You like breakfast?"

"Breakfast," he said, wiping the sleep from his eyes and taking the cup, "what do you have?"

"Rice pudding and fruit."

"What?"

"Rice pudding," he repeated, "hot rice pudding. Doctor Bok show me how this morning. We get sugar from trucks that came yesterday."

"Well," Tommy said, "let's eat!"

After breakfast Tommy plodded down toward the Clinic. He had planned to stop in and say hello to the Doc, but he didn't want to add any pressure to her. She hadn't said anything the night before so was probably still in the processing stage. There were no patients at the clinic when he passed, so the Doc would have time to jump into the research option on native plants. He bypassed the clinic, himself not so sure about the Doc and he and the mission itself and strolled to the crew's quarters to find out what the men planned to do that morning, happy not to think about her for the time being.

When he arrived at the crew area, Barnes and Nuru sat among a small group of teenage girls. The group surrounded a table stacked with a collection of cloth and buttons that had come on the supply trucks. "Barnes," Tommy called, "my man, what gives."

"Window shopping," he said with a smile, "the simplest things fascinate them." Barnes had a way with the girls. Tommy was aware that Barnes, and the crew, had a military background, but in spite of his "Death Before Dishonor" Special Forces body art, the man had a soft side.

Tommy looked around the deserted area. Where is everyone?"

"Blanco took a team out to scout for materials and map the perimeter for a defensive contingency. Page is in town, laying out the new clinic site. We're going to bribe these young ladies to clean the area so we can stake it out."

"Man," he said, "you got an early start today. I wanted to talk to Mike."

"You just missed him," Barnes said, "they'll be back this afternoon."

Tommy said, "are they out scouting for timber again?"

"Sure, timber, stone, whatever. Say," Barnes asked, "throw me a couple, will you?"

"Barnes," he said, "your football days are over,

man."

"Come on, Foster," he said running off to get the ball. Following him, Tommy watched as he pulled the lift open on the tailgate of one of the rovers. A football and a soccer ball rolled out.

"Grab that soccer ball," Barnes asked Tommy. "I've been saving that for the kids. I figured we'd get a game going after lunch."

"Do you play soccer?" Tommy asked him after he retrieved the ball.

"A little," he answered, "but the kids are experts. They were kicking a coconut around the square yesterday, and I've never seen a happier people. They always have a smile on their faces and are always willing to work. Anyway, I remembered we packed some athletic equipment for the school, assuming we'd get around to the school this trip."

"All right, speedy," Tommy told Barnes. "Let me see those legs you are always going on about."

Barnes flipped Tommy the ball and ran a fly pattern along the side of the road. Tommy gave it a heave and found Barnes's hands about fifty yards away, soft hands for sure.

As Barnes jogged back to a round of applause from the village girls, a convoy of trucks rumbled down the road from the north, right at them. A big army rig led the way. After the truck pulled to the side, two heavy ore trucks barreled past, spewing dust everywhere. Several government soldiers stood in the truck bed, covered in red dust. "Watch yourself, Tommy," Barnes told him as he jogged to the camp. "Army regulars are bad news."

"We've been invited," Tommy said. "They should be happy we're here."

"Not these guys," Barnes said, "they still got that Hutu Tutsi thing going on around here."

Tommy watched as the big truck pulled over to the side of the road and in a squeak of brakes, stopped right in front of him and Barnes.

"Hello," Tommy greeted the soldiers as they started to clamor off the truck.

"Hello," a sergeant with a big smile of white teeth called back as he climbed out of the passenger seat of the cab and came around the front of the truck, "Are you Doctor Bok?"

"No, no, I'm Tommy Foster," he said, "Doctor Book is at the clinic."

"Then please," the big sergeant said, "could you call for her? We hear there is a doctor in the clinic, and we need a doctor to look at one of my men."

"Sure," Tommy said, "Barnes, get one of the girls to run and get the Doc, will you?"

After Barnes spoke quickly in the village dialect to the group of girls, Nuru broke away and started out in a run.

"It will just be a minute," Tommy told the soldiers. He counted eight in all, plus the injured man who groaned loudly in the back of the truck. "Would you like to sit and have a cold drink?"

The sergeant spoke to his men in a dialect, and they smiled and gathered around the ice chest. Tommy lifted the top of the chest, and the sergeant pulled out cans of cola for his men. The men found places to sit on crates and boxes and popped the lids and drank from the cans.

The soldiers settled back, talking, and laughing among themselves, but Tommy noticed they kept an eye on the group of teenage girls sitting at the nearby table.

When the nervous girls started to leave, one of the soldiers moved fast and caught one of the older ones by the hair, hauling her against him.

The girl fought back, but the men laughed and began to pass her back and forth between them. Tommy wanted to intervene, but before he could think of what he could or should do, the girl managed to break away and struck the man in the side of his face with her elbow, forcing him back a few steps.

Once steadied, the soldier rushed at the girl, but using a Judo move and the man's momentum, she threw him over her side onto his back. When the other soldiers laughed at the soldier on the ground, he rolled to his feet and stormed toward her. She fended him off, kicking and chopping with her fists, and she landed several punches on the man, including a kick to his groin, which sent him to his knees. The soldier's laughter ended then and two other soldiers stepped in to subdue the fighting girl.

Then, Thema appeared. Looking like fire and glory.

"What's going on here?" she shouted. "Let that girl go. *Immediately!*"

The soldiers paused at her order. With her ferocity, the white coat, and stethoscope around her neck, it was obvious that Doctor Book had arrived.

"What is the meaning of this, sergeant?" she asked the big leader.

The sergeant said something to his men, and they relaxed, but one of the soldiers maintained a hold on the girl. Separated from their friend, the other girls circled behind Thema. The older girl who fought the men shouted something at the soldiers.

"Do not mind my men, Doctor," the big man said with a smile, "they are following orders."

"Well, sergeant," she said, "I would expect you to manage more control over your men than to let them roughly handle anyone they choose. I demand that you release the girl."

Barnes moved to her side. "Take it easy, Doc," he advised under his breath.

"Yes, Doctor," the sergeant said, again showing the big smile. "Take it easy. We only stopped because of our injured man and wanted you to look at him."

He guided Thema over to the truck bed and showed her the soldier who was moaning in pain. Thema looked at the man and immediately understood the pain came from a badly injured leg. A haphazard wrap had stemmed the bleeding. "What happened here?"

"He caught his leg in the machinery at the mine," the sergeant said. "We've no doctor there but heard there was one here in this village."

"Mr. Barnes," Thema asked softly, "could you please find me the crew's first aid kit?"

Barnes retrieved a military grade aid kit from his tent and passed it to Thema. "Sergeant," she directed, "stretch the man out so I can examine his leg."

Once the patient was situated, Thema used a pair of scissors from the kit to cut away the man's pant leg, then she washed the calf wound with alcohol from the kit. When the solution hit the wound, the man yelled out, loud enough to make those in the vicinity wince in sympathy. Once she cleaned the wound, it bled less but the leg looked severely damaged, and the man continued to moan.

She quickly dabbed the wound from one end to the other with more alcohol. Then, using a roll of constricting bandages, she wrapped the man's calf tight from knee to ankle. As she wrapped, Thema paused at intervals to press her hands on the man's leg and hold for a moment. When she was done, the man stopped groaning.

"Here, sergeant," Thema told the big man, handing him a package of additional bandages, "if it starts to bleed again, you can change out the bandage. He might need some stitches, so if he does start bleeding again, you should stop at the hospital in Bandella. They can tend to him there."

"Yes, Doctor," he said. "We heard the supply trucks came, so we stopped for doctor first. It is good there is a healer here again."

She nodded. "I hope I can be of great service to the people of the village."

"Doctor," the sergeant moved to her and leered. "Someone attacked one of our patrols two days ago. We heard there was a new mission here, so we wanted to stop and make sure you are safe."

She stepped back, gave him one of her stern doctors looks. "Sergeant, do we look like we are in danger?"

"But why have you come to our country?"

"The current administration invited us to come and build a clinic. That is our mission."

"You haven't treated any wounded rebel soldiers?" the sergeant asked, moving to the girl who was still in the grasp of the soldiers, and grabbed her chin in his beefy hand. "Any wounded girl soldiers?"

Pulling back her shoulders, Thema spoke slowly, carefully. "I have not seen, nor treated any wounded soldiers."

The sergeant nodded. "Are you sure?"

This time, her spine went arrow straight, adding—

in Tommy's opinion—a couple more inches in height and in stature. "Of course, I'm sure. Now, is there anything else?"

"No, Doctor, this is all for now. If my men need any treatment, we will come back."

The sergeant said something to the two men holding the girl. They tried to load her into the back of their truck, but she fought them, with such force that two other men had to step in to subdue her.

"The girl, Sergeant," Thema asked, "will you let her go?"

"We will bring her back, Doctor Bok," he said with a smile, moving around to the opposite side of the truck, "after we question her."

"Sergeant," Thema said, again slowly and carefully, "surely a child is of no importance to you."

"This girl is a soldier, Doctor," he said, nodding at his men to put the girl in the truck bed. We need to question her about her activities."

Before they could put her in the truck bed, Tommy quickly moved to the man holding the girl. Stepping to the soldier's side, he body blocked him, putting the man on the ground and momentarily setting the girl free. A soldier nearby reacted just as quickly and swung the butt of his rifle at Tommy's head, but he ducked under that and with the man pivoting away he set his hip under the man's waist and hauled him over and to the ground.

Another soldier charged Tommy. Using the man's momentum, he flipped the man over his shoulder and onto the ground as well. Two soldiers halfway into the truck stepped off and charged at him at the same time. The first swung wildly; Tommy feinted away from the blow and with his forearm blocked the blow around and into the path of the second man and both stumbled and fell in a pile. Tommy had managed to fend off five of the soldiers without really striking any of them. Just as the five men started to gather themselves and the others started to climb out of the truck to join them, a loud crack from a pistol exploded in the air.

"Okay, okay, soldier," the sergeant shouted above the ring of the weapon he held high over his head. "You put on good show for my men." He moved around the truck and stepped between Tommy and his men. "But now, you must *take it easy*." Shouting something to his men they gathered themselves and started to get back into the truck, hauling the kicking girl with them.

Tommy watched helplessly as the men scrambled laughing onto the back of the vehicle. They picked the girl up and put her in the big truck bed. The sergeant climbed into the cab and the army truck started and then lumbered off, slowly negotiated the narrow bridge over the Kagera River, and drove away.

Barnes quickly pulled another of the older girls aside and gave her instructions. She took off, running west through the village and quickly disappeared into the forest.

"Where's she going?" Tommy asked.

"I sent her ahead to warn the other nearby villages. These thugs will stop and do more damage before they are through."

"Tommy," Thema shouted, "what the hell happened?"

"Nothing, Doc," he said, "we were just tossing the ball when these trucks came by."

"It's my fault, Doctor Book," Barnes explained. "I invited the girls to come, to show them some of the stuff we got in."

"I'll say," she cried. "There is no telling what will happen to her now."

"Let's go after them," Tommy said.

"Hold on, Mr. Rambo man," Barnes said. "We need to take it easy. They are better armed, and we're outnumbered. Let's see what happens down the road."

"Who was that girl?" Tommy asked the group of girls. "She really fought off those men."

"She, Sauda," someone in the group answered.

"She didn't seem afraid of them," Thema said.

"Not all the villagers are submissive, especially the Buta," Barnes said. "Many of these girls have seen tough times. That one who fought back, she's probably a rebel fighter, just in town to visit her family."

"A girl rebel," Tommy repeated, stooping to pick something off the dirt.

"You bet," Barnes affirmed as he headed toward his tent. "If you want to survive around here, you have to learn how to fight."

"What do you have there, Tommy?" Thema, asked.

"Some kind of charm. The girl must have lost it in the scuffle."

"A girl fighter," Thema said again.

"Yeah, a girl."

Tommy took a good look at the charm before handing it to Thema, and recognized it was similar to ones he'd seen worn by other villagers.

"But a girl?" Thema asked again, examining the charm, bringing it to her breasts.

"I guess the locals are fighting with what they have."

"Speaking of fighting," Thema said, gazing at him, reaching out and taking hold of his arm. "Thanks for trying to help. You could have been hurt or…"

"Now, don't worry about me, Doc. I can take care of myself. That's why they brought me along."

She looked at him a bit more closely than he liked. "I thought they brought you to build the clinic?"

****

Brother Denis read the text message from Frank Barnes on the satellite phone. At first, he couldn't believe their good luck, but with not much time they needed to act. With Masango ten kilometers away by road, the convoy would be to the bridge over the Juarzon in fifteen minutes.

"The boys, Mustafa," Denis shouted, grabbing his rifle and jumping over the short wall of the palaver hut. "This is no drill," he said looking at his watch and checking the time. "We have fifteen minutes to get to the bridge. A convoy and army patrol is coming."

Mustafa shouted something in the native dialect and everyone in the group took their weapons and quickly moved off. They entered the jungle trail in single file with Sekou leading the way.

The young crew had practiced this run many times. More times than not, they made the run in less than twenty minutes. The group moved steadily and after a time increased the pace. Brother Denis began to breathe heavily and forced himself to slow to a jog. They needed to conserve their energy for the coming fight.

"Sekou," he called ahead to his young leader, "run in front. There will be three trucks but the first two will pass before we get there, but you must stop the third. If the troop truck gets there before we do, open fire and pin them on the road. It will take them a while to regroup. By then we'll arrive. Assume a position on the opposite side of the road and when we get there, we'll join in a crossfire."

Denis kept a steady tempo with the boys, but Sekou quickly increased his pace and pulled away on the path and quickly disappeared ahead of them. He would get there three minutes before they could and should beat the patrol truck as well. He'd be on his own for a minute or so, but the faith of his ancestors lived within him and would sustain him.

****

"What the hell is an army patrol doing way up here?" Tommy asked Barnes when he rejoined them.

"Administration soldiers guard the gold convoys along this road."

"Gold?" Both Tommy and Thema asked at the same time.

"Yeah, the mines are just north of here. There are a couple of routes, but they come by here every so often depending on road conditions."

"What gold?" Thema asked.

"The administration's mining operations are one of the main revenue sources, especially with the increase in the price of gold over the last few years. What is it now, two thousand dollars per ounce?"

"Great," Tommy said, "you'd think they could have chosen a better place to build a clinic."

"They'll do anything to keep the mines going," Barnes said. "It's the only way they can keep the lights on."

"That's just great," Thema grunted.

"Look, Doctor Book," Barnes said, "I'm sorry about the girl, but the army pretty well controls things here."

Thema waited for a moment. "Will it be like we've

seen on the news?"

Barnes turned away and didn't say another word.

Thema looked at him and imagined the worst would happen and it made her even angrier. "So, what are we going to do?"

"Don't worry, Doctor Book," he said, "The other villages along the road are less accommodating than Masango. Let's just wait and hear what happens."

****

Brother Denis checked his watch, and taking a quick look around stiffened as they prepared to exit the heavy bush ahead. He held the boys back to a jog and then a silent walk as they came to the edge of the forest. Just as they made the trail's end, he heard Sekou begin to fire on the advancing convoy, the rat a tat sound from his weapon filling the surrounding air. Denis didn't hear any of the big diesel engines and when he came out of the woods, only the army troop truck was at the bridge, the ore trucks having already crossed and traveled away. Sekou fired on the lone troop vehicle from a prone position behind a log. His first rounds took out the front tires of the truck, forcing it to plow into the bridge buttress and coming to a rest to the side of the bridge. Sekou continued intermittent bursts from his weapon, pinning the soldiers in a vulnerable position in their truck.

With Sekou directly across the road, firing a consistent one-man barrage of heavy rounds, Denis motioned for the remaining group of rebels to spread out to his left. The boys and girls quickly fanned out behind the cover of the roadside drainage trench. The soldiers began jumping out on their side of the truck, away from the steady fire from Sekou's weapon, but directly in their own sights.

Brother Denis didn't wait for the soldiers to regroup. As soon as his group settled into their prone firing positions, he gave the order to open fire. The distinctive sound of the AK- 47s filled the air, and the red-hot rounds caught the administration soldiers by complete surprise, cutting into them before they could accurately return fire. The sound ripped through the air and blue smoke poured from the barrels of their weapons.

The last few soldiers got off a round of fire from their weapons that raked the boy's position, but moments later the whole administration army squad lay on the ground.

"Hold your fire," Mustafa shouted above the din of the automatic fire, "hold your fire," he said again and also signaled with a wave of his hands.

The young crew ceased fire and Sekou left his position and ran across the road to make sure the soldiers were dead. When Sekou got to the truck he found the big sergeant still breathing, hanging halfway out of the truck cab. Sekou put a burst from his weapon into the soldier's chest that threw the big man back and into the cab.

Brother Denis approached the truck and looked into the back of the bed. The village girl sat tucked safely behind a couple of fifty-five-gallon drums. Denis smiled at the girl and offered her his hand. "So, what's your name, my darling?"

The girl looked back and forth between the men and boys, and seeing only smiling faces, said, "Sauda."

"Well, Suada," he said, "welcome to Bonga."

The boys smiled wide and laughed, though surprised the girl was there. Somehow, in the excitement, Brother Denis forgot to mention her.

Chapter Nineteen

By early evening, Doctor Book had enough. Her vision was blurred from the reading she'd done. She had stayed busy, grinding and mashing the various native leaf and root varieties trying not to think about the girl, Sauda, and what might be happening to her.

Thinking research might be the cure to her fretting, she started identifying plants with the most healing properties. She sent Zuma out several times to get more samples of the fauna familiar to the village and continued right through lunch and to the dinner hour. Earlier, Nuru lit the kerosene lamps in the room.

Finally done for the day, Thema directed Zuma to lock up, but Nuru entered the office and said something to Zuma who did the interpreting. "Nuru says there is a woman patient here."

"What woman?"

"Nuru says it is Chief Kulu's wife, Nyarai."

Surprised, she asked, "Chief Kulu's wife? Then, I guess you'd better show her in."

The woman entered the office with a large bandage wrapped around her eyes and led by one of her daughters.

"Nyarai, what seems to be the trouble?" Thema asked with Zuma translating.

"She says her eyes hurt?"

"For how long?"

"For not long time now," Zuma answered.

"How can you say, Zuma, you haven't asked her yet?"

"This woman is Chief's first wife, Doctor. She blind for some time now."

"Blind?" Thema asked.

"Yes, one time when she wakes and eyes hurt. Then she blind."

"Well, let's examine her."

Thema carefully unwrapped the cloth from around the woman's head and exposed the woman's eyes. The woman flinched at her touch but as Thema held the woman's face in her hands, the woman stopped moaning. Thema shifted the lamp's position across the desktop and the woman seemed to notice the movement.

After the first inspection of the Chief's wife Thema diagnosed *acute angle glaucoma*. "Ask the chief's wife how the pain started."

Zuma asked the question and replied that the pain started quickly.

Thema gently tilted the chief's wife's head so she could get a good look in the bright light. The woman's eyes were obviously infected. The eye's conjunctiva was swollen red, and the pupils of both eyes were dilated. Using a handheld monocular scope with light, she inspected the optic nerves in her patient's eyes. "Ask the chief's wife if she was sick before the trouble with her eyes began."

Zuma questioned the woman; with a low groan she answered. "She say that yes, she been sick to stomach and vomit," Zuma repeated.

Thema held the woman's head in her hands for a moment and she stopped moaning. The symptoms were certainly associated with glaucoma, unfortunately Thema didn't have a local pharmacy to acquire the would-be prescribed eye drops to reverse the optic pressure.

But she did remember something from that afternoon's reading.

"Zuma," she asked her assistant, "bring me that box of seeds we collected today."

****

Brother Denis sat across the palaver hut from the young lady whom they'd rescued earlier. The light from the fading day threw shadows on the faces of the boys gathered around the young girl, but she smiled at them and bantered back and forth about the whole adventure.

"Don't worry about them," Denis told her. "They've never seen anyone as pretty as you.

"Mustafa, my friend," Denis directed, "get our young guest something to eat, I'm sure she is hungry."

Mustafa ordered one of the boys to his feet and he dashed off in the direction of the other huts in the village.

"Brother Denis," Sekou, the boy leader, called out. "Can you come take a look at this boy here?"

"What's wrong?"

"He is wounded."

"Why didn't you say something before?"

"Boy strong, he no say something before, but now I see he lose blood."

Brother Denis knelt where the boy rested, and kneeling saw the boy's bloody abdomen. "This is a serious wound, Sekou, very deep. See—" he pointed, "— the bullet entered there, but it came out in the back, there."

"Can you fix him?"

"Not me. The bullet probably tore the muscle on its way through," he said, and moving back to the hut began gathering some gear together.

"So, just where are you going?" Mustafa asked Brother Denis, watching him pack.

"The boy needs help, my friend, more than I can do, and it is time that I go walk about."

"Where?"

"We'll carry the boy over to Masango to Doctor Bok. Then, I think I will visit the Mt. Kizi people."

"Mt. Kizi?"

"I want to drop in on my friend with the Buta."

"She will not speak with you!"

"I think she will now."

"Now?"

"There is more at stake now and we can use the help," Denis said, pointing to the little group of boy and girl fighters.

"I still think you are wasting your time."

"You don't think she'll come? She *is* your mother."

"Well, good luck with that."

"You can't stay at odds with the family matriarch forever."

"She is too cautious for me," he said, turning from his friend. "Waiting on a miracle."

"It has worked out for her in the past."

"Has it? Besides, we don't need her men. We'll get what we need from right here."

"Well, my friend," Denis said putting the last of his gear into his backpack. "Let me try. In the meantime, keep gathering more fighters. Although we might have enough men to start this war, we will need more to finish it."

"How long will you be gone?"

"One day, maybe two."

"Will you need more than two boys for the litter?"

"No, two are enough," he said, motioning to the two teens to get the younger boy loaded up. "Make sure you get our young lady back to the camp tomorrow," Denis said as they moved off into the gathering darkness of the forest. "I'll leave the boy in Masango before continuing north. You can retrieve him when you take Sauda to Masango and do me another favor?"

"Yes, my brother?"

"If I miss the next skirmish, try not to get yourself killed."

****

After the clinic cleared out, Thema grabbed a beat-up clip board holding a writing pad with notes she made during the long day and headed out the clinic door. The last rays of sunlight had long disappeared, and full moonlight filtered through an open spot in the surrounding forest. The slightly sloped trail seemed steeper to her just then, but she trudged along. Nuru quickly walked ahead and darted to the house. Thema looked forward to relaxing in one of those big, deep comfortable chairs in the parlor and getting little Nuru or Alex to make her a cup of tea.

At the top of the path, she turned around and looked out over the village. She couldn't believe she was in Africa where her ancestors had lived for thousands of years. Other western country's histories couldn't compare. She really hadn't quite grasped what everyone meant when they spoke about African home. How many times did she hear classmates talking about heritage and roots, and she never understood or even cared really.

How silly it was for her to deny the obvious until now, with it staring her in the face.

"What are you thinking about?" Tommy asked her as he came from behind her.

"Oh, I guess I'm feeling a little at home," she said, "with this place, these people."

He laughed. "You mean city girl, born and raised, Doctor Book has found a home here?"

"Yes, Doctor Book has found a home here," she said and smiled broadly. "Of course, I've been saying and spelling my name wrong all these years."

"What do you mean?"

"Haven't you noticed the different sounds when the villagers speak to or about me?"

Tommy nodded. "Well, to be honest, I did, but figured it was the language difference."

"I did as well—at first," she said. "But Zuma tells me my last name isn't 'book' like in something you read, but is Bok, as in *balk*. That's the way they say it anyhow."

Thema led the way into the parlor and noticed a delightful aroma in the air. "What's that?"

"Soup, Doctor Bok," Alex said.

"Yes, we know," Tommy said, "but what kind?"

"African Soup."

"Well, it smells just delicious, is it ready?"

"Yes, Doctor Bok," he said, "please to wash and I will serve."

After Thema and Tommy washed in the basin under the water faucet in the spartan bathroom, she grabbed a towel to dry off, then said to Tommy, "I'm sorry I shouted at you this morning."

"Forget it," he said, snatching the towel from her

"I'm sorry it happened."

"So, did we hear anything on our little friend?" Thema asked.

"Nothing yet. I'm very sorry I didn't act quicker at the time."

"You gave it a shot for the good it did."

"Just trying to help."

"I've been thinking about that."

"About what?" Tommy asked.

"That big sergeant dude, what he said."

"What did he say?"

She gave him a hard look. "He called you a soldier."

Tommy hesitated. Thema was beginning to look at their mission in a different light. "Aren't we all ex-soldiers of some sort?"

"I guess," she murmured.

"I think Barnes told me he was ex special forces or something," Tommy said. "All those guys served in all branches of the military at one time or another."

"I can't get my head around these girl rebels."

"If they're like Sauda, then they might be on to something."

"Strange country," she said, "all this natural beauty and brutality at the same time. Life brimming in every crevice, yet danger thrives here as well. This is a land of contradictions and mystery, but at the same time, blatantly honest."

"Only in Africa," Tommy said.

"Yes, and the place is beginning to grow on me. Come on, let's eat."

They sat at the small table where Alex set out enamel plates and metal spoons for dinner. Nuru came over and placed several covered dishes on the table and put out two bottles of water. Tommy helped Thema with her chair and taking his seat started to dish rice onto his plate.

"What is this?" Thema asked, opening one of the lid-covered bowls.

"Soup," Tommy said, lifting to lid on the rice bowl to check it out.

"Yeah, but what kind?"

"African soup," he said, "just pour some over the rice and eat the whole mess. You are supposed to mix it all up, but I like mine a little separate."

"Oh, yeah, of course."

"Look, Doc," he said, "I think it'd be better we don't ask too many questions. Besides, it's good stuff. Be careful of those little red peppers though, or you'll be popping hot gas all night."

Tommy and Thema finished the rice, and a bit of the soup, after which Thema showed Alex and Nuru how to brew tea.

"Those two are pretty smart," she said, returning to the table, balancing two cups of tea. "Shall we take our tea in the parlor?"

"Okay," Tommy agreed, moving to the worn but soft sofa, "but let's think about getting to bed early."

"Why?" she asked, putting the cups on a table and sitting a bit away from him. "Do you have early rounds or something?"

"No," he said, inching closer to her, keeping the distance between them close, "but we might…"

"What?" she asked, sliding toward him along the sofa.

"Don't you feel we should be working on forming a closer working relationship?"

"I think I've heard about your working relationships, Foster."

A loud knock on the screen door interrupted them. "Who's there?" Tommy called from where he sat.

"It's Willy," came the reply, "Willy Gray."

"Come on in," Thema invited, straightening up. A little disappointed at the intrusion.

Willy came into the room and took off his fatigue cap.

"What's happening, my man?" Tommy asked.

"Did you two eat dinner already?"

"We did and now we are kicking back and digesting."

"Well, I guess it's been a long day for everyone."

"Sure has," Thema agreed. "So, what's up?"

"Well, I was wondering…"

"Wondered about what," Thema asked.

"Well, Doctor Book, would you mind coming down to the clinic?"

"What?" Tommy said, sitting up.

"The clinic, Doctor Book. Someone just came into camp bleeding awful bad. I tried some compression bandages and direct pressure, but it's a deep wound. I think he might need some stitches."

"Are you sure?" Thema asked.

"Yeah, pretty sure. I'd do it myself, but it's been a while since I tried to handle anything like that, and I think this might call for some internal stitches as well and I didn't want to take a chance and mess it up. Internal bleeding requires a delicate touch I don't possess."

"Okay, let me change my shoes and shirt."

"Willy," Tommy asked, "isn't this something that can wait until morning?"

"Tommy," she said to him, shaking a finger at him, as she dashed into the other room to change. When she returned to the men, she found Tommy giving Willy Gray an angry look, but Willy had turned his head as if he didn't want to make eye contact with the man.

"Don't wait up, Tommy," Thema said as she gathered a few things into a bag. "It could take a while."

****

When Tommy awoke on the third day after arriving in Masango, he recognized his bed. Sweat soaked his collar and the back of his shirt, and he was alone again. He slipped under the mosquito net and stumbled into the bathroom to wash up.

After putting on a clean T-shirt, he found Thema sitting at the table drinking coffee. "Doc. What time did you get in?"

"I guess after midnight," she said, smiling at him.

"Long hours."

"I enjoyed doing a little ER medicine for a change."

"I waited awhile for you."

"The wound required more than a band aide. It took a while to clean it out and then stitch. Young boy, ten or eleven. I was lucky to get it to stop bleeding."

"Did he tell you how it happened?"

"No, he wouldn't say," she said, straightening up. "He lay there the whole time, didn't say a word and it had to hurt. He didn't blink an eye during the whole procedure."

"What was it?"

"A deep abominable wound. I put ten stitches inside and another ten on top, plus I gave him a unit of saline."

"Is he going to be, okay?"

"I think so," she said. "I left him with Willy Gray.

I've seen some wounds like that before."

"Yeah?"

"Sure."

"Where?"

"The ER back at Mercy," she said, then took a sip of coffee."

"I thought you were one of those family medicine types. I didn't know you worked in the ER too."

"All family practice residents do an emergency med rotation. You never know what might walk through the doors." She shrugged. "No big deal, I assure you."

"So, what kind of wound are we talking about?"

"Well, I'd say a bullet wound."

"Bullet wound?" Tommy repeated, like he didn't hear right—and worried the doctor would inadvertently stumble upon the mission's hidden agenda.

"Yes," Thema confirmed getting to her feet. "By the look of it, I'd say it came from a very big gun."

"Wow."

"Yeah," she said. "I'm heading to the clinic now to check on him."

Tommy watched the wonder woman doctor leave. He was amazed at the lady's energy. He hoped she'd save some of that energy for the coming night.

When Alex came into the room, Tommy said. "What's for breakfast?"

"Fruit, Mr. Tommy."

"Alex, my man," he said, "can you fix anything besides fruit and rice pudding for breakfast?"

"I can make you a soup."

"No, no soup!" he said, "Hell no."

"Then what, Mr. Tommy?"

"How about some eggs?" Tommy suggested. "I saw

some chicken's running around loose. There's got to be some eggs in this village if there are chickens."

"Yes, Mr. Tommy, there are eggs. But chicken eggs cost money."

Tommy dug into his pocket and pulled out a hand full of coins and put them in Alex's hand. "Get us some so we can make ourselves an omelet. Money's no problem?"

"Mr. Tommy," he said, gawking at the pile of coins in his hand, "what is omelet".

"Get the eggs and I'll show you."

Tommy watched Alex skip out and cross the village. He should be hustling to the work crew's camp for a briefing on the day, but he didn't. They were going to lay out the foundation today, but he already gave them the dimensions yesterday and he didn't think they would need another hand to hammer in four corner posts.

Even at the early hour, the village appeared alive with activity. A group of women passed by the house, looking to be headed to the river. They balanced large baskets of what looked like laundry atop their heads. They smiled and laughed as they trudged by.

"Morning, ladies," he said, nodding in their direction. Another group of women busily worked, hoeing in the village garden.

When Alex came back with the eggs, the size of robin eggs, Tommy showed him how to make an omelet, without his usual favorites of mushrooms, onions, cheese, or bacon bits. After breakfast, Tommy sauntered to the crew's camp, the sweat already beginning to soak the back of his shirt and drip from under his hat. He found Willy Gray organizing a bunch of crates. "Good morning," he said to the big man.

"Good morning."

"The Doc says you helped patch that kid last night."

"Me? No, I'm clumsy when it comes to surgery stuff. But Doctor Book...I mean she's something special."

"Yeah, I can see that."

"Not just that, Foster," he said pausing and smiling at him, "I mean in the operating room. I've never seen anyone work so fast and delicately at the same time. She was in that kid's gut so fast, tying things off like I've never seen. She stopped the bleeding before I realized it and cleaned the wound out and closed in no time."

"I hear the training back at Mercy is pretty good."

"It's more than that."

"What do you mean.?"

"I mean, that kid was dead when they brought him in. I've seen battle wounds and that boy's was about as bad as it gets. Even under the best of conditions, he would have died, but not last night."

"What are you trying to say?"

"I'm saying Doctor Book is a miracle worker.

Chapter Twenty

Tommy took a break from drawing plans to go outside and stretch his legs around the perimeter of the village. A light cloud cover tempered the heat of the sun to tolerable levels. As he drifted to the forest's edge, a path broke the line of underbrush. He stepped onto it and within ten steps, found himself completely engulfed. The path appeared well worn from constant use. Looking back in the direction he just came from he could still hear children playing but the thick bush blocked the town from view.

As he made his way down the path, the bush thickened and the sounds from the village faded. He shouldn't be out by himself, but he wanted to get out and enjoy the sights. He tripped over exposed roots several times and reminded himself to keep his eyes on the path or he'd end up doing a face plant.

When a moth with a wingspan of two hands crossed in front of him, he followed its flight, entranced with the wonder of it all—and while wondering at the size of the thing, he tripped again. This time he tumbled in a heap and rolled off the trail and down a steep incline. When he tried to get up, he felt a sharp twinge in his knee. A familiar pain remembered from his playing days—and not a good thing.

He was at the bottom of a short bank and momentarily lost his sense of direction. He had fallen from the steep rise, but he couldn't place the trail as to his left or to his right. He scooted up the bank to his left but after a few feet didn't find the path. Thinking he had gone the wrong way, he plowed back into the bank through a buildup of decaying leaves and limbs to scramble to the other side, but he didn't see the path there either. Turning about again he paused and took in the forest scene. He'd only fallen a few feet. The path must be just at the top of the bank across the little ravine. Once more he hobbled down into the thick bush and slugged his way to the opposite bank, this time going deeper into the underbrush, but he still couldn't find the path.

He'd read enough about getting lost in the woods, so he wasn't about to go charging off in random directions. Still, his breathing came in gulps and his heart pounded in his chest as he tried to remind himself to stay calm. Taking his bearings again he was about to jump into the gorge one more time when voices from the woods drifted to him.

Pivoting, he followed the sounds. When he got close enough, he recognized that the words being spoken…were in Chinese.

He went to his knees to creep through the thick bush and found two Chinese men dressed in military garb standing with two native men. The soldiers spoke softly while pointing in the direction of the village.

Tommy quickly and quietly backed away, and when he did, he crossed the path he'd used before that led to the village. There, English conversation and laughter wafted to him. Mike and his crew were striding on the path a few steps from where he stood.

"Tommy," Mike shouted, "what are you doing out here? Are you lost?"

"Just stretching my legs, a little," Tommy said, but before he needed to explain further, he noticed the men were guiding someone. A young girl. Sauda.

She smiled brightly, stood tall among other boys and girls, jostling with them. Looking none the worst for her ordeal. "Is that Sauda? Where did you find her?"

"Over in Bonga."

"But how…"

"Look Tommy, if you don't mind, I'd love nothing better than to chat, but we are beat, and we'd like to get back to camp."

As Blanco and the men marched off, escorting the girl to town, Tommy was right on their steps. When they came out of the woods at the edge of town, several villagers saw the girl and started a round of shouting that skipped from hut to hut. Thema came out of the clinic and Nuru shouted a few words out in native dialect and several village girls answered back excitedly.

Thema quickly started down toward the group as they entered the crew's camp, Tommy watched her break into a run. "Sauda, Sauda, is it you?"

"Sure is," Mike said, as the teenage girl ran into Thema's arms.

"Where'd you find her?" Thema asked, releasing the girl from the fierce hug for a second to hold her at arm's length and look her over. "I'm so glad to see you in one piece," she choked out, then turned and gave Mike a big hug.

"She was over in the neighboring village," Mike said, stroking one large hand up her back.

"So, you mentioned," Tommy said as he moved closer, surprised when Thema brought Sauda into a group hug with Mike and her. "What happened? Did the army let her go?"

"Not exactly," Blanco said, still holding tight to both.

"Then what?" Tommy snapped, peeved with the home coming show.

After Mike released Thema, Tommy waited for him to tell the story. "We weren't there ourselves but seems like there is a rebel group camped over in Bonga."

"Bonga?"

"It's a small village, ten huts or so, a quarter the size of Masango. It's about ten kilometers from here, on the Juarzon River."

"Yeah, okay. Bonga…Wait, isn't that where that brother Denis dude is staying?"

"Well, yes, so there's this group that…"

"What group is there?"

"Freedom fighters," he explained.

"Fighters?"

"Right. Freedom fighters," Mike retorted, putting an edge of snark into his tone—like he was talking to a dummy. Fighters who have been at war against the Hutu for years. No cease fire for them."

Tommy cocked a hip, stuck out his chin. "Oh yeah? How'd they come across our friend, Sauda?"

"As luck has it, they were there at the bridge over the Juarzon when the truck with those soldiers pulled in. I guess they tried to hassle the boys, and when Sauda called out for help, a ruckus started. It's my understanding the fight was short but intense. The girl's safe enough though."

"A fire fight?" Tommy asked, worried about what he feared he was about to hear.

"Yeah, I think everyone on the truck was killed.

That's how they got the girl away."

"*Everyone*?"

"Yes, but they got the girl away, right?"

"Yes, but everyone on the truck?"

"It was them or the girl," Frisco said, interrupting.

"Damn straight," Page said, pushing through the crowd and moving to the cooler, "That girl was dead meat the minute they left here," he said, pulling a cold drink from the box. "It's a miracle she lasted as long as she did. We should be right happy those freedom fighters were Johnny on the spot."

"Doc," Tommy said, "are you hearing this?"

"Well," Thema said, looking deeply at the young girl and hugging her again. "She is safe."

"Doc!"

"She is," she argued, "safe and sound right here." Then she added, "I don't care what happened to those soldiers. The way they treated Sauda and how they looked at the girls. We are lucky those fighters were there."

"But those were administration soldiers," Tommy insisted. "Don't you think they'll be missed?"

"Mike," Thema asked the crew leader, touching his shoulder, "will they be missed?"

"Oh, I'm sure they will, eventually. Course it will take a day or so before the word reaches them. But no worries, we didn't take part in the fight."

"That's it then," Thema ended the little inquiry, "the girl is safe so let's move on."

Tommy watched as she took the leather charm from her pocket, the same one the girl had lost the day before and placed it around the girl's neck. The group drifted toward the clinic. Mike and Thema walked together, with

Sauda between them.

At the rise, a group of women joined in the line and holding each place the line began to move in unison and sang in celebration of Sauda's return. As the women danced, drums played, and men sang. Mike and Thema joined in the dance.

Tommy didn't know what everyone was so happy about. A bunch of dead army men didn't seem like a reason to celebrate. He didn't think this was exactly the mission he signed up for, fighting in a rebel civil war. This verged on armed resistance, way beyond a protection detail. He hoped it didn't get back to them because they didn't have the manpower for that kind of action.

In the middle of the celebration, one of the Chief's wives stumbled into the crowd. Tommy thought she was joining the homecoming party, but Thema started waving her hands and motioned for the group to stop. She ran to the woman who held her hands up to her eyes and shouted out something above the noise.

Chief Kulu must have heard the commotion because he came into the group and raised his arms, and the village became silent, but his oldest wife, who now captured the attention of the village, shouted out, *"Tichaona, Tichaona."*

"What is it?" Thema called out to Zuma who immediately came to her side. "What is she saying?"

"Old Nyarai say, she can see!"

Thema put her hands on the woman's face and cradled her cheeks in her palms. She turned the woman to the sun, and the woman winced away from the bright light, as if in pain. *"Tichaona!"* the woman repeated again, then said something to the crowd who began to chant and shout in a different beat.

"What did she say?" Tommy asked Alex above the gathering noise.

"The woman say she can see. She say, '*she was blind and now she can see*'."

Chief Kulu waved his hands again, bringing the crowd to another silence, and walked closer. When he joined his first wife, he raised his hands to her face, looked closely at her eyes, and asked her something.

"What did he say?" Tommy asked Alex.

"The chief asked how this happen?"

The woman shouted something, and commotion broke out in the crowd at what the answer was.

"What did she say?"

"She say, Doctor Bok made her well," Alex said, bug eyed and entranced with the action. "Doctor Bok brought back the sight!"

The crowd grew quiet, and they moved apart making an opening in their ranks as someone walked among them.

"Who's that?" Tommy asked Alex about the thin old man making his way through the crowd.

"That's Imamu Neo."

"Who?"

"Medicine man, Mr. Tommy," Alex said, again speaking as one might of a holy person.

Imamu Neo approached Nyarai. The crowded square parted as he passed and grew quieter still as he examined her. The Imamu said something to the chief and nodded his head.

When Chief Kulu turned to face Thema, the village crowd paused. Watched. And waited for what seemed like hours when actually it was probably seconds.

Finally, Chief Kulu extended his hand and placed it on top of Thema's head. He spoke a few words, and the crowd burst into shouts of joy. The dancing and drumming started up more boisterous than before.

"What did the Chief say?" Tommy asked Alex.

"Chief say, Doctor Bok is *Sihiri, Sihiri Tinashe.*"

"Tinashe," Tommy repeated. "What is that?"

Alex said, "It means *God* is with her."

The women in the crowd began to jump, then dance to a new rhythm from the drums. The chanting grew into a rhythmic chant with the women shouting, *Thema, Thema.*

Tommy watched Mike and Thema dance away and realized he was jealous. He also realized with the excitement that he forgot to tell Mike about the Chinese dudes he saw.

Chapter Twenty-one

Tommy took refuge in the shade of the mission house for the rest of the afternoon as the celebration eventually subsided and the daily rhythm of the village returned to normal. He sat at the kitchen table trying to work but images of his friend, Mike Blanco, with the Doc continued to interfere with his concentration. He'd known the mission could be physically dangerous—but not dangerous to his heart.

He tried to sketch out some of the new clinic design elevations, but the mental picture of the Doc in Mike's arms and dancing with the man shouldn't have bothered him. The Doc and him had not formed a *relationship*. Not really.

No one had said anything about a *relationship*.

Tommy went into the kitchen to brew a cup of tea. So, they'd had sex. No big deal. It wasn't like love or anything. More a factor of the whole African thing and being thrown together in stressful circumstances. When he took the job, he never envisioned more than a working relationship between them, so he was still no farther along in a rapport. Still, he was jealous. Big time, he could admit without choking on it.

That didn't mean he liked it.

He left the kitchen and walked over to the front screened door with his tea. The air just turned a shade cooler, and he stepped out onto the porch. The sun began to set over the tree line, casting a brilliant red hue between the tops of the surrounding trees and the just appearing moon.

A few steps beyond the porch, he saw lights come on inside the clinic—a sign that the Doc would be working late tonight, though on what he couldn't imagine. Up to now, the villagers hadn't exactly rushed in for treatment.

Usually, the village was quiet at this time of the evening, though tonight there was a lot of activity with people walking about and shouting at each other. He wondered what was up.

****

Tommy slept terribly. The next morning, his head ached like he was hung over although he hadn't had a drop of anything stronger than water the night before. He pushed his way out from beneath the mosquito netting and slipped into his sandals. Plodding out into the other room he found the Doc stretched out on the sofa, dead to the world.

With Alex nowhere to be found, Tommy struck a match to start a burner on the stove and put a kettle of rainwater on. It took a while for the big kettle to get to boiling. Every day Alex boiled several pots of captured rainwater, then ran the water through a ceramic water filter. The filtered water was then used for washing dishes and cooking. He could only guess that the process worked since he hadn't gotten sick yet. To be safe, he kept a full case of bottled water handy for drinking convenience.

Tommy then lit a second burner and put the percolator on. He scooped coffee grounds from a can into the basket, then fixed the lid. The water quickly started to boil, and the pot began to perk. Once the kettle began to whistle, he turned the flame down.

He then took two mugs from the dish strainer and added a tiny bit of sugar from a glass mason jar to one of the mugs. The bare breakfast reminded him how easy it was to get a nice fresh raisin and cinnamon bun from the corner bakery back home, and how it would taste right about then.

"Umm," Thema groaned from the sofa. "Smell that coffee."

"Almost ready," Tommy said as he watched the glass bubble above the pot begin to splash with coffee colored drink. He pulled the pot from the burner so the coffee wouldn't go bitter and poured two mugs full. He kept the one with sugar for himself and took the other to the just awakening Thema. "You put in a long day yesterday, Doc," he said and handed her the coffee. "What time did you get in last night?"

"We got a slew of patients late yesterday, so I stayed late to tend to them. After I got in, I meant to just relax and rest my feet. The next thing I knew was the smell of perking coffee. Thank you, Tommy."

"Can you tell me what that was with the chief's wife?"

"Sure," she explained as she took the first sip, "I treated the woman yesterday afternoon."

"Was she blind?"

"She had what is known as closed-angle glaucoma. It can affect the sight, even result in sudden temporary blindness."

"What?"

"Glaucoma," she said. "It is caused by blocked drainage canals in the eye, resulting in a sudden rise in the pressure inside the eye with very noticeable symptoms. It's rare but treatable. I was reading about it just the other day."

"Why was that?"

"When I walked with Imamu Neo, we stopped at his home site, and he shared a few things with me including some Calabar beans.

"What kind of beans?"

"Calabar," she explained. "They grow along the river here, on long vines, with a pretty purple flower."

"Calabar beans?"

"Right," she explained. "The Imamu showed me the beans and also some powder he made from the seeds."

"So, the medicine man understands about the healing power of this stuff?"

"Not exactly," she said. "I read that the tribes in this area have been using this stuff for years—only they use it as a poison."

"Poison? What, are you nuts?"

"No, no, you see, in a low dose the tribes use it as a truth test of some sort."

"Like a truth serum?"

"Well, I guess, but the point is when I was reading about the Calabar bean itself I discovered that an extract of the bean is an alkaloid physostigmine."

"Speak English, okay? What is this physio thing?"

"Physostigmine, an alkaloid. The article I read said that alkaloid crystal made from the extract of the Calabar bean is a miotic. I figured if I could make a solution from the extract, I could treat the glaucoma. The standard treatment for glaucoma is eye drops, but the nearest pharmacy is a little far away, so this was the next best thing."

"Miotic?" Tommy asked.

"That just means it affects the eye. In the case of glaucoma, it can relieve optic pressure and reverse the blindness.

"You made eye drops from a bean?"

"It was easy, really. Imamu Neo had given me the dried Calabar powder, so I prepped it in a solution which I heated and ran it through a filtering solution and then put it through a coffee filter I had. Once I separated the alkaloid, I mixed it with alcohol and cleaned it again. I took the clean diluted solution and washed Kyarai's eyes a couple of times. She noticed a lessening of the pain right away and I sent her away with instructions to wash her eyes with the solution a couple times a day. It worked better than I'd hoped. Thank God."

"Actually, Doc," Tommy said, "did you hear what Chief Kulu said?"

"What?"

"He said, *Tinashe.*"

"What does that mean?"

"God is with you."

"Well, it wasn't me," she said, "just the solution."

"The details might have gotten lost in the translation. I think you just performed a miracle these people will be singing about for a long time."

"You think?" she asked with a big yawn. "Well, that's well and good but I've got to get dressed and get to the clinic."

After what happened yesterday, he was sure the village people would start to come to the clinic. Thema was going to be a popular person now.

The last time some dude cured the blind, he got to be God.

****

Mustafa woke his young soldiers, making sure they checked their equipment over. Then he woke Brother Denis who had come in late the night before. "Did you speak with her?"

"No, we trailed her in the mountain but lost her along the rim."

"I told you it was useless."

"No, we left word with everyone we met. She will find out what's going on. So," Denis asked when he saw the activity in their camp. "What is happening?"

"We got word a patrol is on its way."

"Oh…"

"Yes, it seems our little unexpected encounter has drawn some expected interest."

When ready, Mustafa led them out of the village and onto the forest path. They set out at a walk this time, in no hurry to meet their glory. After this week the people would hear of the army of Mustafa, especially the Mobassi administration.

The band of young people came out of the jungle right at the trail head where they'd fought in recent days. The burned-out truck still sat off the road where it crashed. The bodies of the soldiers lay along the road's edge, bloating in the hot sun. Mustafa calculated they had an hour to dig in at the bridge before a new patrol arrived. Amid the thick bush running along the red clay road, he spread one half of his band of young soldiers, covering as much ground as possible between a sharp bend in the road and right before the narrow bridge. The other half of his soldiers filed across the road to lie in wait on the far side of the bridge. Though worried about their woefully thin line, Mustafa remained confident they would fight to the end.

"What's the plan?" Brother Denis asked.

"Intel report says two trucks. When the first ones drives onto the bridge, you take out its wheels and disable it there. I'll take out the second, trapping it behind the first. Then we'll blast away."

"That's your plan?" Brother Denis asked.

"Have you a better one? All we need to do now is wait."

During the interval several ore trucks thundered past their position with a rumble that shook the ground. The trucks didn't slow at the remnants of the earlier fire fight. A thick red dust billowed into the air with every passing vehicle and settled on the bodies of the dead.

The sun rose higher over the western horizon of treetops and the rebel group waited in silence. The two teams remained hidden and even for those used to going without food many were more than hungry and thirsty. Finally, in the distance, a heavy rumble along the road swept toward them.

"It is time," Mustafa whispered to the first boy on the line, "The trucks are coming. *Kali Kann*, he said to the boy on his right and the boy turned and repeated the command to the next boy, and he to the next, and on along the line. The fighters raised their heads and shook off just enough dust to clear their hands and pull thatch and leaves from the tops of their weapons, which rested clean and sheltered from the steady storm of the road's dust clouds.

"*Ya mi da,*" Mustafa commanded an older boy who jumped to his feet and crossed the road to a position opposite the hidden team. The dust dropped from him in layers as he covered the distance in just seconds. From that angle he could spot the coming trucks and would be the first to fire.

All eyes stared down the big bend in the road where the approaching column careened their way. Mustafa observed the line of his soldiers and smiled. These children became fighters as soon as they were old enough to lift a weapon, so they would fight well here. He wondered if they understood the end for them could now be counted in days instead of years. He wondered if they understood the speeding change that was coming.

Mobassi would not like to lose a platoon. He couldn't afford to have a bunch of children running over his military columns and still keep face. His pride would force him into reckless decisions.

The trucks stormed toward them, now only a hundred meters around the bend. The waiting party heard the sound of the engines growing loud as the column approached, but the trucks were still out of sight. Their eyes rested on the lone sentry across the road. When he raised his rifle, the boy and girl rebels prepared for the fight ahead.

****

It didn't matter whether his plan worked as it had been designed, the rebel force took the administration's army patrol by surprise at the river crossing and most of the soldiers were killed before getting off the trucks. After disabling the first vehicle on the bridge, the truck immediately behind it, became stuck. Before it could back out of the trap, its wheels were taken out by rebel rifle fire, leaving the administration soldiers trapped in a deadly crossfire.

"Gather every weapon," Mustafa shouted to his young soldiers after the firefight ended. "Leave nothing behind."

"We were lucky," Brother Denis said to Mustafa when he joined his friend at the bridge.

"Yes, we caught them by surprise."

"Yes, and we get a surprise bonus as well."

"Oh?"

"Yes, the two trucks stuck on the bridge make for a nice roadblock. Any later patrols will find the way through most difficult. At best, they'll have to ford the river north or south. We can defend from the riverbanks."

"Brother Denis," Sekou called. "We have wounded."

Brother Denis knelt by their wounded comrade at the side of the road, evaluating then tending the soldier's injuries.

"Is it bad?" Mustafa asked.

Denis looked up. "It looks like we will have to visit the good doctor again."

Mustafa nodded. "Then it is probably best if I went along and spoke to her."

"Do you think it's time?"

"The sooner we tell her the better for all."

"I believe you're right."

****

Brother Denis and others came out of the forest into town and made their way to the clinic along with two boys carrying a litter.

Seeing the commotion, Tommy thought, *Now what do we have? Instead of a protection contract, it was looking more and more like an offensive operation. If it kept up like this we'd be in an all-out war, and I don't think Mike mentioned that when he talked me into this gig.*

Jumping to his feet, he hurried to the clinic. "What happened," he asked as the group headed to the treatment rooms.

"I'm afraid one of the local rebels has been wounded in fighting," Brother Denis said, "and it is critical. A bad chest wound."

Thema walked into the room. "A chest wound?"

"Yes," Brother Denis said, "I'm afraid the rebel group over in Bonga got into it again with an army patrol. There was only the one casualty this time."

"On the rebels' side," Tommy clarified.

"Yes, on our side."

"What about the soldiers?" Tommy asked.

"None of the other side will be needing a doctor," Brother Denis said.

"What are you saying?" Thema asked after directing the two bearers to lift the stretcher onto the operating room table. As she was getting a good look, the boy awoke, moaning in pain.

Above the moans, Tommy said, "I guess what the good brother is implying is that everyone on the opposition side was killed."

"What have you gotten us into?" Thema demanded as she began to unwrap the bandages from the boy's wound. "I don't think they brought me way over here to be a battle surgeon."

"Planned or not, Doctor Bok.," Brother Denis said loudly, above the groans from the wounded boy, "that's what you are now, and you need to help this child."

"Oh, I'll help." Placing her hands directly on the boy's wound, she closed her eyes. "But this will be the last time." When the groans stopped, Thema turned to the men. "This fighting has got to stop."

"I'm afraid it's only the beginning," the tall man standing at Brother Denis' side said, looking at her.

"Just who are you?" Tommy asked, just as Mike Blanco entered the clinic.

This is Mustafa Bok," Mike said. "He is the leader of the area's rebels. His family goes way back around here."

"Is this the guy we came all this way to protect?" Tommy asked. "By the looks of things, he doesn't need protection. It looks like he is quite capable of protecting himself. He and his little band of rebels."

Brother Denis said, "It was his, *little group,* as you say, that saved Sauda, and it is his rebel boy and girl soldiers that are fighting against the administration."

Thema said, "You said boys and girls?"

"We will fight with who we have," Mustafa said. "If men join us, then we will fight with men. If we have only children, then we fight with children."

"But why are you fighting?" Thema asked, stepping to one side to scrub in a small sink before putting on a surgical gown. "Why?"

"For freedom, Doctor." Mustafa's strong, impenetrable voice seemed to fill the room. "We've been at war for some time. Since I was a child. We won a small victory today. My little band faced the administration's soldiers and beat them."

"You mean, killed them," Tommy said. "This isn't some game where you just beat the other side and win a trophy."

"No, it is war, and it will only get worse," Mustafa said. "The platoon we hit today will soon be missed. The administration will send another column to find out what happened."

"Mike," Thema asked Blanco, "is that true? Will the administration send more soldiers?"

Blanco looked like he wanted to speak. Mustafa nodded at him to go ahead. "Yes, my guess is once they realize their patrol is missing, they'll send another patrol to check. Probably on its way right now."

"And that will mean another bloody fight?" Thema asked.

"Most definitely," Mustafa said.

"That will be on you," Tommy said. "It may be your war, Mustafa, but it isn't ours."

"I'm afraid you are wrong about that," Brother Denis said.

"What do you mean?" Tommy asked.

"There's more at stake than you realize," Brother Denis said.

Tommy said, "I realize one thing, I don't think my contract to provide protection calls for me to get involved in an outright war."

"That's enough, you two," Thema bellowed. "Your presence in this room is compromising my patient's life. Get out. Now."

Tommy took a step back, hands in the surrender position. "Look, Doc, I'm beginning to think we made a mistake taking this job. Maybe we should think about getting out of here."

"What I need, Tommy, is for everyone to get out of my way so I can treat this boy."

"Doctor Bok," Denis said, "I might be of assistance."

"Scrub up!"

****

As soon as the wounded boy was under anesthetic, Doctor Bok began to work. Brother Denis watched, and aside from passing her a random sponge or instrument, she needed little help from him. After stopping the bleeding, she closed the boy's wound with what he considered many stitches and oddly placed her hands on the boy's wound and held them there. After, she applied a compression bandage and gave him a shot of antibiotics.

Thema finished and walked out onto the clinic porch, with Brother Denis following.

"How is he?" Mustafa asked.

"He is stable," Thema said, taking off her face mask and gloves, "and should recover."

Brother Denis said, "Doctor Bok is much too modest, my friend, in fact, her doctoring skills verge on the miraculous. I'm sure the boy will be up and around in no time. Doctor Bok is *Tinashe.*

"Why do they say that?" Thema asked. "It is only my experience that saved the child."

"No, when they say, *God is with you*, Doctor Bok," Mustafa said. "They mean it. They believe your skill is God given. Many Imamu from here have had special healing powers and you, as well possess this gift."

"No, no," she protested, raising a hand, "it was just my training."

"Look, dude," Tommy said to Mustafa, "the Doc has been trying to fit in here. Sure, she's practicing native medicine and all, but she doesn't belong here. She came over like on vacation. That's it and I think maybe she should get the hell out of here before it's too late. Fact is, I'm thinking I made a mistake signing on for this and maybe I'll get out of here too."

"Doctor Bok may have come on vacation, my friend," Bother Denis said, "but she'll stay because she belongs here."

"Look," Thema said, "I get that I share a name with many in the village, and I admit I have grown fond of the people and feel a kinship with them, but I am only a visitor. Here for one year like my contract states. That's all."

"But you are much more than that," Mustafa said, moving to stand and tower over her. "You see, you are Thema Atsu Bok, of the Bok clan."

She did not back down. But tilted back her head and looked at him straight on. Unafraid, not intimidated in the least. "How can that be?"

"Because you were born here."

Chapter Twenty-two

"Doc," Tommy sputtered, "what's this nonsense about you being born here?"

As soon as the words left Mustafa's lips, Thema knew it was true. It also explained a lot about her innate medical skills. She'd excelled at her specialty rotations, but never more so than when she was in the ER. Some of the supervising doctors even recognized her work as miraculous.

Could it have been the connection to the village and the Baobab tree's ancestry? Though she'd gravitated to family medicine for a specialty and found success there, it was always her critical care cases that showed the greatest success. Could it really be her connection to the village? Could it be the village's connection to the tree of life?

Tommy repeated, "Doc, what's this guy talking about?"

"Doctor Bok was raised in America in the foster care system," Denis said, "but she was born here in Masango."

"I don't understand," Tommy said. "

"Just after she was born," Mustafa explained, "civil war broke out in our country. Many of our people escaped to the States. A group of refugees landed in Miami only two days after Thema's birth and took her to the community hospital to have her checked. They told the hospital staff she'd been born at home. It was late on a busy weekend night at the hospital and Thema was small and looked like a newborn baby. So, believing she was the product of a home birth—not uncommon in those days and that neighborhood—the staff admitted her for observation. After she was found to be in good health, they discharged her in the usual process and sent them on the way with a birth certificate. Just like they do with all deliveries."

"What happened to her real family?"

"At that time, there was much strife on Miami's streets. A turf war ensued; over time, many were killed, including some of her family who had escaped to the States. Eventually, she was placed in foster care. When she turned sixteen and could understand, her foster parents told her she was the child of a single mother who had given her up. Once she started college, she was on her own."

"At the time," Denis added, "her people wanted to protect her. Sending her away from the danger made sense. As the family was wanted by the government, they were forced into hiding, To protect her, they sent her to America.

"Thema was born here in this village," Brother Denis continued, "and her heritage is rich with customs and practices of the area. Her grandfather was paramount chief for this whole region, and very influential. That was why the family was forced into hiding."

"But we are done running," Mustafa said. "From this point forward, we are standing our ground and will fight right here in Masango."

"Dude," Tommy said, "how are you and a handful of kids going to fight a war against the current administration?"

Mustafa said, "We will get more boys and men to fight."

Brother Denis said, "Men will come because Thema Atsu Bok is their queen. That's what her name means."

Tommy said, "Look, guys, let's be serious. The Doc may be a lot of things, but a queen?"

Mustafa said, "I think Doctor Bok can feel it is true."

"Doc," Tommy said, looking at her, but she had lowered her head, not making eye contact with him. "Listen, Doc, you don't need all this. I'm thinking about getting out of here too. We can leave together now. Give it all back and get out before it's too late."

"It's already too late," Mike said. "Boy, this war is just getting started. There'll be another administration patrol along shortly, maybe two. They'll have to be stopped, just like the last one."

Tommy gave it one last shot. "Doc, we didn't sign on for this. Let's pack our bags and go home."

After a long pause, Thema gazed at him, and said, "Apparently, I'm already home, Tommy."

****

Just before evening, Mustafa and his band of boy and girl rebels met another administration convoy at the Juarzon Bridge. With accurate intel from the Agency's contact in the capital, the quickly planned ambush took the administration's soldiers by complete surprise. Unable to cross the bridge still blocked from the previous firefight, an officer led his men on a poorly devised attempt to cross the bridge on foot, thereby trapping them in the middle of a crossfire. The bottle neck of disabled trucks and dead bodies was too much of an obstacle.

After the brief exchange, Brother Denis walked

along the road's edge, ensuring no one in the column was still alive. He came to an administration officer who'd fallen alongside his men. Going through the man's pockets, he found his identification papers which listed his age at twenty-five. Brother Denis studied the soldier as he stuffed the papers into his breast pocket. Looking over the scene, and satisfied that no soldiers survived the surprise attack, he gathered his gear and darted into the jungle as his retreating band of teens scattered in the bush.

Lugging heavy ammo cans and a thirty-caliber machine gun, scavenged from an administration's abandoned truck, a small group hiked through the thick bush to Bonga. Several boys slowly limped along because of wounds and two older boys hauled the lone serious casualty on a rough litter while Brother Denis yelled instructions for the young men to not jostle their patient. "Pretend you are carrying precious cargo there, not a lump of old laundry."

Twice the uneven terrain forced them to stop and to start out again proving more and more difficult. "Almost there, now," Mustafa said to them, "just around the next bend in the trail."

When the group came out of the woods and onto the edge of the village the boys placed the stretcher in the palaver hut. Brother Denis asked Mustafa and Sekou to light the lamps and to get a fire going for a pot of hot water. Brother Denis pulled an old first aid kit from his bag; cotton bandages and thick gauze, and he laid out one of his own clean sheets across the rough-hewn tabletop in the hut. He took his own mosquito netting and told Sekou to string it above the table, draping the table and keeping the swarming insects attracted by the bright light at bay. He then got the men to lift the patient onto the tabletop, so that he could get a good look at the damage.

"Is it bad?" Sekou asked.

"Let's just say it is a good thing our young charge passed out some time ago."

Denis pulled the tattered shirt from the wound. "Well, the wound was caused by a single shot, thank God. The round left a good bit of cloth material in place where it clotted and slowed the bleeding. It is a pretty nasty wound, to say the least," he said to Sekou, using a rounded pair of surgical scissors to cut away pieces of the shirt where he could.

"What can you do?"

"Not much," he said, "bring that light closer."

Once Sekou held one of the lamps right over the table, Denis was able to inspect the extent of the wound. "The round tore through the stomach area here, but it's impossible to tell how serious the damage is without digging into the inner abdominal tissue. "It is hard to say whether our patient has bled out or if the bleeding has just slowed," Denis said, straightening up. "He needs fluid replacements, perhaps blood as well. There could be damage to the intestines which is never good and means many doses of powerful antibiotics."

"Can you do all that?" Mustafa asked.

Denis shook his head. "Not half of what's needed, even on a good day. We need a doctor for this, a proper doctor, a surgeon. There might be a chance then," he said, "otherwise…"

"Yes, Doctor Bok, is only a short walk away. We should take our patient there."

"No, at night, being bumped along on a carrier during the trip. That might not be the best idea. Our young soldier might die on the way there. No, it's best we keep our patient quiet and resting right here."

"Then what do you suggest, my friend?" Mustafa asked.

Denis said, "I guess one of us should take a little walk through the woods and check if the good Doctor Bok might come out for a house call."

"I'll go," Mustafa said, "you need to stay in case something happens."

"No, I should be the one, Denis said. "I might have to do some explaining about what is happening. Her heart is in the right place, our Doctor Bok, but you never can tell. Then of course there is Mr. Foster."

"Oh?" he asked, "will he be trouble?"

"I'm not sure. Sometimes I wonder why Mike brought him along."

****

Thema poured soapy water from a bucket over the operating table and scrubbed. Zuma and Mudiwa washed the floors and walls after the day's work, but she always cleaned the table since the chance for infection centered there.

She stepped onto the porch and shuffled to the clinic office where she took off her white coat and tossed it into a basket filled with dirty linens. Since Zuma's duties included taking care of the wash, she didn't need to say anything.

Thema clutched the clip board with the day's makeshift charts, making notes of the patients they'd seen. By late in the evening, she'd lost track of the numbers when a woman presented needing an emergency appendectomy. So, it had been back to surgery.

But she needed to check the notes one more time and make additional comments of what she remembered. The detail would help her be more proactive in the care of her patients.

Thema walked down the steps of the clinic and turned to take the short hike to the mission house. Someone had left a lamp on in the house. A dim yellow light shone out of the front window, and she couldn't wait to get home. Her stomach began growling for food late that afternoon and hadn't stopped since.

When she entered the room, she found Tommy sitting at the table. There was a bowl of rice and a bowl of soup resting in the middle of the table and a burning candle gave off romantic vibes. He stood when she came in and pulled her chair out for her to sit. "What's all this?"

"I just wanted to apologize about this afternoon. I know you have found a home here among the natives, and well, I just wanted to say I just got caught up in the fighting. I understand how you feel."

"Since when?"

"Look Doc, I just want you to know, we're in this together."

Wondering about his change of heart, Thema gazed at him. She hadn't heard about this side of Tommy Foster and wondered if this was an aspect she should look into. "So, this is some type of peace offering?"

"Is it working?"

His grin sent a zing through her system. *Yup, maybe I should look a little deeper.* "I'll let you know."

During dinner, Tommy didn't mention fighting or child soldiers but encouraged her to tell him more about the Baobab trees and all their healing properties. When they finished, they stepped out on the porch to enjoy the quiet night. The sky filled with stars and a half-moon caused shadows in the village. She noticed a lot of activity with people congregating in the town center and when she leaned out over the railing, she could hear Chief Kulu making some kind of speech.

"I'd like to know what's going on down there?"

When Tommy moved to her side he said, "I'd like to know what's going on right up here."

"What do you mean," she asked as she let him circle her waist with his arms.

When she didn't push him away, Tommy tried to kiss her, and she surprised herself and let him.

"Slow down big guy," she told him, leaning slightly away. "Remember, I've heard everything about you from the nurses at Mercy."

He stroked her cheek with the tip of one finger. It felt warm and soft and caring. "Now, are you going to listen to rumors? I'd think a person of science like you, who is interested in the effect of nature on a person's health, would want to investigate for yourself."

Being in his arms felt… good, safe. Right.

She leaned into him. "Maybe I should."

****

Thema didn't think she had been asleep long when the bright blast of lightning from a midnight squall produced a silhouette of someone standing at the foot of her bed. "Who's there?" she asked, through the mosquito netting.

When the figure said nothing, she repeated, more loudly, "Who's there?"

"Sorry," came the graveled Irish brogue, "It's me, Brother Denis."

From his spot on the bed next to Thema, Tommy stirred. "What the hell, Dude? You scared the shit out of us."

"My apologies," Brother Denis said.

In the flashing lights of the outside storm, Thema followed the man's movement around the bed as he struck a match and lit the bedside candle. The dim light shone on Brother Denis and Mike Blanco.

"It couldn't be helped, Thema," Mike said, rainwater running off the brim of his floppy camouflage hat. "We need a minute with you."

"What?"

"I wonder if we might speak with you for a minute," he said, unsmiling, his arms and body covered in a long dark rain poncho.

Tommy sat up, covered his lower parts with the sheet. "About what?"

"This doesn't have anything to do with you, Tommy."

"The hell it doesn't. Last I knew I'm a member of this team."

"Then act like it and stand down."

"That's enough, you two." Thema scolded the two men. "Now, Brother Denis, what's this about?"

"I've just walked over from Bonga," he said, as if entering a bedroom and finding two naked people to be an everyday occurrence. "I've come to ask if you would mind coming with me to examine a young, injured villager over there."

"Injured villager?" Tommy asked, "what kind of injury?'

"Oh, it's quite a stomach wound. I tried to patch it with my own paltry experience, but I'm afraid the injury requires much more then my feeble skills."

Thema climbed out from beneath the netting, wrapping a sheet around herself as she did.

"It is a deep wound in the abdomen area, right through here," he continued and demonstrated moving his hand across his midsection. "I'm afraid there is extensive damage."

"A bullet wound?"

"Yes, and I didn't want to chance a long rough trip through the dark jungle," he said, moving back around to the foot of the bed just out of the cast of light. "No use taking chances."

"Dude," Tommy said, "it's the middle of the night. Can't this wait until the morning?"

"I think Makena might be dead by morning," Denis said, "but if Doctor Bok could come and take a look...well, it might make the difference."

"Look, Brother," Tommy said, "I'm sure..."

"Makena," Denis said.

"What?"

"Makena," he repeated, "the patient's name is Makena. It means, happy one." Wiping rain from his face, he said, "One of the local chief's children, and full of life."

"Okay," Tommy said, looking at Thema, "okay, we get it, a nice kid, but..."

"Tommy," Thema said.

"No, Doc," Tommy started again, "you are not going wandering around in the middle of the night."

"Don't tell me what I'm going to be doing."

"And we won't be wandering," Mike said. "Brother Denis will be leading us."

"It's pouring out there," Tommy said.

Mike said, "It's always pouring somewhere out there. It will stop soon enough."

Tommy said, "Doc, I don't think you signed on for this kind of medicine."

"What kind of medicine is that?" she asked. Then shifting her gaze she asked Mike, "Is this about the freedom fighters over in Bonga?"

"Yes, it's about that group."

"And you, Brother Denis," Tommy asked, "are you with them as well?"

The Brother paused before answering, "Well, I am sort of an advisor."

"Advisor," Tommy repeated.

"You understand my meaning."

"So, this Makena, got shot during another confrontation?" Tommy asked.

"Yes, as we figured, the Mobassi Administration sent a patrol to look for the last patrol. We skirmished with them there at the Juarzon Bridge. They were caught by complete surprise, just like the previous column, but our poor Makena ..."

"How many men are we talking about here?" Tommy asked.

"Makena is the only serious casualty."

"I mean," Tommy said, impatient, "how many of Mobassi's men did you kill?"

"Does it matter?"

"It matters to me," Tommy said, glancing at Thema who sat on the edge of the bed slipping on a pair of socks.

"Well, about thirty in all," Denis admitted. "I didn't stop to count."

"Thirty people?" Tommy asked. "Brother Denis, you killed thirty people. Who do you think you are?"

"That's enough, Foster," Mike said, cutting him off."

"No," Denis said, "It's okay. I want to respond. These were not people, Foster, these were Mobassi's henchmen. These were not even proper soldiers. You saw how they treated the girl, Sauda. They'll do the same to anyone that gets in their way."

"So, you take the law into your own hands?"

"We will do what we must when no law is present."

"We," Tommy said, "who is this *we* stuff? From where I stand your skin looks a little white for *we*."

"From where I stand, Foster, I could say the same about you."

"Okay, you two," Mike said, "This isn't getting us anywhere. Doc, what about it?"

"Let me get my things."

"Thema," Tommy said, "you can't be serious?"

"I have to go," she said. "Brother Denis, go to the clinic. I'll need some help with the supplies. Mike, if you can wake Willy Gray in the crew camp, he might be able to help. Tell him what we are going to do, and he can gather what we might need from the medical supplies that came in. I'll meet you there."

"Doc," Tommy said after Brother Denis and Mike left, "you are not thinking about going out there in the night with those fools?"

"I must."

"Doc, this Denis guy is a kook. He's liable to get you killed."

"Nonsense," she said as she scrambled around to finish dressing and putting on her boots. "Mike will be with me. And you heard him, they took care of them."

"That's the point, Doc," Tommy insisted. "You are

going to get yourself in a war here."

"I've been worrying about that for a couple of days," she said. "But these are my people, and they need my help. I can't turn my back on them. I thought you understood."

"I do understand, but we didn't sign on to get into the middle of another country's problems." He moved closer, tipped her chin up. Looked into her eyes. "What about us?"

"I can't think about us," she said, taking her bag and heading for the door, "I can only think about my people and the work I must do."

Chapter Twenty-three

Mustafa waited up through the night; morning came in a bleak gray dawn. He expected Brother Denis and Doctor Bok with the first light and sent a boy to meet them on the trail. The boy came back a short while later with Brother Denis, Sekou, the Doctor, Mike Blanco and another man who was dressed in fatigues.

"Greetings, Doctor Bok," Mustafa said when the group came out of the forest and entered the small village. "Welcome to Bonga."

"Good to see you again, Mustafa," Doctor Bok answered. "This is Willy Gray," she said, introducing the crew member in the fatigues.

"You made good time."

"Yes," Mike said, "we hiked straight through. I hope our efforts were not wasted."

"How is our patient?" Brother Denis asked.

"He slept through the night," Mustafa said, "but it is good Doctor Bok is here."

Thema peered into the darkness, "So, where is the patient?"

"Over in the far hut, resting," Mustafa said.

Thema and Willy Gray walked to the hut and got to work. Thema got a good look at the patient. "This is a girl!"

"Yes," Brother Denis said, "Makena is a girl."

She looked to the ceiling. "I still can't wrap my head

around girl soldiers fighting here or anywhere."

Mustafa said, "there are a great many girls among our little army. Your Sauda is one and there are many others. They are quite capable."

"But girls?" Thema repeated.

"Yes, yes, quite brave and capable. They show little fear in a fight, very capable in fact."

Staring at Makena, she hesitated for just one moment then, with a nod of her head, started to work. She congratulated Brother Denis for stabilizing the girl. She told him the fluid feed he'd given the patient likely saved the girl's life.

The other boys crowded around the outside of the low built palaver hut. Brother Denis directed one to restart the fire and boil water in a big pot. Thema gave Willy a handful of instruments to sanitize and used sterile towels to drape around Makena's wound. She poured alcohol across the girl's abdomen, then located the entry point for the wound.

"She's lucky," she said to Brother Denis, "the bullet ripped through the flesh, but passed out the back. There's muscle damage here, but based on the location of the entry wound, it looks like it missed her intestines, otherwise, given the time that's passed since the firefight, she'd be dead, or close to it from peritonitis."

While Mustafa and Brother Denis moved away from the area to allow Thema and Willy Gray some room to work, Mustafa asked, "Did you encounter anyone on the trail?"

"No," Denis said. "Why do you ask?"

"We've had a few more of the Mt. Kizi men come in."

"How many?"

"Two," he said, "and another group came from the Kagera Village. The bodies floating in the river caught their attention, so they sent a runner. We told them what was happening, and they started coming in twos and threes."

"Twenty more?" Denis asked. "This is great news. It's a good thing and just when needed."

"What has changed?" Mustafa asked.

"Mobassi will be serious next time he sends troops.

"What makes you say that?" Mike asked.

"There was a young officer killed at the bridge today."

"Yes?"

Brother Denis said, "It was one of Mobassi's Chinese advisors."

"Well," Mike said, "that will be the Agency's headache, not ours."

****

The high sun hammered the little village. Sweat poured from every boy surrounding the hut, but they still didn't move, their eyes fixated on Doctor Bok as she and Willy Gray worked on Makena, cleaning, sponging and suturing until she was able to bring the bleeding under control before she bandaged the girl's wound.

Thema leaned over and placed her hands on either side of the girls midsection. She closed her eyes and breathed deeply, and felt the familiar heat build in her palms.

"Doc...Doc." Willy said, touching her shoulder after she had stood over the girl for a minute without moving. "Are you okay?"

"I'm fine," Thema said, standing straight for the first time since they started, shaking her head to clear her mind. For the moment the girl was stable. "Thanks for your help, Willy."

"That's some great work you did, Doc," he told her as he washed his hands off in a bucket of water sitting in the corner of the hut.

"Thanks, I like working in tight places," she said, checking the IV bag, then preparing another.

"I never assisted anyone who worked that hard for so long."

"I'm sure, Willy."

"No kidding, Doc," he continued, "even the Marine doctors I worked with never put out the energy like you did this morning. Of course, they were mostly Navy."

She took time to do a few stretches to loosen muscles cramped from standing in one position for too long. "Once I get going, I can't slow my momentum. Thanks for your help. We can use you up at the clinic."

"I don't know, Doc," he said, gathering his gear into a big green duffle, "you keep long hours."

Over forty young boys and girls and teenagers, standing three deep had gathered to watch her work through the morning. Mustafa came over to the hut and chased the crowd off, telling them to go and get some rest because they would soon need it. They turned and marched off with an older boy sounding a chant that the whole group of boy and girl soldiers responded to in rhythm.

"What are they saying?" Thema asked Mustafa.

"They say you are *Sihiri,* Dr. Bok"

"What's that?"

"Magic."

"No, no, it is medicine."

"For them it is *Sihiri*, Yes, they say you are one with

Baobab, heal the sick, and bring to life the dead."

"The tree?" Thema said, gazing up into the branches of the mammoth tree.

"The tree spirit, the *Sihiri,* one and the same.

"The girl was not dead, Mustafa."

"To these boys and girls, she was dead when she was shot—but you saved her. That's the song they sing, *Atsu Sihiri*. This thing you wear," he said, moving closer to take hold of the leather amulet hanging from her neck. "Where did you get this?"'

"I've had it since I can remember. I think my mother gave it to me. It was with my things as I moved between foster families.

"It is *Sihiri*, only those with *Sihiri* wear it."

Mike Blanco and Brother Denis joined them. "How is she, Doctor Bok?" Denis asked.

"She lost a lot of blood, but I think once her system gets back to normal, she should come out of it."

"I'm glad the girl's going to pull through," Mike said.

Gathering her supplies, Thema asked, "Are there others?"

"You'll have a few drifting into your clinic today, I'm sure," Denis said. We don't have a centralized command so many of our lads are in the bush, but I suspect when the *Sihiri* word spreads about you, they'll start showing up."

She held deep feelings during the healing process of her patients, but she wouldn't describe it as magic. "What is this *Sihiri,* the boys and girls are saying?"

"Oh, well, a bit of folklore; juju, hoodoo, that kind of stuff."

"But you don't believe in that?"

"Doesn't matter what I believe, Doctor," he said, sitting on the low wall surrounding the hut. "It only matters what they believe, and they believe you are one with Baobab and the *Sihiri* of life, strong medicine. The Tree of Life, the tree with strong Sihiri. The charm you wear is made from the bark of the tree. They bind it with the leather to lock in the Sihiri."

Sitting next to him she said, "I've seen a number of these in the village."

"Yes, the Sihiri is strong within the village. There are quite a few curing qualities behind the folklore."

"Yes," she said, bending over and picking up a bit of bark that had fallen off the tree. "I've done some research."

"Yes, the magic is grounded in some science and there's a blurring of the line between fact and the magic."

Thema scanned the village and the people still celebrating. "Shouldn't we explain about the real medicine here?"

"No," he said, taking hold of her shoulder and squeezing. "Let them believe. We'll need all the help we can get."

Thema said, "So, what about this conflict with the Mobassi government?"

"The locals don't appreciate the current administration's heavy-handed rule. They believe in self-government and not a dictator ruling the land."

"Have they tried a meeting to have a conversation?"

Getting to his feet, Denis said, "Oh, sure, been a lot of talk, but I'm afraid the time for talk is over."

Rising, she reached out to him, taking hold of his arm, "Is there no alternative?"

"I'm afraid not," he said, sadness in his voice. "The

time for talking ended long before you got here."

"Is it that bad?" she persisted. "Is armed insurrection the only alternative?"

"It is," Mike said, as he and Mustafa joined the conversation, "and made all the more possible with you."

"You mean a doctor to tend the wounded?"

"Are you are getting the feeling your mission was not just designed to build a clinic?" Mike asked her.

"I'm getting that feeling."

"Yes," Mustafa said, moving to the wounded girl and studying her. "We needed a doctor for the wounded, but not just that, you mean more than just bandages and shots. You heard the boys, and they are not strangers to death. Many of their friends have died fighting this war so more casualties would not deter them, but you saved Makena, *Thema Sihiri*."

"Mustafa," Thema asked, nearing the man, "you are a leader here. Who are you and what is your fight in this?"

"I am from Masango," he said, turning to her, "although from long ago. I have been fighting with the freedom fighters since I was a boy. I have spent my youth fighting for the same basic right all men want, freedom. The four previous administrations have ignored our situation here, but this time, with a different leader, we hope a different spokesperson will make a difference and bring real change to the region."

Thema said, spreading her arms in wonder, "But what person can do this thing?"

"Brother Denis," Mustafa asked, "you didn't tell her?"

Denis said, "The village meeting ended late."

"Tell me what?" she asked.

"This person is you, Thema Atsu Bok," Mustafa said.

"Me," she said. "What are you talking about?"

"The people of this region met and voted last night. You are to be the new Paramount Chief."

"Don't be funny," she said, her smile faltering. "Chief Kulu is the chief."

"Kulu is the chief for Masango," he said. "Just as Mekena's father, Tariro, is chief for Bonga. There is a chief for every town and village, but only one paramount chief who represents the whole region. Bonga and Masango initiated the process for the election, and you were voted to be the Paramount Chief."

"Don't be ridiculous, Brother Denis," she said, not smiling at all. "How can I be a chief of any kind?"

"Because of your heritage, Doctor."

"What heritage?"

"Your grandfather was Paramount chief here fifty years ago. The right of succession is strong in the heritage of your people. Your ancestry goes back several hundred years. Plus, I might add, your visibility as a returning home native and miracle worker helped your cause and swayed many voters."

Chapter Twenty-four

After returning to Masango, Thema went to the clinic while Mike Blanco and Brother Denis met with the crew. Tommy was quick to ask about the plan to protect the asset.

"Look, Tommy," Mike said, when he gathered the crew around their bamboo table and a map of the area. "We're putting this together on the fly, but I think this is the way it is going to go down, so it's time to put up. We didn't drag your ass all the way over here for nothing.

"What do you have in mind?" Tommy asked.

"We just heard that Mobassi has sent a company of men to confront the increasing resistance in Juarzon. The kid soldiers over there number about fifty, with a few grown men thrown in and hoping to get more. Thing is," Mike said, pointing down at the map. "I don't think they can hold off a company of regular army, no matter what plan they have. They got lucky the last couple of firefights, things broke their way, but not this time. A new company won't be making the same mistakes. I need every man on this."

"Where are you getting this intel?" Tommy asked, not feeling good about any intel that wasn't rock solid.

"The Agency has assets in the capitol with eyes on the military's movements. It's solid. This time, whoever they send will know there's a formidable opposition here and will be prepared to fight. Hell, just the smell of the dead will be enough to convince them. This time, I think they'll break through at Juarzon."

"Then what?" Tommy pressed.

"Couple of things," Mike said, indicating a spot on the map. "One, they could chase those boys back to Bonga and take out the whole village. If they do that," he said, sweeping a finger along the map, "they could then move cross country and attack us from the rear. I wouldn't like that any, because we're vulnerable at our ass."

"You don't think he'll do that?" Tommy asked, leaning over the table to get a closer look at the map.

"No, his men won't want to fight a bush war."

"What's the second thing?" Bobby Raines asked.

Mike said, pointing to the road on the map, "They come straight down the road and hit us direct."

"Direct on the town?" Tommy asked.

"That's it," Mike said, nodding. "A direct hit on the village and clinic."

"What are our options?" Jimmy Phillips asked, stepping to the table.

"The only option we have is to meet them at the Kagera Bridge, right here," Mike said, pointing at the map. "The water is deep here, they just can't walk across. We could put together a pretty nasty welcoming for the guys. Only…"

"Only what?" Tommy asked.

Denis said, "Only you'll need more men. I like Mike's summary. They'll be better prepared next time. I expect a direct hit. A hard one."

Tommy twisted to face the brother. "Why are you so sure?"

"There was a Chinese advisor with that last patrol

the boy rebels took out," Denis said, taking off his cap and wiping sweat from his brow. "I imagine they are anxious to set things right for losing a fellow comrade."

"Shit," Tommy said. "I forgot to tell you, Mike. The other day when I was out in the woods, I saw a couple of Chinese guys scoping out the village.

Mike glared at Tommy. "You could have said something before now."

Brother Denis said, "Don't worry about it, Mike, it wouldn't have changed a thing. In fact, it might have helped."

"What do you mean?" Wade Billups asked.

"If they got a look at the village set up, they're probably thinking it will be an easy action. They won't know about our capabilities. That might be enough to give us an edge."

"We still need some more manpower," Mike said. "Oh, we can put out some C3 and mine the road, and we've got a couple of machine guns packed away somewhere as well, but we need manpower to man the perimeter."

"So," Tommy asked, standing straight, "just how are you going to get the manpower?"

Denis regarded the group and smiled. "Actually, with her new position as Paramount Chief, Doctor Bok can call upon the towns to send their men to fight."

The men stood quiet, digesting what the brother said. Finally, Marc Frisco said, "And the men will come just because she calls?"

"The chief calls and the people will come."

"Brother Denis is right," Mike said. "They want to fight. Just dying to, but her call to arms is the best excuse to join. We need Doctor Bok to put out the word, ASAP."

"And if she won't?" Tommy asked.

"We don't stand a chance without at least another fifty men," Mike said, "We have plenty of weapons and ammo, but if we don't get the extra men, well, let's just say it won't be pretty around here."

"You got to realize, Foster," John Page said, "we are the only thing standing between this village and a horrible death for every man, woman, and child in this village. If we don't stand together, we'll die together."

"And if you don't mind," Bobby Raines told Tommy, "I didn't come six thousand miles to die in some shithole of a village."

Tommy said, "What makes you think it will come to that?"

"Mobassi will be out to get her," Mike said. "And we've got a contract to protect her."

"I thought Mustafa was the future leader we came to protect."

"No," Mike told him, "we came to protect Thema Atsu Bok, the woman who would be queen."

****

Tommy and Mike Blanco intercepted Thema on the clinic breezeway as she examined a group of wounded boys and girls. Deep in her work, she looked to have her hands full. Tommy hated to give her more, but she needed to understand what was happening.

After a deep cleansing breath, he said, "Got your hands full?"

She only glanced at them, her attention on her work. "Some wounded fighters just came in."

Mike said, "We wondered if you could spare a minute to talk before you get busy."

She sighed. "Guys, I need to scrub for surgery."

"Can we tag along," Mike said, "it's important."

"Come on then," Thema said, "you can pour the water."

The trio weaved their way between the wounded. Boy and girl soldiers sprawled along the stone porch in a variety of positions.

A small sink occupied one corner in Thema's office. She went over and poured hot water from a kettle into a big pan before starting to scrub her hands and arms. "So, let's have it," she said. "I've got work to do."

"The team sends their congratulations about the chief thing," Mike said. "They are a little surprised but they're for it if it will help us out.

"Tell them thank you, weird as it is," she said. "What else?"

Mike said, "We've been wondering if you can put out a call to the surrounding villages in your domain."

"A call...a call for what?" Thema asked, continuing to wash her hands and arms.

"Soldiers, my dear Chief," Tommy said. "Soldiers to defend the motherland."

"What makes you think I can put out such a call?"

Tommy said, "Ah, that chief thing the village did last night."

"Wasn't that for like a spokesperson thing?" she asked.

"I guess it means you can speak for war type stuff, too. Doc, if you haven't noticed we are in an ass kicking war."

"I know, Tommy, I'm not dumb. Come and pour the rest of the hot water over my hands."

Tommy shuffled over and taking the kettle off a kerosene burner poured the water as directed. "Listen,

Doc," he said, "this is no exaggeration. We are into some wild stuff here and it's about to get really heavy."

"Tommy," she said while blotting her hands on a clean towel, "I've been up to my elbows in blood, so I understand the gravity of the situation."

Tommy looked intently at her, "Some people would call that collaboration with the enemy."

"I can't let these children go untreated."

"Doc, I hear you, but we got a crazy man in the capital and he's hearing about is some fool woman in Masango who tends the sick, cures the blind, giving her people hope, And, all of a sudden, she's elected Paramount Chief for the whole region—but every time he sends soldiers to check things out, they get their asses kicked. How does that look to you?"

"I see."

"And don't forget," Tommy continued, "he needs to control the roads up here to keep the gold ore flowing. I don't imagine he's happy about you interfering with his gravy train."

"I hadn't thought about that," she said as she stepped to the doorway.

"Thank you!"

"So, Mike," she hesitated before backing out the door, keeping her hand and arms away from surfaces, "what's this thing about putting out a call for men?"

"We have information from our sources in the capitol, who say a company of Mobassi's finest men are headed this way."

"What sources? Who else is in on this?"

"The Agency," Mike said. "They hired us to protect you. The crew, including Tommy here, we're all in on this."

"The agency?" Thema asked. "What agency?"

"He means one of those secret type agencies," Tommy said.

"The Agency has field officers from one end of Africa to the other." Mike said.

"I thought this was a MAM thing?"

"MAM is a front for the Agency."

"So, you need help because the administration is sending more soldiers?"

"That's right, Chief," Tommy said, "in fact, Mike tells me they'll roll in about lunch time."

"This afternoon?"

"Yep."

Thema paused before asking, "So how many soldiers does your source say are coming?"

"About two hundred and fifty men, maybe a few more"

"How many do we have?"

"We don't have any," Tommy pointed out, "but those poor fools over in Bonga have about fifty or so teenage boys and girls, counting those scattered about the clinic here."

"That's not many," she said. "Is that what the word is supposed to do, bring in some more men to fight?'

"We need every fighting boy, girl, woman or man we can get."

"These people aren't fighters, Mike. These girls, boys, and teenagers aren't soldiers."

"You'd be surprised, Doc. These people have been fighting off and on for the past forty years. I bet everybody here knows how to handle a rifle."

"Tommy?"

"That's the deal, Doc. So, your first official act as

the new Paramount Chief is to institute a draft and get everyone pissed off."

"Do I have a choice?"

"Like I said, let's get out of town before it's too late."

Hands still in the air, she took a step back. "You can't mean you want me to just leave?"

"Yes, I do. Things are a lot different than I figured. Let's get our skinny asses out of here before we get a lot of people killed."

"Leave or not," Mike said, "lot of people are going to get hurt today if we don't get some more men in to help defend the village."

"I can't leave, Tommy, things are different now."

"Listen, Doc, this is serious. There's a company of soldiers on their way right now and the only thing standing between that army and you is a crew of out of shape mercenaries."

Thema had started to back out of the doorway but stopped. "Tommy, I've got to get into surgery. The boy in there has taken a good look at the face of death and he's fighting back. It's a fight for all these people. From what I see, just living day to day is a fight and I am not going to run from this fight."

"It will be a massacre," Tommy said. "How can a handful of ex-marines that have seen better days hold off an army."

"That's why we need the extra men." Mike said.

"How many more do you need?" Thema asked.

"I'd like to have fifty, but I'll take a squad of ten if that is all you can round up."

"Okay, I'll send Alex and Kimo out to the surrounding villages and spread the word, we'll find out how many are willing to fight."

"Make sure you send someone to the mountain, the Buta region."

"Why, who's there?"

"Older group, been at war with whoever is in charge for a while. They are of the Bok clan but have been hiding out for some time. We've got a few of them in already, but there are a lot more available."

"Doc," Tommy exclaimed, "you're not going to listen to this guy, are you?"

"Mike," Thema said to the man, "are you sure about this?"

Looking at her, Mike said, "About as sure as I've ever been about anything."

Thema looked at Mike for a long minute. "Okay, I have to stay with my people. We'll need to get everyone inside the village and arrange our last line of defense right here."

"Are you nuts?" Tommy said. "If those soldiers find the village guarded, it's finish time for everyone."

"No, Tommy," she said, backing out onto the porch walkway and heading for her OR, "Let's give the surrounding men a chance to heed my call. They've got as much to lose as anyone. Mike, you tell the crew that Thema Atsu Bok will send out the word. I'll get more men even if I go village to village myself."

****

Tommy and Mike tramped to the crew's camp and found the men packing up.

"What did the king say?" Raines chuckled.

"That's queen, dumb ass," Mike said. "She sent Kimo and Alex out to spread the word to the surrounding villages. We'll see how many people come in. In the meantime, we move out."

"What do you have in mind?" Tommy asked.

"We need to mine the east road at the Juarzon, and we need to put some demo out here as well."

"Here?" Tommy asked. "Right in the village?"

"Not in the village, out on the road, on the bridge, and I'm thinking on the banks of the river too."

"You don't think the boy soldiers can hold them at the Juarzon do you?" Tommy asked.

"I'm not sure, but if they break through, there won't be anything between them and the village except us, and I want to be prepared. We'll be outnumbered, but if we prepare right, we could hold them off."

"That's a pretty tall order," Tommy said. "What, two hundred to eight?"

"We'll get more men by then."

"And so, for what," Tommy asked, "how long do you think you can hold out?"

"Until the cavalry comes."

"What cavalry? You think John Wayne is going to come over and save your white ass?"

"Something like that."

"Boy, don't hold your breath."

"Listen, sunshine," Frisco said, moving by Tommy and bumping him out of the way. "I'm about sick of your optimism. Are you always this positive or is this a phase?"

"Look," Tommy said, "I don't mean to trash your little parade here, but we are talking some serious shit. Some tyrant is about to send a two-hundred-man column up here and the only thing between them and the Doc is a bunch of teenage soldiers and a few old mercenary dudes who have seen better times and wars too long ago to inspire much confidence. So, I'm sorry if I'm not jumping on your band wagon."

"These old soldiers might just save your ass, Foster boy."

"Now don't get defensive. I'm sure you were a hell of a Marine in the Afghanistan or wherever you were, but I am more concerned about here and now, and right now I don't like the odds."

"So double down on your bet, Tommy boy," Frisco said. "What say you help us out instead of giving us this quitting crap you are shoveling."

"Still some pretty long odds," Tommy said. "What makes you so sure this will come out good?"

"Because this time we are going to stay there and fight right alongside our teen troopers, and that should give them the edge."

"What's he going on about?"

"We are going to even the odds a bit" Mike said. "C3 is a great equalizer and I'm taking Frisco, Barnes, Raines and Billups to form a welcome party along the Juarzon Road. After they prepare, they are going to stay on and back the boys, just in case."

"That's not security, Mike, that's offensive. Does the contract include offensive measures?"

"I've got leeway to make the call. From what I see, a little offence is needed to provide the protection."

"Your call, I guess."

"Right. In the meantime, we are going to lay some charges here, wire the bridge, and dig in along the riverbank. Defensive measures. We get any volunteers from the village, we'll deploy everyone we can along the perimeter and everybody will dig in."

Tommy studied the men in the crew, one by one.

"You boys are nearing the point of no return."

Frank Barnes said, "We passed that when we signed on."

"Well, not me," Tommy said, "I don't remember reading a death clause in my contract."

"Oh hell," Frisco said, "quit your bellyaching. I never heard so much crap."

Tommy watched Blanco and the four from the crew head out, and the three rovers disappeared around a bend in the road. Richards and Phillips grabbed a couple of heavy duffle bags and started off to the bridge. Going to wire it, Tommy assumed. He wondered if there would be enough time for Blanco to hustle back to the Kagera after the fight at the Juarzon. Mike was a good friend, and he wanted them to succeed but, in a way, he hoped for their failure.

Chapter Twenty-five

Mike Blanco sped along the rutted dirt road, avoiding as many potholes as possible, the accelerator pressed to the floorboard. Timing on the action was critical in order to take advantage of the situation. They would hear from their contact in Bandella when the military column passed through; that would give them a time frame in which to expect their guests.

"Who's that?" Billups asked from the front passenger seat. Scanning the road ahead of them he saw a band of delinquent boys in the road, kicking a ball around and jostling with each other.

Mike said, "It looks like Mustafa and his kid army got a game together."

Mike slowed and rolled to a stop near the boy leader who stretched out prone in the tall grass in the shade of a wide Jackal Berry tree. "What's going on," he asked the young leader.

"You can't smell the stench out this far," Mustafa said from beneath his floppy hat.

"That bad," Blanco asked, watching Mustafa's unit of about twenty young boys and girls kick a ball around.

"I've never seen a worse scene. I didn't want the boys to wait among the smell, so we got away from it for a while."

"Where's Brother Denis?"

"He kept his group there. He claims the sense of

smell fades; after a few minutes you wouldn't even notice the stink."

"Well," Mike said, "we are going along and make some preparations for our guests."

"A warm welcome, I hope," Mustafa asked.

"The warmest we can arrange. Better get your team ready." Mike said, pulling away and watching the boys continue their game in the rearview mirror.

Blanco drove another hundred meters and came to the road bridge. As the men piled out of the two vehicles, the stink from bloated bodies rotting under the blistering noon day sun hit them hard.

"Smells like Fallujah the week after we took the city, remember?" Billups said, pulling equipment from the back of the rover.

"Heads up," you guys, Mike told them, "reminisce later. Frisco, you and Billups get busy across the road. You'll want to set the charges just south of the last ones. The column will be going pretty fast until they spot the first blown truck. After you are set, get back and dig in on the south side of the bridge. You can cover the far side of the bridge from there and if you have to, you can get out using this gully for cover as you withdraw back to the rovers.

"Raines, Barnes, you two take the big gun across the road, behind that thick tree. Dig in so you can cover anything that comes across the bridge. Don't fire unless they make it across. I don't want you exposed until it's obvious the boys can't hold them. It should be a big surprise to the Mobassi army if they run into a couple of big guns just when they think they have gained the upper hand. If they still come across, you'll have to boogie back to the rover and hit it back to Masango. Park your rover around the bend there, just out of sight. That will give you about a fifty-meter dash if they over-run the bridge."

"Except we'll be carrying that gun."

"Most definitely, don't take off without it, we'll need that later."

"What about our young friends," Billups asked as he watched Mustafa's unit drift back to their position south of the road.

"They're on their own if they don't stop them at the bridge. No telling how many will be left but they'll take to the jungle. I don't think Mobassi is coming all this way to chase a bunch of kids through the woods. The real danger to his administration is in Masango."

****

Over the mid-morning hours Tommy watched as an assortment of village men and women slipped into the village. By noon the town burst with activity. Kimo came in, leading a bunch of men Tommy didn't recognize. He soon realized that these must be the other men that the doc called for.

"Kimo," Tommy called out to the man, "how many have you brought in?'

"I not sure Mr. Tommy, many come."

"*Many*?"

"Yes, they hear Doctor Bok call for men, so they come."

"Just like that?"

"Yes, she called, and they come."

"But why?"

"She chief."

Tommy didn't know if he'd ever get use to Thema being a chief of anything, much less a war chief. In his mind the doctor bit and the chief thing just didn't mesh. He watched Kimo lead his group off to the town center. It looked like the new arrivals were gathering to wait— for something. He counted about fifty teenage boys and girls and an assortment of men and a few women. A more ragged army he couldn't imagine.

Chief Kulu came out of the crowd and spoke to the people, getting them riled up. Tommy didn't understand any of what he said but it sounded like a locker room pep talk.

Then Thema walked out of the crowd and took a position in the center of the new recruits. An immediate cheer rose from the village. Tommy got that feeling in his stomach that told him they were at the point of no return, again.

Kimo translated while Thema spoke to the crowd though Tommy didn't care to hear what she said. Whatever she told the men, he knew in his gut it had nothing to do with saying goodbye.

****

Brother Denis's mother used to say he could hear a mouse in the potato cellar. From where he sat on the fender of one of the burned-out trucks that blocked the Juarzon Bridge, he heard the far-off rumble of motor vehicles. "They are coming," he said to Mike Blanco sitting next to him.

Denis took out his whistle and gave it a short blow. The ringing surged alongside the road and echoed off the trees. He then ran over to the south side of the road and motioned for his unit to spread out along the ditch there. He hoped the boys would perform their roles like the previous encounters at the bridge. For most of them now, this would be several battles they faced off against

Mobassi's army units and so far, they counted success at each meeting. He hoped the success rate continued.

The Americans ran toward him at full speed, dodging dead bodies—or jumping over them—as they cut the distance between the approaching trucks and the cover of the bridge.

"You get the charges laid?" Mike asked his men as they came across the bridge.

"Enough," Frisco answered, breathing hard.

"You hear the trucks?" Brother Denis asked.

Barnes nodded. "We felt the rumble along the ground. Sounds like a big column."

"The more the merrier," Frisco said. "I'm tired of messing with these dudes. I'd just as soon have it out here, once and for all."

"Let's be patient, my friend," Denis said. "Your time will come soon enough."

When Denis looked up, Mustafa and his boy unit arrived back to the bridge area. He signaled for the boys and recruited men to spread out along the bottom of the roadside gully, then sent his top boy, Sekou, across the road with a small squad to guard any advance from the south and to fire on any retreat from the bridge.

Denis watched Blanco order his men into their two key positions and then they waited. The sun began to sink past noon on the horizon, but time remained in the day for the task at hand.

"Are you staying with us?" Denis asked Mike.

"No, I'm heading back," he said, "I've got some preparations to make so I'll have to hustle along. Good luck to you!"

"Same to you," Denis said as he watched the American leader jog over to his vehicle and drive off.

Denis took a pair of binoculars from his rucksack and focused the strong lens on the other side of the bridge. He expected to hear the explosions of trucks hitting land mines. Instead, only silence came from the road and the low persistent chant of jungle life emanating from the thick forest that surrounded them.

After several minutes Denis caught the first glimpse of an administration soldier. Three of the soldiers made their way along the tree line using the many wide tree trunks as cover. The trio crossed the road and stopped atop a rise behind a thick stand of trees. Denis wasn't quite sure, but it looked like the men were staring back at him through their own binoculars.

A few minutes of silence passed and then a high squeal filled the air above them. Unsure for several seconds, it wasn't until the round exploded on the ground that he understood—*mortars*. The blast rocked the bridge road although the rocket itself landed fifty yards short. Denis waited a minute and feared for the expected to come, and he dreaded the unexpected turn of events.

The second round landed on top of the bridge with an explosive force that lifted one of the abandoned trucks clean in the air before it settled back remarkably close to its original resting place. Another minute of silence followed, and the dust began to settle before Brother Denis heard what he most feared. This time the whistling from high in the air came in waves, as mortar rounds zeroed in on the bridge.

All too late, Denis figured the trio of men in the trees were spotting for a mortar battery, located farther back from their position and well out of sight. Worse, he realized, they appeared to be spotting accurately.

****

Under the continuing heavy barrage of mortar rounds, Brother Denis crawled over to Mustafa's position, "We can't hold them," he shouted in the ear of the man as the firefight raged on in a thunder of weapons fire accompanying the deadly mortar attack, "we should pull back into the cover of the forest."

Although prepared, the small unit couldn't hold the bridge under a heavy bombardment. The Mobassi forces forded the river south of the bridge and flanked their position and started coming at the boy unit from different directions.

"We can stop them," Mustafa shouted back, over the sound of the gun fire from both sides, unleashing another volley of bullets from his own weapon.

"No," Denis shouted again, over the sound of the weapons going off around him. Boys and men began to drop at regular intervals. "There're too many, save whom we can and fall back to Masango!"

Mustafa ignored him and in a crazed state continued to fire.

Denis grabbed his friend by the shoulder and shook him. "Now. Before it's too late!"

He continued shaking Mustafa until his old friend halted his firing to view the surroundings, and their precarious position. Realizing what was at stake he lowered his weapon and nodded his head in agreement. Denis took out his whistle and blew long and hard and the signal brought the boy's shooting to an abrupt end.

"Carry the wounded," he shouted above the gun fire. "Leave no one behind."

Raines and Billups continued to use their machine gun to rake the far side of the road, pouring red hot rounds into the administration soldier's position, providing covering fire until the boys in Denis's unit pulled out and retreated back into the forest. When it was clear, Frisco and Barnes withdrew to their Land Rover. Once the boys in Mustafa's unit were clear, Raines and Billups grabbed the big gun and ammo and ran along the roadside gully heading back to their rover. Weapons fire from Mobassi's soldiers followed the men as they retreated. Bullets pelted the ground around them. Raines tossed the hot gun onto the floorboard and climbed into the driver's seat while Billups dove into the vehicle. Raines started the engine and putting it in gear the rover lurched forward and barreled away, up the road to Masango, following behind Frisco and Barnes.

"Shit," Raines said to Billups when they were out of range, "what a fucking show!"

"Fuck yeah," Billups said coughing deeply, "I just wish I'd gotten another shot at them."

"Don't worry," Raines said, turning to look at his friend, "we'll get another chance soon enough."

Billups didn't answer.

****

Tommy Foster watched as the men of the construction crew placed charges in strategic locations on the Kagera Bridge where the river ran wide and deep beneath. As far as he could recall, it was a good two times as wide as the Juarzon and much deeper

"You put enough C3 under there?" he asked Page as he crawled out from beneath a bridge abutment. In response, Page glowered at him.

"Just making sure."

"Sure, of what? Sending it into outer space?"

"No," Mike said, stalking across the bridge, "but we do want to make sure no one gets across, at least not by using the bridge."

"Oh, I got it," Tommy said. "If you blow the bridge, they have to wade across the river."

"That's the idea. The water will work as the equalizer we need."

"You sure it will stop them?"

"Probably not stop them," he said, "but it'll slow them down."

"And they'll be sitting ducks while they cross?"

"That's the idea," Blanco said.

"Don't you get tired of trying to figure out new ways to kill people?"

"No."

Shaking his head, Tommy walked away from the bridge, amazed that men could speak of death so coolly. It had been a while since he served in combat, but he remembered that even then there was some concern for life. Even the enemy's life. Tommy had served with some bad dudes back then, but these guys had them beat. Worse, they were licensed. He couldn't believe he had thrown in with them.

Tommy walked back toward the town. People had been coming in all morning, and they gathered in the square. Thema spoke with each group while Willy Gray and Phillips took the men aside in threes and fours and made sure they were already armed or gave them a new weapon for the battle to come.

"Tommy," Thema called during a lull in the training, "where've you been?"

"At the crew's camp," he said, shuffling up to her. "Big planning going on there."

"When do they plan to blow the bridge?"

"You heard about that?" Tommy asked, stopping

near her.

"I've heard the talk," she said, taking Nuru by the hand and leading her away.

"Talk," Tommy said, "like talk about the town?"

"Yes, talk," she said again, moving in the direction of the clinic, "everyone is worried, so there's been talk."

"I'm glad someone else is worried around here," he said, following her. "I was beginning to believe no one in this whole damn town was worried."

"Of course, people are worried, Tommy," Thema said, turning to face him. "It's only natural, but we still need to get ready. All the worry isn't going to help anyone right now."

With that, she took off again, but Tommy followed. "Is that what you tell these poor men who come in to fight for you?"

"They don't come in to fight for me, Tommy," she said, reaching the clinic steps. They come to fight for themselves."

"Is that what you say?" Tommy asked, reaching out and stopping here from moving farther.

"I don't say a lot, but I do tell them why it is important to fight for their homes."

"And that's enough? Enough for them to maybe get themselves killed?"

"Yes, it's enough," she said, "of course I also tell them I'll be standing with them."

He couldn't believe what she was saying. "Doc," he said, moving closer, holding her in his arms, "we don't need this, we don't have to be a part of this."

"But that's the problem Tommy. Can't you see I am a part of this?"

"Doc, two weeks ago, I bet you couldn't find

Masango on a map. I know I couldn't. Yet today you are willing to get killed for this place."

"Tommy," she said, putting her hand up to his heart, "being here, living here, attending to the sick and the wounded, I'm seeing things differently. Don't you feel the same?"

"Doc, I want too but I'm having trouble seeing the good in this."

"Look," she said, breaking away from him, "I told you, these people are my people. I can't let anything happen to them. They are depending on me. I need to be here. Whatever happens today at the Juarzon bridge, I need to be here. It's my job now to be with my people and I won't leave them. We need to do whatever it takes to keep this village safe and if that means blowing a bridge or two or calling for more men to fight to get it done then you'd better stay out of the way because I'm all for it."

Tommy wanted to continue the argument, but Kimo came up them. "Doctor Bok, more men have just come to fight. You must speak with them."

"Absolutely, Kimo," she said, turning and walking back the way she had come. "Let's talk to them about how important it is to fight for home and freedom."

"Doc," Tommy said again, before she got away, "it's not too late. We don't owe these people anything. Let's get out of here. You and me."

"I can't Tommy, these people need me."

"Thema, two weeks ago you never even heard of them."

"Things are different now," she said in a calm, clear, convincing tone. "These people are my family."

Chapter Twenty-six

Unsure of the merits of her actions or her beliefs, Tommy watched Thema walk away. Just coming to this new country to help people would be enough for anyone to grasp. But now, with the knowledge of her family roots tossed in, he couldn't imagine what she must be going through. He didn't know if there was a chance for Thema and him, but he did know they stood a better chance if they weren't being shot at.

At first, he didn't notice the change in the crowd. The noise ratcheted up several notches, then a new excitement took hold of the group. Looking past the crowd as they swarmed to the road, he saw the crew's rovers coming over the bridge.

Tommy rushed to the bridge, his bad knee throbbing, and got to the road's edge just as the rovers pulled up.

Mike Blanco ran to greet them. "What's the score?" he asked the men once they came to a stop and the doors opened.

"We struck out," Raines said, climbing out of the driver's seat of the second rover. "I'm afraid Billups's bought it."

"No, way," Mike said, moving to the passenger side door and opening it. Billups's limp body confirmed the bad news.

"He took several rounds during the retreat and bled

out before we got back."

"Hell no," Phillips swore.

"So, what happened?" Mike asked, still kneeling at the rover's door.

"They had a mortar squad, and they really punished those boys."

"Mortars?" Tommy asked, hoping he hadn't heard right.

"That's right, big ones," Raines said, leaning back against the rover hood. "Probably our damn M224 American made, 60 mm by the look of the craters."

"Accurate?" Mike asked.

"I'd say, the column stopped a half mile back of the bridge and lobbed the bastards in on us. They had a spotting squad zeroing in on our positions and must have dropped four or five dozen shells on us."

"How many of the boys did they get?" Tommy asked.

"I'd say fifty percent casualties," Frisco said, "maybe more."

"Where are they now?" Mike asked.

"We held them at the bridge for a while," Barnes said, kicking out at the ground, "but with our numbers low we couldn't cover the area. They got a unit in the water to the south of the bridge and flanked us. They hit Mustafa's boys pretty bad."

"Did he get out?" Tommy asked.

"When he realized we couldn't hold them, he made it to cover, and they withdrew into the forest," Barnes said. "We ran back and got the rover, the rest of them scattered in the bush, but I imagine they'll make their way here. They should arrive with the wounded anytime."

"You and the rest, okay?" Mike asked.

"Yeah," Barnes said, "but we were lucky."

"Mike," Raines said, thumbing toward the road, "that was some shit back there. It looked like a whole fucking company."

"How many men?"

"Hard to say, they held a bunch back in reserve, but I bet we got at least fifty of the bastards."

Mike walked off and gazed in the direction of the Juarzon bridge. He looked like he expected to find the soldiers coming. Turning back to the men he said, "Come on, on the double, get Billups out of there."

"How many village men came in today?" Raines asked as he and Frisco pulled Billups from the vehicle and gently laid him on the ground.

"Maybe fifty or so," Mike said.

"Did the Buta come in?" Frisco asked.

"No," Mike said, "and no telling when they'll show. They might not understand the circumstances here."

"That's comforting," Frisco said.

"No, it's going to be okay," Mike said. "These new men are not just farmers, they know how to fight. Most came in with weapons and ready for action. Don't forget they've been at war for a long time."

Tommy stepped forward, "Wait, you guys think they are definitely going to attack the village?"

"That's a sure bet, wonder boy," Frisco said, "these guys are all business, and it looks like their company commander is well trained. He didn't just walk into the trap, and he avoided our mines as well. Then he put that flanking action together and came at our exposed weak ass. Yep, this guy's trained, probably Chinese trained."

"Great," Tommy said, feeling worse, which he

didn't think possible.

"That's probably why he just didn't follow us straight away," Frank said. "He's probably regrouping, seeing what he has left."

"Did he spot you guys?" Mike asked.

"That's a negative, Mike," Raines said, wiping his face with a big handkerchief. "I could hardly see anything myself between the mortar's shit and the smoke."

"If he didn't then we'll still have the surprise here. He might be thinking we are just a sitting duck of a village, now that he took out the main boy unit."

"Mike," Frisco said, "don't make book on that. I'd say this guy is experienced."

"I'm counting on that," Mike said. "I think he'll regroup, count his dead, check equipment and all, before heading this way. Anybody in command would do that. Are they still on foot?"

"Definitely," Barnes said, smiling wide. "They can't clear that bridge without heavy equipment."

"Okay," Mike said, with a burst of energy." I'd say we have a couple of hours before they get here, maybe more."

Then, Thema walked into the crowd of men and asked, "What's the situation?"

"They broke through at the Juarzon, and are headed this way," Mike reported, a little enthusiasm draining from him. "Billups got hit, I'm afraid he didn't make it."

"No," Thema cried, going to the man and kneeling to examine him.

"How can you be sure they'll come here," Tommy said.

"I'd bet my life on it," Mike said. "Billups just did!"

"Are you going to bet ours too?" Tommy said.

"That's enough, you two," Thema said from where she knelt next to Billups. "How many casualties did you have?"

"Besides Billups," Frank said, "the boy unit probably sustained fifty percent."

"Doesn't that cut into your force, Mike?"

"We'll be a little thin. That's why we asked you to send out the word."

"You did send out the word?" Frisco asked her.

Of course!" she confirmed, looking at Billups a final time and getting to her feet, "Men have been coming in all day."

"You talked to the Buta people as well?" Frank asked.

"We sent boys into the mountains but have not heard back."

"Did you tell them Thema Atsu Bok is calling them to service?"

"Yes," Kimo confirmed, "I tell them to say this."

"We'll have to wait on them," Mike said. "In the meantime, we'll fight with what we have."

"Where are the wounded now?" Thema asked.

"They are heading this way," Raines said, "through the bush, they should start shuffling in any time."

"So," Thema said, turning to address Mike, "what's the plan?"

"We've wired the bridge with enough C3 to blow it in two," he said, pointing at the big stone bridge. "Now, I'd like to wait to get half the administration's advancing men across before we blow it. The initial blast will take out some, and in the confusion, we should be able to take out the soldiers that get stuck on this side. We've got the two machine guns we can station on the high ground, he explained, pointing, "over there and right here. "That should take care of a big chunk of them."

"How many will they have?"

"Our intelligence said they had about two hundred and fifty men when they left the capital, but Raines says they lost about fifty at the Juarzon River."

"So," Thema repeated, surveying the area, "you plan to cut that in half when you blow the bridge here?"

"That's right," he said, "once we divide their strength, we'll have two actions. We can take care of the first half that's cut off and then face the second wave after they wade across."

"What do you say, chief?" Frank Barnes said.

"Well, sounds like a plan," Thema responded.

"Mike," Tommy said, "this can easily go the other way."

"No guarantees, Tommy boy."

"That's what I mean," he said. "Look, Doc, we can still get out of this. You really want to save your village? The best thing is to get out of here."

"How's that going to help?" Thema asked.

"If we head west out of here, they'll follow us and leave the village alone. You're the target here, not these villagers. If you get out, they'll follow you and leave the village."

"You'll get caught out in the open," Mike said.

"We've got the rovers, and we have a head start. Plus, you said they're on foot now. If we head east, we'll be way gone before they can catch us."

"East," Mike said, "to the border?"

"That's right, to the border, out of the country. When the administration army gets here and you're not around, they'll bypass the village and chase us."

"What about my people?" Thema asked.

"Come on, Doc," Tommy said, kicking out at a big wooden crate. "These people are hardly yours."

"My family—my people," Thema repeated, turning to look at the faces of the gathered crowd who were listening to the discussion.

"Okay then, look," Tommy said, thinking fast, "we've got the rovers and the panel truck. Get your twenty or so people together and we'll take them with us."

"What about the rest?" Thema asked.

"They'll be fine," Tommy said, exasperated. "They can go back into the jungle and hide out."

"But this is their home," Thema said. "Even if we got away, won't the soldiers still come and attack the rest? Mike, what do you think?"

"If they don't get you, they'll take it out on the village. If for no other reason than they don't want witnesses."

Thema nodded, once. "Then we can't leave." She moved to stand among the gathered children, and gently placing her hands atop several heads. "I could never live with myself if I left now."

"Look, Doc," Tommy said, "you've become attached to these people, I get it. Now, with you being born here, even more so, but there is no guarantee you can fight off this approaching army. And even if you do, will it stop there? Mobassi appears to be a real blood thirsty dude. He'll probably just send a whole other company, what about that?"

"I can't say Tommy, really," she said. "But I can only deal with one emergency at a time. Now, we are going to be getting some wounded soon, so the ladies and I are going to get ready at the clinic and these men need to prepare. It seems like there's plenty to do. Only question is what are you going to do?"

Tommy looked around the gathered crowd. The children, women, Blanco and his men, "You are all crazy. I didn't sign up for a massacre." Looking at young Alex he said, "I'm going to pull out, and I'm taking Alex with me."

"Pull out how, boy?" Frisco asked.

"I'm taking one of the rovers and anyone who wants to come."

Mike looked over at Thema. She barely nodded her head in agreement. "Take Nuru with you," she said.

Mike dug in his pocket and took out a set of keys and tossed it to Tommy but said to his men. "Come on guys," he said, smiling at Tommy, "the chief has spoken. Let's get Billups wrapped and get into position."

Tommy caught the key ring with his left hand. Thema smiled weakly at him before spinning around and rushing to the clinic. He watched her stalk off and didn't take his eyes off her until the little group disappeared behind the clinic walls.

"Mike," he said to the man before he strode off, "you can't be serious about this."

"Dead serious," he said.

"You can't win this thing."

"We'll make a go of it, if the Buta fighters show up."

"And why should they bother?"

Mike said, "The leader of the Buta has family here. Mustafa is her son for one. Offspring always provide incentive."

Tommy's eyes followed the man as he plodded

away with the other crew members carrying Billups with them. "Come on, son," he told Alex. "I've got to pack a few things, and you need to find Nuru." Then, looking out over the village he said, "We're getting out of here."

Chapter Twenty-seven

Tommy limped to his room in the mission house and put a bunch of stuff into a duffle bag. He grabbed his passport and the wad of American money he had stowed in the toe of an extra pair of shoes. He was at his door when Thema came out of her room.

She smiled at him and asked, "All packed?"

"I've got what I need," he said and noticed she had changed into fresh scrubs.

"I'm glad you're getting Nuru out of here."

"Doc, think about Nuru. You can still come with us."

She reached up to take him in her arms. "Nuru doesn't need this. I can't leave but she can."

He closed her in his arms, knowing it would be the last time he'd hold her. "I wish you'd come with us."

"I know, Tommy," she said, cupping his cheeks in her palms. "Under different circumstances, I would."

"Doc…"

From outside the building someone called her name. Hands dropping to her sides, she murmured, "I don't have time to explain it all. I don't even know how. Just keep Nuru safe."

Tommy came out of the house and watched Thema march down the path to the clinic. He shook his head in wonder but determined, he stalked over to town looking for Alex. When he got there a crowd with Kimo, crossed the village square. "What's going on?" he asked Kimo.

"Some fighters arrive," Kimo said, out of breath, "there are many wounded."

Tommy flowed with the crowd and came to the forest's edge where they met Mustafa coming out of the dense underbrush, carrying a young girl in his arms. Several boys carried wounded in on makeshift litters. Others limped into the town clearing.

"Doctor Bok?" Mustafa asked, somewhat out of breath.

"She's at the clinic," Tommy said, "they're expecting you."

"She has heard then?"

"Yes, the crew came in some time ago and they told us what happened."

"And she still stays?"

"Yes, I can't believe it myself."

"Doctor Bok is a remarkable woman; we are lucky to have such a sister to stand with us. I must take the wounded to her."

Tommy grabbed a handle of the next litter and helped a young boy carry a wounded friend the last one hundred paces to the clinic.

"Kimo," Tommy said, as they struggled, "better run to the crew's camp and ask if Willy Gray can lend a hand." Kimo jogged away looking for the corpsman.

At the clinic the boys and men began to line up on the porch and Thema worked her way down the row of young wounded, appraising the severity of their wounds. When she found Mustafa among them, she said, "You don't look too good, are you okay?"

"I'm fine. You need to look after the others before you worry about me."

"Dude," Tommy said, "you do look a little pale for a brother."

"I am fine," Mustafa said while rocking to his left and losing his balance.

"Whoa," Tommy said, catching the man before he hit the ground, then lowering him to the covered porch floor. "Oh yeah, you are just fine."

"What's wrong with him?" Thema asked.

"He just keeled over."

"Did he say anything?"

"No but he carried a wounded girl out of the jungle. I figure he's just worn out."

Thema kneeled at the man's side and gave him a quick look over and spotted a wet spot on his pant leg, "It's his leg."

Tommy raised the man's pant leg and saw a bloody mess. "Is he shot?" Tommy asked.

"I don't think so," she said after a quick exam of the wound. "Likely it's shrapnel from the shelling. There are quite a few shrapnel wounds among the boys and girls."

"Is it bad?"

"No, he'll be okay," she said, taking her stethoscope and listening to his heart. "He's exhausted like you said. He's lost some blood too, but his heart is beating strong, he'll come around shortly."

"Well, good, he's a good man."

"Yes, he is. So," she asked, studying him, "did you find Nuru?"

"Alex is out looking for her. We'll be shoving off soon."

"Keep her safe," she said, continuing to work and not looking up. "When you get cell service, please contact the embassy and tell them you made it. I'll get in touch with you through them."

After the Doc scrambled off to inspect another injured kid, Tommy knew it was the final signal that she had really made up her mind to stay. He was disappointed but he could not fight her passion for the people of the village.

As he started to walk away, he passed several wounded boys and girls resting on the porch. He couldn't imagine what the clinic would be like in twelve hours. Although he felt guilty about leaving, he still went off in search of Alex and Nuru. Saving them seemed like the next best thing.

****

Tommy met Alex and Nuru coming across the square. "You guys ready?"

Nuru carried a basket of clothes atop her head and held Alex by the hand. The Doc loved the young girl, she said to him as much. She found out that Nuru was orphaned some years ago after the village was hit by the previous administration's troops, so she had kind of adopted her. Somehow, feeling a kinship. Tommy recognized there were needs there, he just didn't think they could be met by inciting a civil war.

Tommy hustled the two onto the path to the crews camp. The area stood empty with most of the crew working on the defense of the village, but Richards greeted him. He had pulled one the rovers to the back of the van and was filling it with gas.

"You'll need a full tank before you drive out of here," the big man said as he used a hand pump to draw gas out of one of the fifty-five-gallon drums that made the trip up with the other gear. "There are no gas stations along this road," he said. "Hey, pull a couple of those five-gallon cans over and I'll fill them up too."

Tommy grabbed two of the heavy empty gas cans. "I appreciate this, Richards."

"Ah, I like these kids too and I'm glad some are getting out. Not everyone is as gung-ho as Frisco and Page. To hear those guys, you'd think this war was being fought on their doorstep back home."

"You should come too."

"No, a contract is a contract. We've been through a lot together. Nuts as they are, I couldn't leave these guys."

Tommy opened the rear door and put Nuru inside. He tried to take the basket from her to stow in the back, but she kept a tight grip on it, so he just let her keep it as it seemed to keep her settled. Alex climbed in the front seat.

Once Richards finished filling the rover's tank, he started on the two spare gas cans. "You have to strap these two in the rear braces there," he pointed. "Don't ever put gas inside a vehicle," he warned. "Smells like hell and would put you to sleep if you sucked on those fumes long enough.

"So how far will I get?"

"Oh, let's see, thirty gallons on board, at about fifteen miles to the gallon, plus the two five-gallon spares, oh I'd say about six hundred miles. Take it slow and maybe a little more. The border is less than fifty miles away by road. It's closer overland but fifty miles or so along the road."

"Great, Richards, thanks."

"Well," Richards said, holding out his big right hand, "good luck to you."

"Same to you," Tommy said, shaking his hand and

getting in behind the wheel and cranking the engine. "You guys get in touch state side when this is over."

Tommy started to back the Land Rover onto the road when villagers started drifting from the town to the bridge. He pulled to the side of the road. Looking back through the rear-view window he could see the village men and boys taking positions along the road and the river. He touched the gas pedal and steered onto the road just as he saw Mike heading his way and stopped when the man raised a hand.

"All set?" Mike asked, peering through the passenger side window.

"Yeah, got the kids in and all."

"Did Richards fill your tank?"

Tommy hesitated, wondering about whose idea it was to give him a full tank of gas. "All full."

"Good, you should be okay. Once across the border, there's a pretty big town, almost a city actually, Goma, about two hundred miles in. How's your French?"

"I got some high school stuff I remember."

"You'll need it there," he said. "And whatever you do, don't give them your passport at the border. These clowns at border crossings always want to take passports. Put an American fifty-dollar bill on the first page of your passport before you hand it in, and they should just stamp it and let you by. You think of a good story why you are crossing over?"

"No, will I need one?"

"Better think of something," he said smiling at Nuru sitting pretty in the back seat. "Tell them you are taking the girl to the hospital in Goma. That should work."

"Thanks," Tommy said, surprised at the helpfulness of the man.

"You dug in well?" Tommy asked.

"Frisco fixed us up. He wired the explosives to the bridge, and we can set them off from the one spot. When they reach the road, and we can hit them before they get across."

"I hate to say it, but I wish you guys luck. I hate to think of anything bad happening to the Doc."

"Well, I might visit the clinic," Mike said, smiling wide. "To see how Thema is doing."

"Don't go to any trouble, man."

"No trouble, big guy," he said, smiling at Tommy. "Don't worry about her," he said, winking at him, "she'll be in good hands."

"Come on Mike. No bull. What do you think your chances are?"

"We've just got to hold them until the cavalry comes."

Tommy watched the man head to the clinic. *What cavalry,* he wondered. Taking his foot off the break he inched forward, still thinking about Thema when he saw Willy Gray stroll his way.

"So, you're really getting out?" Willy said, looking into the cab of the rover.

"All packed," Tommy said, "Are you going to the clinic?"

"Yeah, Mike said to find out what I can do. Are you sure you don't want to hang around? We could use the help."

"I don't think so."

"Man, I can't believe you are chickening out like this."

"Well, believe what you want."

"What about the Doc?"

"She could have come."

"Oh, man," he said, shaking his head, "you the blindest dude around. She couldn't leave. These people chose her as their leader. What do you think it would look like if she skunked it out of here with you? How can you leave? Don't you have a thing with her?"

"I guess not enough," he said, nodding in the direction of Mike Blanco hiking up the hill to the clinic. "She made her choice."

"You mean with Mike? That's just business, man, just the duty. And speaking of duty, she is stuck here just like the rest of us, at least until the cavalry gets here. Nothing personal."

Tommy watched Willy walk away, but the man paused in mid step and stared at the sky.

At first Tommy didn't understand what he heard. It could have been a far-off train whistle, but before he could think it through, the ground around him began to explode in a deafening fury. Mortar rounds rained out of the sky and began to chew the ground in deafening explosions along the town side of the road. The force of one blast knocked Willy Gray to the ground, but the big man rolled to his feet, and he rushed off toward the clinic.

Tommy hit the gas and drove far enough away to escape the falling rockets. Smoke and flying debris filled the air and people screamed from hidden positions along the bridge and riverbank.

Tommy watched the well-planned defense of the town begin to crumble at the bridge. After the second wave came through, he recognized the rockets came in a sequence of three. He figured Mobassi's troops must have three of the mortars positioned somewhere back from the bridge and were lobbing the shells in waves.

The fourth wave whistled from above and Tommy squinted and waited for the bombs to hit. The first hit just beyond the end of the bridge and the consecutive explosions worked their way west from there.

Through the smoke and dust, Tommy saw Mike running toward the dug-in position where Frisco had set the charge detonator. A pause brought seconds of quiet which let Mike get into the fox hole, but another wave of bombs soon exploded about ten meters from their position. Then another rocket in the sequence landed closer to the men. The force of the explosion threw the men into the air and out of the hole. When the dust settled the two men lay motionless in the rubble and Tommy realized with Mike out of action, the plan to blow the bridge was in serious jeopardy.

At the same moment the administration soldiers from the column came around the bend and rushed the bridge. Barnes and Page, manning one of the machine guns north of the bridge, opened up, laying a steady stream of heavy rounds. On the south side of the bridge Raines and Phillips manned the second gun and they also began firing on the advancing soldiers from their raised position. The combination of lethal fire from both big guns brought the advance to a pause but didn't stop it.

The advancing troops congregated at the opposite end of the bridge. Then, using the bridge's thick stone railing as cover, the soldiers made their way forward, staying beneath the heavy fire and gaining position to return fire. Mike had been right about this. He figured the advancing soldiers would get across, but if they blew the bridge at the right moment, half could be trapped on this side and half on the far side. With the troops divided they could concentrate fire on the soldiers that made it across and take care of the rest later. But right now, that plan was in trouble with Mike out of action and the other men too busy to realize the predicament.

Another wave of mortar rounds screamed overhead and headed to the bunker positions. The first wave in this group landed north of the bridge with blast after blast working their way to the machine gun position manned by Raines and Phillips. That wave ended short of the men but right after another wave followed and it carried all the way to the men's location. At the last second the men jumped from their position and escaped the pounding explosions where one shell made a direct hit on the machine gun site, taking it out of action.

Fire from the mortars shifted to the south. As if guided by a wire the next two waves of blasts worked their way toward Barnes and Page. The last rocket in the sequence found the shallow bunker. Tommy watched the explosion flatten the little bunker and he looked away before the dust cleared.

The remaining crew members fired away on the advancing troops that kept coming. From where he sat, Tommy didn't think the men could hold much longer.

He turned to Alex to tell him to hang on because they were getting out of there before they got killed, but just Nuru stared back at him with wide frightened eyes.

"Where's Alex?" Tommy asked the girl.

Nuru motioned at once out of the rover toward the bridge. Tommy climbed out of the rover and saw Alex running in the direction of the battle.

"What the...Alex!!" he yelled at the boy, but the screech of another round of incoming mortar shells drowned out his call.

The incoming shells fell between Mike's blown out

fox hole and his position away from the main action. Alex appeared to run inside the targeted area, but the exploding earth made it hard for Tommy to see.

"Stay here," Tommy told the girl who crouched on the floorboard. "I'll be right back."

He started out with a limp but broke into full speed when a break in the earth showering mortar rounds gave him an opportunity to advance directly to Mike's location. Taking quick steps, he reached the fox hole where C3 detonation lines were set up. Sliding on his backside, he fell into the shallow depression in the ground.

Mike and Frisco had been blown several feet away and he couldn't tell their situation. He wanted to go to them, but the sound of advancing administration troops came from the bridge. If he wanted to stop the surge of troops across the bridge, he needed to act quickly.

The simple configuration of wires and the detonation device seemed in place. Tommy had seen enough training movies to know all he had to do was twist the knob thing, and he was happy the charge unit and wires were still in one piece. He took hold of the wind key and cranked the unit several times setting the charge. When the key stopped turning, he took it out of the charge slot and put it into the red detonate slot. He glance quickly at the administration soldiers spilling across the bridge and Tommy realized there was no other option, so he ducked in the bunker, took a breath of air, closed his eyes and turned the charge key in its socket.

The charge clicked off but nothing more. Tommy peered over the edge of the ditch again and saw more soldiers streaming across the still standing bridge. He pulled the key out of its socket and reset it. He ducked and turned the key a second time and again the charge clicked off but nothing else happened; no explosion. Tommy panicked, but when he rose to scan the expanding battle, he saw Alex standing about ten meters away. Alex held two loose ends of wire, one in each hand.

"Watch out," Tommy shouted at the boy. He climbed out of the fox hole and scrambled to the boy. Pulling him close he dragged him back for the hole. "Boy, you're going to get yourself killed out there."

"Mike needed help," the boy said, handing him the two frayed wires.

"Damn, one of those shells must have hit the line. Thanks," he said as he grabbed the bare wires and started to twist the lines together, "but don't you ever do anything like that again?"

"Anything like what?"

"Anything that could get you killed," Tommy said, pushing little Alex's head down. "Fire in the hole," he yelled out as he turned the key and this time the line sparked.

A second later the charges under the bridge exploded in a spectacular show of power that rocked the village from one end to the other. The big bridge buckled up in one movement, the momentum of the structure pausing at the apex of its rise and then it fell, with a snap that broke the bridge in two. The remnants of the concrete structure crashed into the river below. River water splashed over the banks on both sides of the Kagera. A wave of steam and debris filled the air above the village with a thick cloud.

The sound of the exploding bridge made everyone in the village stop and turn to the road. When Tommy peeked out of the hole, he could see that Frisco was an expert. The bridge was cut in half, and the remaining men were withdrawing. With a portion of the soldiers cut off the Americans and villagers opened fire on the troops caught without cover and choking in a thick dust cloud. The weapon rounds from the remaining crew tore through the troops leaving the area covered in bodies.

He waited until the last of the small arms fire ended, then getting to his feet, he grabbed Alex by the hand intending to run back to the rover, but the sound of approaching mortars stopped him. He didn't want to be caught out in the open, so he retreated to the little bunker and waited it out. Administration rockets began to pound the riverbank from north to south. The volunteer villagers who came in to join the fight took the brunt of the blasts as the mortars pulverized the riverbank driving anyone who could flee out of their cover and back to the village proper.

Administration soldiers charged into the river. It appeared when the bridge collapsed it also dammed the river's flow, and the water shallowed downstream to barely a trickle. Something no one anticipated, and the soldiers began to cross the shallowing flow with ease. The mortar bombardment ended, and the soldiers piled out of the river and climbed its bank. The Americans waited and began firing at the first head over the bank, but with both machine guns out of action the light small arms resistance couldn't hold the advance.

Phillips signaled to the team to withdraw, and Tommy watched as Phillips, Richards, and Raines pulled back in phases, working their way back to the town proper. The soldiers continued a steady stream of weapon fire as they drove the Americans and any villagers with them back to the center of town. Tommy stayed in his hole and watched as the Americans took refuge behind the thick foundation walls of the still to be finished clinic. Situated on a little rise at the end of the open square the Americans and the last of the villagers fired on the approaching administration soldiers.

For a moment it appeared they would hold them there, but as more and more troops crossed the choked river and joined the soldiers already across, Tommy doubted they could hold them off for long.

The administration troops split their numbers, and one group headed for the clinic building. Automatic weapon fire came from the clinic. The wounded Mustafa and his injured boys and girls took positions behind the stone walkway surrounding the clinic and fired on the advancing soldiers. With two fronts to attack the administration soldiers stalled but reinforcements continued to cross the shallowed riverbed.

Amid the continued battle, a squad of administration soldiers broke away and approached the clinic from the blind side. Mustafa's men continued to fire on the opposite end but didn't react to the flanking action. Tommy wondered what would happen when he realized the squad was not headed to the front of the clinic, but they were climbing on top and looked to be planning to enter through the thick thatched roof. Thema would be caught by surprise.

Tommy turned to young Alex. "This time, I want you to stay here. Not like last time, but stay right here, understand?" When Alex nodded, Tommy jumped out of the bunker and hobbled toward the clinic, crossing the open area in seconds. He maneuvered through the fallen soldiers and just stepped onto the clinic path when his bad knee gave way, and he collapsed. Rolling over he bent his knee and felt the damage. He figured the last of his ligaments just torn loose, but he could still move. He grabbed an abandoned AK-47 and using it as a cane, got to his feet. Hobbling, he approached the left flank of the advancing troops. They were making steady progress toward the clinic, so he shouldered the weapon and squeezed the trigger. Rounds fired off in the direction of the soldiers.

Caught by surprise on their flank, the troops dropped for cover and returned fire. Tommy fired point blank at the soldiers as he limped on until he ran out of ammunition, and dove for cover. He crawled off under the fire and made his way around the clinic. The squad in the rear of the clinic had made their way atop the roof. Using their rifle butts, they dug into the layers of thatch trying to get through. One lone soldier stayed on the ground. The man stood staring at his comrades, not paying attention. Tommy decided to take a chance and pulling himself to his feet and gathering his remaining strength, he charged toward the man, ignoring the pain, hoping his knee would hold for one last play.

Chapter Twenty-eight

With the noise of the raging battle covering his stumbling steps, Tommy crossed the space with some momentum and crashed shoulder first into the man. The crunch of the man's back and the grunt of air told him the man wouldn't be getting up. When the soldier fell, he dropped his weapon. Tommy grabbed it, swung it up, and took aim on the four soldiers on the clinic roof.

Sighting along the barrel of the weapon, he put his finger on the trigger but couldn't pull it. The men's backs were to him, and he couldn't bring himself to fire on them like that. He started to lower the rifle, about to call out to make them turn and defend themselves. Before he did, one of the men saw him and let out a shout. The soldiers whirled and started shooting.

Tommy fired the weapon and swept the roof with automatic rounds. After the men dropped in unison, he lowered the rifle. He didn't feel proud. His action actually surprised him. It had been a long time since he had killed anyone. It was one of the things he hated about the army. Although he had been in intelligence he still had to patrol on occasion and even then, he didn't particularly like taking the life of a man.

Tommy limped around the clinic and continued onto the porch, diving for cover among Mustafa and his boy soldiers as they continued to fire on the troops. Peeking above the stone rail he saw the administration soldiers being reinforced again from the rear.

"Good thing you came along when you did, my friend." Mustafa smiled at Tommy. "I was worried we couldn't hold them."

"Dude, I don't think this one gun is going to make much of a difference."

"One more than we had before you showed up. Are you okay?" he asked.

"Yeah, I'm fine, just this bum knee here, how about you?"

"Yes," he said, looking out over the porch's stone wall and firing off a long burst from his AK-47, "I'm feeling much better now."

"Well, that's great, because you look like hell."

"Thank you, my friend," he said, preparing to fire again, "but as they say in America, do not judge a book by its cover."

Tommy looked over the stone railing and watched as the soldiers moved forward, cutting the distance between them and the clinic. He was thinking what he could do to stave off the pending assault when he heard a different volume of fire power rise over the village. Brother Denis and his little band of boys came out of the woods. Pouring from the trees along the east end of town, they engaged the tail end of the advancing troop and forced them to stop.

"It's your man, Brother Denis," Tommy said to Mustafa. "Better late than never I guess."

The man struggled to his feet and finding his footing he opened fire on the advancing soldiers catching them in a brief crossfire. The action raged on in a stalemate with ammunition running low. Brother Denis's unit held the east flank, the American crew and village volunteers were pinned behind the new clinic foundation in the north, and Mustafa's squad, though depleted, held the high ground around the clinic on the west. Unfortunately, the administration's soldiers kept swarming out of the south in unending numbers.

The group on the clinic porch continued to fire on the stalled administration troops, pinning them where they took cover. In the midst of the exchange of rifle fire Thema screamed from the OR, twenty paces away along the porch. Tommy turned in the direction and realized she must be under attack. Struggling to his feet he started in her direction. Mustafa called out to him to take cover, but Tommy, with one thing on his mind, didn't hear him.

When Tommy got to his feet the movement drew every soldier's attention and a stream of rifle fire followed him as he lumbered along the companionway, the rounds tearing into the mud walls behind him, driving him forward.

Thema screamed again and Tommy plowed through the OR doorway. When the screened door burst open, he raised his weapon into a shooting position and just before raking the room with hot rounds he yelled, "Everybody down!"

The rounds from the AK47 splintered the walls above the operating table, killing two administration soldiers who had just entered the room from the roof above.

Thema knelt at the operating table, with one hand in a patient's chest and the other holding on to the table, keeping it steady. Two soldiers sprawled in odd positions where they fell after being shot. Willy Gray was on the floor where he held another soldier in a choke hold. Once the man stopped moving, Willy got to his feet.

Tommy scrambled across the room to Thema and pulled her up and to him. She only had one free hand but managed to hug him. "Do you always try to impress the girls with this last second rescue thing?"

"Well, Doc, you know me. Always got to make an entrance."

"What are you going to do for a second act?"

Tommy was trying to think of something clever to say when shouts from Mustafa's men and an escalation in the furor of the battle drew his attention back to the porch. "I might have an idea about a second act. I'll have to tell you about it later."

"Oh, does this mean you are going to stay around?"

"A little war isn't enough to keep me away from you."

Leaving Thema to continue her work, he turned and struggled to the porch. The administration troops, solidly reinforced from the rear, began their biggest assault yet. Advancing in lines, the troops moved forward, yard after yard, their weapons pouring automatic rounds into the solid stone front porch of the clinic.

Mustafa's little band fired back, as the administration's men raked the clinic in heavy fire. Tommy saw the boys and girls hit one after another under the barrage from the advancing troops. He scrambled and took a position along the stone porch and began firing at the approaching men as they attacked the short rise. He reminded himself to make every shot count but could tell it would just be minutes before they overran the clinic. Unless something changed.

Tommy fired off his last round but didn't have time to worry because just then a big soldier in the administration's army scaled the porch at the far end and started toward them. The first boys he came to offered little resistance, and he tossed them aside. With no ammunition the boys were forced to tackle him and fight hand to hand. Tommy hopped to his feet and on his bad knee he lurched toward the man, praying his knee wouldn't collapse when he needed it most.

****

As he neared the soldier, Tommy increased his pace and lowered his shoulder for the collision. The big administration trooper had just shaken off a stubborn boy soldier who held tight to the man's leg in an attempt to keep him from continuing toward the helpless wounded. The boy hung on and the soldier tripped and had to pry the boy off his leg with his rifle. The struggle turned him around and his back was now toward the rushing Tommy. Bracing himself for the impact Tommy closed his eyes and let out a scream. At the last second the soldier pivoted, and Tommy hit him in the midsection like he had tackled the practice dummies many times during his playing days.

Churning his feet, Tommy drove the man back into the low wall. Under the combined weight they both surged over and fell ten feet to the ground below. Tommy landed on top of the man as the man hit a section of the rock foundation. He heard the crunch of the man's back and rolled off and gained his feet.

For a few seconds, he stood over the man in silence. The brief fight between the men and the villagers caused a momentary lull in the battle, but when the other administration soldiers saw their sergeant killed, they began the fight again.

Shots began to explode around Tommy, and he dropped to safety behind the fallen sergeant. When the last of their ammunition ran out Mustafa passed the word along the line to be ready. Some of the boy soldiers pulled big knives from packs and belts and fastened them to their rifle ends. Others prepared to use their rifles as clubs. Without a knife, Tommy grabbed the trooper's rifle. He figured the rifle's clip had some ammunition left and he'd get off a few shots before it ended. A shout from the administration's men filled the air as they charged the clinic.

Tommy kneeled over the man to face the onslaught and started squeezing off single shots. Picking out clear targets he hit one, then two, then a third charging soldier before the last round clicked out. Tommy got to his feet and raised the rifle to his shoulder and prepared to fight hand to hand, but just before rushing out, other shots from the rear of the administration's soldiers rang out, and a group of men and boys swarmed out of the jungle and attacked the administration's troops from behind. Sekou and what was left of his boy fighters, arrived out of the thick forest on the south side of the road and joined the fray, firing on the advancing troops.

The soldiers stopped the clinic charge and taking new positions, turned to face the new assault. For the moment it looked like a standoff again, but more administration soldiers surged over the bank of the river and positioned themselves to flank what remained of Sekou's unit.

Exposed from the lack of cover, several in Sekou's unit crumpled immediately. At that rate the group would not last long. From the low hill of the new clinic site Tommy saw Phillips jump over the wall, leading Raines, Richards, and the rest of the villagers in an attack on the right flank of the administration soldiers.

Tommy took a deep breath and charged from his position and joined the fight. He met the first soldier with the butt of his rifle. He caught the second soldier under the chin with his right fist and hit across another soldier's face with the rifle barrel. He gang tackled three other soldiers, and they crumbled to the ground in a heap.

Tommy wondered for the hundredth time that day, *this certainly is no vacation!*

****

Up to then, the VSI crew and the boy soldiers had fought well but the likelihood of a win seemed improbable. Brother Denis' boys had managed to keep the administration's troops pinned on the east, but Tommy and the others began to lose the hand-to-hand skirmish in the middle of the square. Tommy's arms began to feel like lead as he fought off two administration soldiers at once. He landed a hard blow against the temple of one of the soldiers, and taking the man's weapon, he fired at several others and drove the small group back. A soldier whacked Tommy in the back, sending him to the ground. Tommy watched the soldier raise his weapon in preparation to crush his skull when a fresh torrent of weapon fire sprayed over the compound and took out the soldier before he could land the lethal blow. Other administration soldiers crumpled in the new hail of shots and their attack faltered again and the soldiers fell back.

Tommy rolled over and squinted through the haze of gunpowder. A fresh force of men charged into the village to join the fight, saving him. A woman led the fifty or so reinforcements out of the north woods. Phillips rushed to Tommy, pulled him up, and wrapped an arm through his armpits. Shouldering Tommy's weight he half carried him to the clinic to join the last of Mustafa's men.

"Wow, that unit came along just in time," he said to Mustafa when he saw the administration soldiers hunkered below the new steady incoming fire.

"That's my people from Buta."

"And who in the hell is that big Mama leading them? She's a force by herself!"

"Um, yes, that's the leader of the Buta, we've been waiting for her to come and join the fight."

"Hey," Tommy added, "better late than never, right?"

"Yes, for a moment there I didn't think we'd be able to hold the clinic."

"What do you think the administration's men will do now?"

"Maybe they'll surrender?" Phillips joked.

"Look!" one of the boy soldiers shouted pointing at the administration troops that began to withdraw to the river.

"Hey, look at that!" he shouted out, "They're retreating."

Others among the exhausted village troops stood and joined the celebrations. Shouts of joy filled the air.

****

With the pause in action, Mustafa ordered the smallest of the boys and girls off the porch walkway and to crawl out into the battlefield. "The boys will scavenge for ammunition among the fallen soldiers out there," he explained as he stretched out and closed his eyes. "There's plenty about."

Tommy watched the boys and girls crawling among the fallen soldiers, scavenging ammunition, and needed weapons as well.

When his little group was re-armed, Mustafa rose to his feet and shouted an order. Boys and girls struggled to their feet and then they charged down the rise and with the newly arrived Buta, they attacked the administration's position.

What was left of Brother Denis's group and Sekou's little band swarmed altogether toward the remnants of the administration's army. Under attack from all fronts, the administration soldiers only hesitated seconds before they abandoned their positions and scrambled away to the shallow river and slogged across. On the other side, the soldiers scurried up the far bank and scattered, dropping weapons and equipment in their hasty retreat.

"Look," Mustafa said at the edge of the river, jumping in celebration. "The great Mobassi army!"

"Should you be moving like that," Tommy asked, concerned about the man's wounds.

"My friend," Mustafa smiled as he limped, using his rifle as a crutch, "I am feeling well."

"Where do you all think you are going," Tommy yelled at the other girls and boys as they limped off heading to the river for the victory celebration. "You'll be bleeding all over the place if you don't watch it."

"I guess that's it," Willy Gray said as he plodded behind the last of the crew.

"Willy, my man, you made it! How is the Doc?"

"She's okay," he said, sitting heavily on a corner of the stone foundation, "still working. I heard the shouts of celebrating and had to take a look at what was happening."

"The cavalry came just in time?" Tommy said.

"We were waiting on them," he said, taking a

checkered handkerchief and wiping his face. "Say," Willy grinned, "you made a pretty good cavalry by yourself."

"Yeah, well," Tommy started to explain, then he saw Richards and his group running to the bridge, and he remembered, "Mike Blanco." Tommy said, "Mike's fox hole took a direct hit. Come on."

Breaking into a limping jog and chasing after the men, he arrived at the first machine gun position where several villagers had already pulled Barnes and Page from the mortar crater. The two were wounded but alive. Richards stopped to minister to them, but Tommy and Willy ran on ahead to Mike's position. A crowd had already gathered, and they were blocking the view, but he pushed his way by them when he got there. When he muscled through, he saw both Mike and Frisco sitting on the edge of the mortar hole, dazed, but alive.

"Damn," Tommy said to Mike, "you're a hard man to kill."

"I try to keep it that way." Opening his shirt, he showed him a thick Kevlar vest sporting several smoking shrapnel holes. One of the village women was wrapping one of his legs with a piece of cloth.

"Are you okay?" Tommy asked Frisco, who seemed dazed but unhurt.

"I can't tell," Frisco said, putting a hand over one eye and then doing the same to the other, "my eyes might be going bad. It seems like the last time I saw you, you were heading west. My eyes must be really bad because here you are, and holding an AK-47 in your hand, so something must be wrong with my eyes since I am seeing things."

Tommy looked at the weapon still gripped in his

hand, "Just something I found along the way," he said, handing the rifle to a village man.

Little Alex squirmed through the crowd to Tommy's side. "My man, thanks for helping out back there, that was a brave thing you did during the shelling," Tommy said, cradling the boy's small head in his hand. "Very brave."

"We go to America now?" Alex asked.

"Not just yet," Tommy laughed. "Why don't you go and fetch Nuru, will you?"

"Okay, Mr. Tommy," he said as he skipped off.

Tommy limped across the square to where Brother Denis stood on the clinic steps. As he walked, he passed the bodies of boy and girl rebels interspersed with the bodies of uniform-clad soldiers. Tommy noticed the soldiers didn't look much older than the village boys.

"Cavalry came," Tommy said to Brother Denis when he approached.

"Yes, the cavalry from the north, the Buta people. We were hoping they'd come," he said, taking a handkerchief from his back pocket and wiping his face clean. "They are originally from this town."

"There was no guarantee, right?"

"Oh, in this case, there was no doubt."

"Looks like we are going to be here awhile," Tommy said to Brother Denis as the older man took a seat in a rattan chair. "Are you hurt?"

"No, just worn out, but it was worth it."

"How's your boy, Sekou," he asked.

"He took one in the left arm, but it is okay."

"How so?"

"He is right-handed," Denis smiled.

"What about the rest of the VSI team?"

"Well, tough loss, with Billups," Denis said, "the rest look like they'll survive. What about Doctor Bok?"

"I wish I knew," Tommy said, "I can't get within ten bodies of her."

"I called the Bandella Hospital earlier and told them what was going to go down. They are Tutsi over there so agreed to send their mobile unit to assist. Good people. They'll be a great help."

Just then, Willy Gray and Richards walked up. "Come on, Brother Denis," Willy said, "let's give Doctor Book a hand."

The three men labored up the steps and picked their way over and between the wounded. At the end of the walk, Thema banged her way out through the door and leaned against the porch, catching her breath

"Doctor Bok," Brother Denis greeted her, "Could you use a hand?"

"Brother Denis, yes, yes," she said, turning to greet the men. "That would be great."

"I called for assistance from the Bandella Hospital. Some help should arrive in a few hours. In the meantime," he said, moving past her and into the OR, "we'll stand in with you."

"Well," Thema said, seeing Tommy standing there, somewhat bloodied and ragged looking after the battle, "Are you still hanging around?"

"Yeah, well," he said, then smiling added, "got to be the center of attention."

"Alex and Nuru?"

"They're fine, they'll be along."

"Thanks for staying."

"No problem, chief," he said, giving her a quick salute. "Looks like there's going to be a lot to do for a while. Maybe I'll stick around and see what I can do to help."

"I'm glad you stayed, Tommy, I thought we were goners for sure."

Mike Blanco hobbled up. "Tommy saved the day."

"Did he?"

"Yeah, we might not be here if he hadn't jumped in when he did. I knew there was a reason I dragged his ass along on this mission."

She took a step back. Gave them both the look of a warrior chief demanding the truth. "Don't you think it's time to clear the air about this mission?"

"I guess we can give you the full scoop now. Medical African Missions is a cover for the Agency. They hired us to protect you."

"Me?"

"Yep, the woman who would be queen."

"And Tommy?"

"He's a reluctant recruit to the team, but I'm glad he came along. You had me worried, man, but you came through."

There was an awkward pause among the three, but Willy Gray's call for help from the OR and broke the silence.

"Well," Mike said, "I've got to look in on my men. I'll talk to you two later."

Another awkward pause between Thema and Tommy followed Mike's departure.

"Okay," Thema said, "I've got to get back to work."

"Still curing the sick and tending the wounded?"

"It's what I do."

"I'd expect nothing less from the village doctor. I'll be at the house."

"Okay, I'll join you as soon as I can."
"Don't worry, Doc, I can wait."

Chapter Twenty-nine

Help arrived from the Bandella Hospital in the form of two doctors, four nurses and several orderlies. They also brought a large recovery tent, a generator, and halogen lights.

With her people in good hands, Doctor Thema Atsu Bok left the clinic and trudged toward the mission house. Tommy sat in one of a grouping of chairs arranged beneath the giant Baobab tree that dwarfed the house and watched the Doc pace off the steps toward him in the twilight of what had been the busiest day of his life.

Alex and Nuru slept soundly, stretched out on a bamboo mat on the ground nearby. He was too tired to offer much help to her, but did call out once for encouragement. "Get the lead out, Doc!" Which by the look on her face, she did not find amusing.

"Damn, Doc," Tommy said, "you look like you just founded a country or something."

"Funny man, Tommy," she moaned, toddling into the clearing beneath the tree and moving to a companion rattan chair. "I knew you were a funny man."

"I'd give you a hand, but my ass appears to be stuck on this seat here."

"Don't get up, now," she said, sitting heavily."

"How did you get away?"

"The mobile unit from Bandella arrived, so they fired me and told me to get some rest. They said they could handle things from here on out."

"Thank the Lord."

"The kids look like they had enough," she said, gazing at the two children who had captured her heart.

"Nuru wanted to wait for you," Tommy said, reaching down and patting the little girl's back. "She didn't make it ten minutes before she nodded off. I've just been too tired to take her into the house."

"Well, big guy," Thema said, leaning back her chair, "from what I hear, everyone's saying you saved the village today."

"Oh yeah," Tommy laughed. "In one of my wilder moments in memory I dashed out of my comfort zone and tried to be a hero."

"Tommy?"

"Actually," he said, pointing to the sleeping boy, "Alex bailed us out or we might not be here right now."

"Well," Thema said, "I hear your role was a little bit more than that."

"Just rumors, Doc, just rumors."

"No kidding, Tommy," she said, grabbing hold of his hand in the dark, "I'm glad you stayed. I'm sorry we couldn't work all that out before, but I'm glad you're here."

The two of them sat in the near dark and listened to the laughter and talk coming from the village.

"Ahoy, the house!" Brother Denis called out from the path, holding a lantern out in front of him as he walked toward them.

"Ahoy yourself, old man," Tommy answered.

"Who do you have there?" Thema asked, noticing someone with him.

"This is '*Adana*', of the Buta," he said, stepping

aside, holding the lamp so he could introduce the older woman at his side.

Adana nodded at them, sporting a wide smile and high cheeks that Tommy found familiar. She stood almost shoulder to shoulder with Brother Denis and from the fierce fighting he saw from her, Tommy understood she led by example. The woman carried a vintage AK-47 with wood stock that looked like it had seen a lot of action.

"So, this is the woman who saved our butts just before the final bell."

"Tommy!" Thema scolded.

"I mean," he said, rising and bowing, "thank you for coming to the rescue."

"Yes, Adana is the leader of the Buta," Denis continued, "They are originally from here, but a previous administration drove them north of the border where they took refuge in the mountains. Her father was a chief here many years ago, Paramount Chief as well, before the government arrested and executed him. I'm afraid it has been rough on them these last thirty years. It seems like each new administration gave them a harder and harder time."

"Welcome and thank you," Thema greeted the woman, standing and offering her a hand. "How can we thank you."

"You are welcome, my child," Adana said in clear English, with a bit of British in the accent. "I am sorry I couldn't come sooner."

Thema said, "We are very happy you arrived, as you can imagine."

"Say," Tommy said, studying the woman, "haven't we seen you before, I never forget a face!"

"Perhaps from the night you first came to Masango," the woman said, smiling brightly. "I was part of the welcoming committee."

"That's it," Tommy said, snapping his fingers.

"But another time as well," Thema said. "On one of my first days here, when I walked about with Imamu."

"Yes, we met then, but I don't visit the village often. The administration doesn't appreciate our political stance, and we spend much of our time avoiding an army unit charged with hunting and capturing us. Before today, as a group, we haven't ventured this far south in some time. I only got the word late, that you called the people to arms. We stay some way off, and it took this long to get here."

"Well," Tommy said, "better late than never!"

"Yes, indeed," the woman agreed, taking Thema's hand in both of hers, "this is a moment I have long waited for."

****

Thema held onto the woman's hands, feeling the warmth of her body even through the rough calluses. "Have the years been difficult?" she asked, recognizing a resolute disposition in the woman.

"Yes," she said, releasing Thema's hands to touch and hold her shoulder in a light grip. "Up until now I'm afraid the years have only seen fighting and heartache for us. Our family was torn apart some years ago and we have been fighting since to bring peace back to this region. It has not been a place to raise children."

"But it has been a wonderful day," Brother Denis said. "Newfound freedom has come to Masango and its people."

"Yes," Adana agreed, continuing to hold Theam

with a firm hand. "A day to truly celebrate, a brief time to celebrate ahead of the hard work that will come."

"Hard work is done," Tommy said.

"Oh no," she said, shifting her gaze to him, "the hard work is yet to come. It is easy to start a revolution. All it takes is guns. But to sustain a revolution and build a country," she said while switching her attention back to Thema, "that takes great sacrifice, diligent people, and hard work, but I am truly optimistic this time."

"Why is that?" Thema asked.

"Why, because of you, my child."

"Me…the village doctor?"

"Oh, but you are much more," she said, releasing her and standing tall before her, like at attention. "The people have voted, and you are the Paramount Chief now, a great honor."

"Speaking of this Paramount Chief election thing," Tommy said, "did you have something to do bringing in those votes from the countryside?"

"I was fortunate to do my part," she said, then smiled wide.

"But why would you want me to be the Paramount Chief?" Thema asked.

"These people need a spokesperson, my child," she said, waving her arm out toward the village."

"But I will hardly have much of a chance to speak for them from the clinic."

"Oh, your clinic work will be valuable, but your voice will be more important."

"What do you mean?"

"I mean things will be changing in the government. You'll have an important voice in the discussion about moving the country forward."

"Will there be a new government?" Thema asked.

"Yes, there have been other endeavors to change things and Mobassi is unable to hold his coalition together. Many say his administration will soon fall."

"Is that true?" Thema asked Brother Denis.

"The Agency has been working on a companion operation," brother Denis answered, hanging the lamp from a tree branch and adjusting the wick for a light that covered the area. "I'm not privy to its details, but something is happening down in the capital."

"Yes," Adana said, "change is coming, and, of course, you will represent the people in this whole district now and you'll speak for them."

"I can't do that," Thema said, shaking her head.

"Oh, but you can, and you must," Adana said, "and quite eloquently I believe. The people will now depend on you to represent them. You are our spokesperson now and you will speak earnestly for us, I should think."

"I don't understand."

"Why, you are their hero now."

"Hero?"

"Yes, the woman who defeated Mobassi. That is no small feat."

"The woman who gives sight to the blind," Brother Denis added, "*That* was some feat. I am pretty sure they are making up songs about it right now. Many people across this country will be anxious to meet and support you. Why, you could be president."

"Brother Denis don't be silly," she said.

"Well, who can say," he answered, sitting slowly into a chair, "but the people have spoken, and they will have their say in the government. You will make sure that happens, one way or another. You cannot forget, my dear, that many people died today, just so you would have that voice."

"I'll never forget this day, Brother Denis, the people's sacrifice, but I'm not really part of this country."

"On the contrary, my dear," Adana said, clutching Thema's amulet, and showing her one of her own, larger, but the same in design and wound tightly with leather. "You and the country are one. You are *Sihiri*. That's what this is. A symbol of life for our country, a symbol of a new beginning."

"Yes, but…"

"And" Brother Denis noted, "let's not forget that *miracle*."

"Now, Brother, you of all people understand that was just chemistry."

"Do I?"

"You most certainly do."

"Then there is also your family," he added. "The people recognize your family's heritage and past leadership and bravery over the last decade of struggle."

"My family?"

"Yes, your village family, you have a large assortment of relatives here."

"I sensed as much," Thema said, "only hoped."

"But certainly, a great many, unfortunately, I'm afraid some of them paid the highest price today."

Thema looked out into the gloom, to the village, where drums were sounding out in the night and people were dancing and celebrating.

"Exactly what kind of family are we talking about?" she asked at last.

"Well," Brother Denis began, "I guess there's no

harm in telling you now."

"What?"

"Well, actually…"

"A brother," she interrupted him, "I have a brother, don't I?"

"Yes, and you've met him, a couple of times I think."

"Yes, a brother," she repeated, "I felt it the moment I met him. Mustafa Bok."

"Yes, among other relatives," Denis said.

"Mustafa," she repeated after a minute.

"Yes," Denis said, "your twin brother. I am sorry to say we have kept it from you these past few weeks. But we thought it was safer."

On a hushed breath, Thema repeated, "Yes, I have a twin brother."

****

Thema barely listened to Brother Denis's explanation as she wrestled with the new feeling of having a brother. "Your family here is deep in ancestry, you have many relatives, some already in government. Your blood relations are wide and deep, and you would have family ties over the whole region. It is, matter of fact, quite a large lineage."

"But a brother," she asked, "does he know?"

"Oh yes," Denis said, "he agreed to the secret since his own reputation was sullied by the administration. He is a wanted man and his whole family is at the top of the administration's list of kill on sight. So, it was better to keep quiet about the family connections. Afterward, he saw your willingness to become part of the community, and he relaxed. He told me more than once he is not disappointed in you."

"I treated him this afternoon," she said, taking a step toward the village. "A leg wound?"

"Yes, good job," Denis said, "he has a limp now, but it will heal."

"Mustafa Bok?"

"Yes, a true patriot of the people, he's of the Buta."

"I did feel something the first time we met. A brother, indeed...Tommy?" Thema asked.

"News to me, Doc, I swear. I wasn't familiar with each aspect of the mission."

"Everyone kept the secret, Doctor," Denis said, "the family thought it best for the time being."

Thema turned and looked at Brother Denis. "Where is he?"

"He was looking in on his boys in the recovery area. He's quite a leader, that young man, born leader really, the whole family is like that."

"Yes," Adana agreed, "A true patriot, as you say, I just left him, and he is doing well."

"You sure about this," Tommy asked Brother Denis.

"About what," he asked.

"This brother thing, with Mustafa?"

"Oh yes, it is so."

"How is it possible?"

"They have the same grandparents and parents, my boy. Thirty years ago, I'm sure everyone thought Thema would be safer in America and they were right. This was no place for a baby girl, during those war years. Her right to succession to a leadership position of her people had to be protected. Her brother's destiny was to stay behind with his people and eventually grow and fight this battle here. I'm surprised you didn't figure it out on your own."

"What do you mean?"

"Thema's name, man, her name. *Atsu* ...it means second born twin."

"Wait," Tommy questioned, "you said they are twins?"

"Yes, of course, brother and sister, Thema and Mustafa are twins."

"But Dude..." Tommy started, but lost the words, turning and pointing to the woman, Adana.

"What, Tommy, what?" Thema said.

"Denis...Denis told me earlier that the leader of the Buta is Mustafa's... mother!"

Thema turned to Adana and then she knew.

"You are the leader of the Buta?" she asked.

"Yes, my child, for the past thirty years."

"Then?"

"Yes, my daughter," she said, opening her arms wide, "and I am so proud to call you daughter!"

Thema held her ground for just a moment as she mulled over the announcement, then rushed into her mother's arms.

Mother and daughter held on to each other in a long and vice-like embrace. Thema had a thousand questions to ask but none mattered just then. The only thing that mattered was her mother's embrace.

"Brother Denis," Tommy asked, "why didn't you tell us?"

"The family wanted it this way and the Agency agreed..." he explained, "and for safety reasons we kept it a secret. The Agency wanted to support the Buta and their fight against the administration but with the Chinese here, they didn't have much choice. Mustafa told me about Doctor Bok some time ago, and I told the Agency. As part of the strategy, they hired VSI to

317

provide security, and they hired Thema and lured her here. But I would have thought you would have pieced it together."

Tommy nodded his head, "Yeah, I guess Thema *does* mean Queen," and looking up he smiled, under the *Tree of Life.*

A word about the author...

Ruben was born and raised in East Los Angeles. After college he was with the Peace Corps and spent two years teaching elementary school in a small African village by day and reading and writing by candlelight at night. Ruben's first published work was by the BBC for world broadcast. After the Peace Corps, he moved to North Carolina. Ruben was an entrepreneur for many years owning his own business. He began working with the City of Winston-Salem in 1997. Before he retired from the city, he was Director of Business Development. Now he writes full time and teaches part-time with the local community college system. Ruben has published other books in the mystery genre, but this is the first where the main characters are Latinx.

Thank you for purchasing
this publication of The Wild Rose Press, Inc.

For questions or more information
contact us at
info@thewildrosepress.com.

The Wild Rose Press, Inc.
www.thewildrosepress.com